DANTE'S INDIANA

ALSO BY RANDY BOYAGODA

Original Prin
Beggar's Feast
Governor of the Northern Province

Dante's Indiana
A NOVEL

RANDY BOYAGODA

A JOHN METCALF BOOK

BIBLIOASIS
WINDSOR, ONTARIO

FIRST EDITION

Library and Archives Canada Cataloguing in Publication

Title: Dante's Indiana / Randy Boyagoda.
Names: Boyagoda, Randy, 1976- author.
Identifiers: Canadiana (print) 20210213272 | Canadiana (ebook) 20210213280 |
ISBN 9781771964272 (softcover) | ISBN 9781771964289 (ebook)
Classification: LCC PS8603.O9768 D36 2021 | DDC C813/.6—dc23

Edited by John Metcalf
Copyedited by Emily Donaldson
Cover designed by Michel Vrana
Typeset by Vanessa Stauffer

Published with the generous assistance of the Canada Council for the Arts, which last year invested $153 million to bring the arts to Canadians throughout the country, and the financial support of the Government of Canada. Biblioasis also acknowledges the support of the Ontario Arts Council (OAC), an agency of the Government of Ontario, which last year funded 1,709 individual artists and 1,078 organizations in 204 communities across Ontario, for a total of $52.1 million, and the contribution of the Government of Ontario through the Ontario Book Publishing Tax Credit and Ontario Creates.

PRINTED AND BOUND IN CANADA

For Anna,
my Virgil and Beatrice both,
and for Mira, Olive, Ever, and Imogen,
our stars.

"We made our way, along the brink …"
—Dante, *Purgatorio*

"'The hearse—the second hearse!' cried Ahab from the boat,
'its wood could only be American!'"
—Herman Melville, *Moby-Dick*

1

RIDING THROUGH THE valley, I looked up and lost my way.

From the ground, my bike beside me, I caught my breath and bent my legs. Nothing cracked or snapped or stung. I pushed up, on my elbows. It was midday in Toronto. Late November. A Thursday.

People pedalled and jogged past. Families fanned out along the path with food bags and strollers and toddlers leashed at the wrist. A few people waved, to make sure that I was okay. I waved back. Loose dogs approached, curious, their tails whipping around. Their owners called out treats and punishments and they turned away from me. I slipped back down.

I was alone in the city.

I blinked a few times. Beyond the pencilled high branches, the heavens looked like the greywhite of rainwater in an empty swimming pool.

I was alone in the city.

The demon was still there. It was beside me. The creature squatted on a plinth wedged between the bike path and the murky river. It had bat wings and a dog face. The Thursday before, it hadn't been here; I was certain of that, at least, and had stared at it for far too long. Mid-pedal past. My front wheel went off the path into a slurry of pea gravel. Small stones dug into my skin. Pushing into the earth made them go away. The ground was damp and forgiving.

I looked at the gargoyle again. The battered creature must have been dumped out of some lately condo'd church. Smashed-up bramble and bush ended near its base, rutted lines of dried-out mud that led across the path and up to the main road. Tire tracks. Someone had driven it down from the city proper, unloaded it, right-side up, and left.

A statement? A warning? A joke?

Had I taken a wrong turn, higher up the path?

If they were here with me, we wouldn't lay down and blink and stare. We'd climb and call out and conquer.

Molly left in July, with the children. To stay with her family for the summer. She took their winter clothes.

"Leave you here?"

The driver dropped me in front of the glass-boxed front of my old Catholic college. It was now a condominium and assist-ed-living complex called The New U.

I walked through the airy vestibule built in front of the chipped-brick building. The old hardscape had been torn up and replaced by paving tiles; pitted and silver-grey, they gave off a sheen like old trophies and tea services and baby cups, spoons, shoes in which first steps were taken, decades ago.

"Prin, has the condo board changed the rules and nobody told the guy who has to enforce them? Am I really going to let you go up the elevator with that bike, like that?" said Marcus.

I went over to his desk. The monitors and phones and cardiac-arrest kits were concealed by slatted lengths of amber wood—warm like honey and candlelight, like honey in candle-light. The desk softened the rest of the building's otherwise cold bright bare beginning.

Marcus was a retired soldier. He lined the top of his desk with potted cactuses, a tribute to his late wife, and was beloved by the building's residents for settling daily disputes about party-room bookings and guest-parking.

"Where am I supposed to go then?" I said.

Others were watching and listening. They were always in the lobby, fixed in their places like the unsecured umbrella stands. They carried tablets and e-readers, in case you asked any direct questions.

Marcus tapped and checked a screen. He checked his watch.

"Go to Underground 2. You might hop in the tub with your bike. You have about ten minutes before they start coming back from their dog walks. I'll text you the code. Hurry up so you're not ambushed."

I was too late.

"So, what do you got there? Poodle-Harley mix?"

The other dog-walkers laughed at the old man's joke. I waited.

When I eventually left the dog-washing room, I discovered that I wasn't the only one waiting. The building's elevators, programmed to reach each resident's floor via face-recognition software, weren't working. At every face, the screen flashed "The Terraces."

This had to be an error message.

They all looked to me. I was the youngest resident in the building. I knew "computer." I did have the code for the utility elevator, so I offered to bring everyone back to the lobby. Certain dogs didn't get along. Multiple trips were necessary. I had to make each one. No one believed the code would work for anyone else. No one would chance a trip to The Terraces, the condominium's medical wing.

Thank yous were offered.

Standing in the lobby, I looked through the condo's glass facade. Traffic and the faces of people in traffic; behind them, above them, more condominiums. The sky was endlessly the same. As if grey clouds had worsted the heavens.

"Overcast until evening, then cooler. The same's in the forecast tomorrow," said a voice from the unsecured umbrella stand.

I had to leave the lobby.

Four o'clock was too early for dinner.

For the microwave.

For pepperoncini or hot mustard on the reheated joint.

2

CLASSES WERE JUST getting out on The New U's second floor. The condo's test kitchen was at the far end of a hall that was lined with scholarly books arranged by binding colour.

More than a year earlier, the college had announced it was shutting down—after its plan to open a satellite campus in the Middle East ended with its visiting delegation caught in a terrorist attack at the airport. Two people were killed—a Chinese real-estate developer and a university business consultant, my ex-girlfriend from graduate school. Two survived: the consultant's assistant, a Chinese woman who had since become the condominium's exclusive sales agent, and an English professor.

I remembered very little about the attack.

Flashes of light. Shattering. Footfall. Quiet voices in the dark. Secret voices.

Not just mine.

Smashing. Yelling, calling, screaming.

A final brightness.

Angry men and ringing phones and crying children. A bandage pressed against my bleeding forehead. A blanket that made me shiver. That made me realize I was shivering. Molly, on a phone held to my ear by a gloved hand, crying so hard it sounded like she was laughing. Finally asking her what was so funny. Forgiven that.

I had been pensioned and granted *emeritus* status at the age of forty-one. And while our house was being renovated, I was given temporary use of a free unit in the building, where my divorced parents were also now living. They had quickly established themselves as major players.

Which meant I wasn't just *that* professor; I was also *his* son, *her* son, *their* son. *The son.*

Wasn't he also married to that sweet American girl? Didn't they have all of those wonderful little girls? Where were they?

I was spared direct questions.

My parents must have told them something.

Sins of the heart, sins of the mind, mouth, hands. Yes. Yes to all. But despair is the greatest sin of all. And so solo bike rides and daily dinnertime calls, it was just easier. *It was just easier:* isn't this the surest commandment for any marriage well into its middle age? It doesn't have to mean despair. We weren't there yet.

The other professors at the college were given two options: they could accept a modest buyout from the board and framed final blessing from Father-President, or they could accept a radically reduced salary, access presale pricing for their own units, and also free storage for their personal libraries—provided they offered lifelong learning seminars to fellow residents.

I saw some of them now, in the hallway.

"Prin? What are you doing here, Prin?" said one of my old colleagues.

"Professor, is that an example of chiasmus?"

She didn't wait to answer her student's question. She couldn't. The momentum was too much. She kept pushing on to the elevator like her other exiting colleagues, surrounded by their personal libraries and by grey students asking detailed questions. They would continue with this, day after day, year after year, until they stopped receiving balance-owing statements from the college's loan officer, who was now its only employee.

I reached the end of the hallway, where the books changed from brown to green. The walls around the corner looked burnt orange. Fresh bread was baking. The test kitchen, one of the college's original refectories, was quiet.

The cooking class that my mother and Kareem, her newish, Muslim-ish second husband, were taking involved condo members sharing recipes and stories. Today, the class was led by an older Italian couple, hale and well-dressed. The man had the face of someone who worked with his hands. The woman was splendid. Cadmium hair, down to her shoulders. Her face glowed. Slipping in at the back of the room, I noticed it was shining with tears.

"I'm sorry. I'm sorry, everyone."

She turned to her husband, who held out his hands, smiling and looking sorry.

Useless.

"It's just that, this recipe, it really brings me back, you know? But next year will be our fortieth, and we have seven grandchildren, with another on the way. Things worked out in the end. They worked out wonderfully," she said.

The room was quiet and stayed quiet. But then came a loud crack, and some jumped in their seats. Kareem and my mother were clapping. Others joined in, including the husband. Everyone came to the front and thanked the couple for the baking lesson and wrapped their loaves before taking them upstairs to their units.

I held back, but Lizzie and Kareem saw me. Waving, fanning, they made their approach.

"Ah!"

"Hi Mum—"

"Aahh!"

"Mum, I just—"

"AAAAAAAHHHHHHH!"

"Prin, your mother said AAAAAAAHHHHHHH!"

I rolled my eyes. I sighed. I shrugged my shoulders. None of it worked. It wasn't supposed to work. This was old theatre between us. And it had been a while. And so I opened my mouth and, while the watchers cheered, my wild-winking mother fed me hot tufts of focaccia until I couldn't say anything at all.

And then she nodded, cordially, and left.

She dropped her mother-face and left?

I didn't get the chance to fail to avoid telling her about falling off my bike in the valley?

And since when did my mother have a face to drop?

"You like the bread?" said Kareem.

He'd stayed back.

I swallowed.

"Where's my mother going?" I said.

"Oh, Prin, you know, she's very busy," said Kareem.

"Busy?"

"That's right! Just really busy, you know, with, with—"

"With retirement?" I said.

"You got it! But do you want me to text her for you? You want some more lamb? Maybe mint sauce this time?"

"I can come get it—"

"Just text me first, okay?"

"I can call my mother directly, Kareem. And I can visit her when I want."

"Then go ahead. Call her. Go ahead. Visit her."

"Kareem?"

"So you do want me to tell her you're coming now?"

"No."

"Okay Prin."

***

The hallway was empty now. I took the orange way to the eleva-tors. After I'd first come back from Dragomans, my mother had counted my fingers and toes every time she saw me like when I was first born, as she told me and everyone else. Kareem had worn a fanny pack full of her prescriptions, "just for dealing with everything." But after Molly and the children moved to Milwaukee my mother had only nodded, barely, at my explana-tions (The New U didn't offer family-style suites for temporary residents; I needed to be here to check in on our home renova-tion; it was easier to homeschool in America; it was just easier). In front of others, she was, as ever, "the mother": fighting back tears of pride and sorrow, Sri Lankan Tiger-Balm-Mom supreme. Otherwise? She had become cordial. *My mother*: Cordial.

Of course she'd answer if I called her.

It was a little nearer to five now. I took the elevator down to the gym.

"Six thousand!"

Kingsley was standing at centre court, pickleball racquets in both hands, giving instructions. His red warm-up suit looked a little baggy, or at least a little baggier than the last time I'd seen him wearing it. I waved. He came over.

"What are you doing here?"

"Hi Dad. I thought I'd see if—"

"But you're not supposed to be here. You're supposed to be … aren't you supposed to be somewhere else today?"

"Sorry to interrupt, gentlemen. Hi, Prin. Listen, Kingsley, Luca's varicose veins are killing him. We need a sixth to complete the rung on court three. Can your son join us?"

"Sure. I can do that. Could I borrow a—"

"No. He can't," said Kingsley.

The other players fell back.

"Dad, I can play for a while before—"

"Before what? Before you take another bike ride? At least a kid delivers the papers."

"I'm taking a break, actually. I had a fall, earlier today. I'm fine. Anyway, I just thought I'd say hi. You know, before—"

"Before what? Before you do more of your 'research'? A man your age, Prin, even after what happened, what happened to you ... but this isn't ..."

"Dad, I know what you're trying to say. And you know I'm not allowed to teach as part of the settlement," I said.

"They've been down there for months! You can use my car if you want."

"Dad, I've told you, we discussed this before they moved. I'm going for Christmas, I'm definitely going for Christmas, and I'm thinking of asking her—"

"Molly! Her name is Molly!"

"I know my wife's name."

"Okay. I'll pay for the gas ... *and the oil*."

"Dad, I appreciate what you're trying to do."

"Yeah. Okay. Centre court is waiting for me."

"Okay then. I'll come by later to watch the 6:30 news," I said.

"Dinner?"

"Mom already fed me."

"She fed you? Or Halal Caesar fed you?"

"I'm not hungry. Just a beer. Did you put them in the fridge this morning?"

"Yes. Help me bag the empties when you come."

"Okay."

"You know what I think, Prin?"

"No."

"I'm your father! I can tell!"

"You can tell what?"

"Something's wrong."

"I'm going for Christmas! I'm renovating the house for them!"

"No. You like it this way."

"What? I like it this way? I like this?"

His lips trembled. He walked away.

"Ten thousand steps! I did it!" an old voice called out from the track above us.

"No! The winning number is one thousand! It's just one thousand steps to chapel!" called out another, a new one.

Sister Contra Melanchthon used to teach English and Latin, and when the college closed she moved to a religious house north of the city. She didn't drive, but somehow came to The New U by three o'clock every afternoon, Monday to Friday. She visited with a rolling black suitcase full of metaphysical poetry and shortbread. Every day she would walk through the building, harrying everyone to the 5:15 Mass.

By now, dinner in Milwaukee would be finished. Arguments would have started, about pie now or pie after the dishes. Both. Bets about whether Uncle Patrick would wake up from the dog licking the bacon out of his fingernails.

Kingsley had no idea.

How could I like this?

I left my bike against the handrail outside the chapel, in between two walkers. When the college closed, most of the pews were sold to prop companies and salvage shops. I saw in a magazine that a few ended up as "Come to Jesus benches" scattered around the beanbag lounge of a startup. The nave had been reduced to half its size, and a brick stack had been built directly over the Holy of Holies to protect the unleavened Godhead from seven storeys of padded feet.

An old priest was napping under a Boston Red Sox cap on

the front bench. I didn't look up to see the flame flickering in the red globe mounted between the bricked and bronzed boxes. I knelt for the briefest touch.

I sat and listened to Sister's shuffling in the sacristy, to the priest's sleeping.

"Prin, would you like to serve the Mass? Do the readings? Carry the gifts?" she said.

"I'm not really dressed for it, Sister. And it's just the three of us. Also, do you really think Father needs the help?"

"It's not him I'm thinking about, Prin."

"I think Father wants to begin," I said.

Eighteen murmuring minutes later, on my way out of the chapel, she called after me.

The altar candles flickered behind her as she smiled, then jumped when her phone buzzed. She made a motion for me to wait as she squinched her face and tapped on the screen. I knelt to touch the grey-dark tile. I held it a moment, pressing down, grinding a little to see if there was any pain. If so, I'd hold it until they came home!

No I wouldn't.

But I went upstairs and called. I was eventually called back and passed around the Thanksgiving table.

3

THE FOLLOWING WEEK, I sacrificed my bike ride. I had to go check on our house. The contractor needed to show me something in person, and to discuss the budget.

An Italian builders' association was providing us with a new home. The offer came a few months after I'd been in the news. *The English professor who survived the terrorist attack.*

Theirs was the only offer I'd accepted. For about a month after I returned from Dragomans, assistants to movie producers and interns at motivational-speaker firms and assistant interns from literary agencies contacted me. More than a year later, only one agent was still checking in: Kyle from New York. But he was easy to ignore. They all were. Fending off my parents, my parents *then*, was work enough. And I didn't want to be a disaster celebrity. I wanted to be at home, near Molly and the children, in-between my appointments—trauma counselling, dental work, hearing tests, plastic surgeon. I was also given prescriptions to help with travel and other things. These ranged in need and repair from temporary to permanent, optional to necessary, spoken to unspoken.

Before I could think about money, the university sent its legal counsel to the house.

He was an older lawyer with a boiled, ruddy face and thick flaps of faded blonde hair.

"The man looks like St. Patrick's Day dinner," said my youngest, Pippa.

The children were sent to another room. This was not easy. When I came back from the Middle East, they treated me like I was just learning to walk. Molly treated me like an astronaut. Eventually, she called me an astronaut. Not the hero returned, but the guy still out there, orbiting. I told her it didn't feel that way to me. I told her, in fact, that it felt like I'd fallen to earth. A hard fall. She nodded. She didn't acknowledge that I'd extended her own metaphor to explain myself. She didn't acknowledge that I was trying.

"What a wonderful family! I am here—is this loud enough? Can you hear me? Just nod. Good. Thank you. Here's my card. And unless you're my sainted mother, ignore all the extra O's and I's and shamrocks on the letters and just call me Simon. So, to begin, I am here, on instructions from the Board, to inform you that, first of all, the Board is glad for your safety and sends blessings and best wishes. The Board seeks nothing in exchange for its steadfast promise of continued prayers and good wishes other than your full recovery so that you're happy and whole. Also, until you are informed otherwise, for your safety and that of your colleagues, you are not to communicate with any Board member or employee of the university except me, or through me. Third of all, the Board asserts it is not liable for anything that happened while you were travelling on university business."

"The university takes no responsibility for what happened to him?" said Molly. "You know that everyone thought he was dead? Do you have any sense of what that was like for us?"

"Well, funny you say that. I've been a widower since—"

"How can someone do something like this and not take responsibility?" said Molly.

She turned. I was watching the lawyer pull papers from his boxy black hearse-bag.

"Professor? Is this your signature? Hello? Can you hear me? Is this your husband's signature?" he said.

"No. It's a little computerized checkmark in a box," Molly said.

He pulled out another sheaf of papers.

"Is this your husband's signature?" he said.

"It looks like it, yes," Molly said.

"And that signature, which he provided when he accepted his position with the university, confirms that checking the 'I agree' box on all subsequent agreements, digital or physical, serves *in loco subscriptionis*, including the online waiver he signed before going on his recent trip," he said.

"His recent trip? Didn't you watch the news?" she said.

"The news has become so divisive these days—"

"Did you really come here, come into my home, to say that the university is going to do nothing for someone, someone with children, who was nearly killed because of its stupid ideas?"

The lawyer looked at me. But I was looking at Molly.

Why wasn't she getting mad like this, at me?

The lawyer was looking at Molly, too. He didn't look at me again.

"Look, I don't want to have to use any more lawyer's Latin. Believe me, I can. But if you're open to working out an agreement, then I have good news for you. Shall I proceed?"

"Alright," she said.

"As you know, the university is proud of its commitment to values; a commitment, and also values, that for more than a century have been inspired by the institution's historical identity as historically Catholic—"

"Please," I said.

"Yes," said Molly.

We looked at each other. I nodded.

"Provided your husband agrees not to bring any suit against

the university and agrees to make no public statements regarding recent international initiatives and events associated with the university that he may have witnessed or participated in, the university is prepared to make a settlement that, given its own precarious circumstances—"

"You want me to feel sorry for the university?" she said.

"Molly," I said.

"Do you two need a moment?" said the lawyer.

"Yes," I said.

"No," said Molly.

"Yes," I said.

"No," said Molly.

"Well. Why don't I just leave this with you to look over," said the lawyer.

After he left, Molly called the girls into the living room. They had magic tricks ready and I sat there, picking the wrong hand again and again. Molly went back upstairs. I signed.

A few months later, when the builders' association proposed the design and construction of a new home in recognition of what our family had gone through—and in exchange for testimonials and pictures—we agreed. The girls were getting older. We could use a bigger space. A different space. A change. I inquired about family housing options at the condominium. Molly made plans to stay in Milwaukee for the summer. With the winter clothes.

The four corners of our old house were gone. In their place was a rubble-banked concave pit surrounded by plastic-covered trees and battered waste bins and stacks of near-white wood. Workmen were eating lunch in luxury pickup trucks. Neighbours walked by our corner lot, their dogs sniffing the wrapped-up trees.

"You the homeowner?" said a worker.

"I am," I said.

"Okay. Stay out of the guys' way. You should be wearing a helmet. Code. I'll get Marco for you. Hey! Lombardo, the homeowner's here!" he said.

A man came to me in a cloud of smoke.

"You the homeowner?" he said.

"I am."

The contractor dragged on his cigarette, then exhaled and shook his head.

"Can you tell me what's wrong?" I said.

"Money."

"What we signed with your organization, to build the house—"

"Identifies you as solely responsible for any and all change requests and situations not initially contemplated or reflected in the agreement. Listen, this is an old house, and while we were digging down we hit an old pipe that must have been put in a hundred years ago. Fuck me. Anyway, we need to figure out where that goes before doing anything else and the City's going to want to sign off and, I don't know, there's other stuff too. My concrete guy's being an asshole about the foundation walls. The structural engineer's an asshole too. And assholes cost money. Overruns. Those are on you. Just look at the terms sheet," said Marco.

"I don't need to look," I said.

"Great. You need to come up with $5,000. And if it doesn't happen in the next week, maybe two weeks, the ground is going to freeze and that's it until spring and you're not getting this house until next winter. Maybe. *Maybe*. Remember, we're all doing this as a good deed, and the crews change every month and we all have other jobs, paying jobs. And Christmas is coming. So, I need to deal with this mystery pipe. Can I book my guy? That means you need to tell me right now you can get the money and that you're ready to get more. I can front the first five, but I expect to be paid back in a timely fashion. Timely means two weeks. Can you make that?"

"Can you still do what we were planning? For the backyard?" I said.

Molly and the girls didn't know I'd spent our savings on a backyard pool. I'd never forgotten what Molly once said, about going to a friend's house when she was a kid in Milwaukee. The friend had a pool in her backyard and Molly didn't think such things were possible for people who weren't presidents or movie stars (her friend's father was a regional manager for Sears). She told me how she'd told her sister about this and then, her voice full of longing and frustration, described the hours and hours and hours, the years and years, that she'd spent drawing pictures of her future family's backyard swimming pool.

I'd asked her mother to check the storage bins in the basement. She sent a drawing to me. I would frame it and hang it near the water.

That would show her.

Show her I'd been listening, really listening, all along.

"Yes. We can still do the pool, which is all on you. But it's early enough that you could cancel that. Or do it another time. Then there's lots of money to start dealing with the pipe, and whatever we find down there next," said Marco.

"No. Don't cancel the pool. I'll have the money for you."

"Attaboy."

He clapped me on the shoulder. I didn't jump back. I didn't hit him in his smoking face. I'd taken half a pill that morning. Dealing with things in general.

The next day, I found myself sitting on a chapel bench outside the office of the college loan officer. Through frosted-glass, I could see lamplight, drooping plants.

It was lunch-hour, Friday at The New U: once a week, in the lead-up to iPad bingo, a food truck came to the side street outside the community great room. The hallway where I sat waiting was empty.

I had already decided not to ask my father for the money—if I wouldn't accept his car for a road-trip to Milwaukee, I couldn't ask him for thousands of dollars for excavation and soil remediation—and I couldn't bring myself to ask my mother to ask Kareem.

Not true. Of course I could listen to Kareem lecture me on the Aga Khan's microfinance program. Again. And I could ask Kingsley.

I didn't want to.

But if I didn't keep things going with the house, then when would Molly and the girls come home and move back in?

And *then* what?

The door to the financial-aid office opened and one of my colleagues left, glancing away. She turned hard to the left.

I did not qualify for a home equity loan from The New U's financial partners. The house, in its current state of partial renovation, did not have an assignable, stable value. The bank had already said the same.

As for my salary, it wasn't in an equity category the college's bank recognized. The loan officer agreed it was funny because I was paid by the college, from the same bank. I hadn't said it was funny. I pointed this out. The loan officer noted it. He began clicking through screens, smiling sadder and sadder.

"Prin, I'm sorry. I'm really sorry. I wish there was something else I could do, but … "

Then he waited, sad-sad-smiling, for me to leave.

Fuck buts, I thought.

I left.

I pulled out my phone and scrolled down until I found the New York number that had been appearing on screen for months. I called.

"This is a message for Kyle. My name is Prin. You've been calling me for a while now and now I'm calling you back to— oh, wait, I think that's you, on the other line. Okay."

4

I WENT TO New York in early December. Kyle proposed breakfast at the Princeton Club. I arrived early, well-caffeinated. No after-effects from the pill I took before going to the airport that morning. Kyle texted that he was running late. When the men behind the counter loudly established that I wasn't *the* member, and that I also wasn't a member of one of several hundred worldwide reciprocal clubs—I stopped them at the Capital Club Bahrain—I was given a brochure and asked to wait in the main floor library.

Bronze busts of famous alumni were set up at the end of book stacks like giant pinecones and walnuts. Up close, they all kind of looked like Dwight Eisenhower. I sat down at a library table and took out my book and placed it beside the brochure and checked my phone. Kyle had texted again. He was sorry, but he'd be here soon!

Kyle texted another time, to see if I was waiting in the lounge or the restaurant. Then he texted an apology that I was in the library. The next message suggested he didn't want to waste any more of my time. He asked if we could meet outside the Equinox on Forty-First. It was just around the corner. We could find a place for breakfast near there.

He walked out of the glass-box antechamber of his health club just as I arrived. He was young and quick, his body lean and angular, uncontrollably alive. He swung down his leather gym bag and shook my hand pneumatically until I let go and looked around.

"So, where shall we go?" I said.

Kyle checked his phone. He rolled his eyes, looked at me, and violently smiled.

"Prin, sorry. I. Am. So. Sorry. But I need to make one quick call and put out a tiny five-alarm fire back at the office. Then it's just you and me talking forever about how we're going to take over the world. Okay? Do you mind if I step over there, just for a second?"

I nodded and waited. At nine in the morning, New York was well into its day. The December air was full of sweet and burnt smells. Men and women in suits sat on stone benches near great bare trees strung up in Christmas lights. Black and brown men were everywhere, carrying black food boxes and brown Amazon boxes, stack after stack after stack after stack.

"Okay, I'm putting this away and now it's just us! Where should we go?" said Kyle.

"It doesn't matter to me. I have to be somewhere for one o'clock." I said.

"Oh, okay. Sure. Wait. You're taking other meetings?"

"Why don't we sit down, wherever, and start talking?"

I wasn't meeting anyone else.

"Wait. I know. YES! The Oyster Bar at Grand Central Station won't be too busy this time of day. Have you seen the place? I mean, in person? Obviously you've seen it in the movies."

"For breakfast?" I said.

"You haven't lived if you haven't had oysters for breakfast at Grand Central Station. I think the great writer Frank Capra said that first, in one of those crazy stories of his. But you already know it, right? Come on, let's do this!"

The Oyster Bar at Grand Central Station didn't open until lunch.

"They must have changed their hours," said Kyle.

I followed him upstairs, where he was overcome by the great blue ceiling with its filigreed zodiac of the heavens. He turned around, dropped his gym bag, and thrust out his arms.

"I love this town!"

"Kyle. Kyle? When we first spoke you said you'd tell me about some opportunities if we met. Your website is password-protected, so I wasn't able to learn very much about your services. Don't worry about breakfast. I'm not hungry. I'd like to hear what you have to offer."

"Why not a walking meeting? *Fast Company* says it's super-efficient," said Kyle.

"Why don't we go to your office?"

"Of course. But it's all the way in Brooklyn. Come on, I never get to visit the city. That's why I'm acting like a tourist now, right?"

"My next appointment is in Brooklyn anyway. Let's go to your office," I said.

"Who are you meeting with? I'm thinking I had an exclusive."

"And I'm thinking you're full of shit. This was a mistake. Goodbye," I said.

"Wait!"

He grabbed my arm and I swung around and pushed him and stepped back as he came at me again. Palms up, like he wanted to surrender. My heart was going hard. Pills and coffees and breathing. This wasn't supposed to happen. This wasn't supposed to feel so good.

"Prin—"

"YEAH?"

The transit police arrived. I did more of the breathing,

introduced myself as a professor—"Congratulations. What's the problem here?"—and told them it was a misunderstanding and that I just wanted to get on with my day. Kyle said nothing. He looked terrified. He showed one of the officers his ticket—a bus ticket, return fare.

To where?

We were walked out of the station and pointed in the general direction of the Port Authority. I began walking the opposite way.

He asked me to wait. Just wait.

My fingers felt crushed, hammered and shocked from touching him. Shocked to life. I breathed in and breathed out. I closed my eyes and saw the troll dolls under the bridge.

"We know Prin's scared. We know he knows, because Prin's very good at living in his head. And because he lives in there so much, when he has to come out, when he has to come up from under the bridge, he has to make a decision. Which troll is he? Is he hiding down there or is he waiting down there? To do what? To who?" the therapist had said.

"To whom," I said.

"Thank you for that. Again. To continue: are you original Prin or new Prin? Which original? Which new? And why not just let all life's Billy goats pass by?"

"So that I can keep living under a bridge?"

"Well, not literally, obviously."

"That's not what literally literally means," I said.

"I appreciate your informing me. Thank you. I'm sensing, in your answer to my question, that you're Professor Prin right now. Good. Do you sense that, too? And why?"

"Well, in fact, the college has shut down and the position I've accepted isn't a professorship, exactly, so I'm not Professor Prin now, or anymore."

"I see you're scrupulous Prin again. Remember, these are the names you chose for the different dolls we're working with. And I think spiritual Prin comes next, doesn't he?" she said.

"Not spiritual Prin. I named it metaphysical Prin."

"And now you're scrupulous Prin and Professor Prin at the same time. You're looking at me right now, Prin, instead of at the troll dolls that have been placed between us. Why?"

"Because, if I remember correctly, the last time I saw you, we had this same conversation, and you said the same things, and asked me the same questions."

"Yes, that's right. Very good. Very good, Prin! But remember, I ask you these questions and we have these conversations until we can move on to other questions and other conversations, and my promise to you as a therapist is to never get tired of being here, with you, until you are ready to go somewhere else. Okay?"

"Let's go somewhere else," I said.

"Let's. If you're ready, I'm ready. I'm just checking my notes here. Okay. Here are three other troll dolls: husband Prin, dad Prin, and son Prin. And over here, on the shelf, is astronaut Prin. Can you put any of them somewhere on the table? Can you take off the spacesuit?"

"I'm not wearing one."

"Molly said at one point it felt to her like you were. You shared that."

"Yes. So. Where should I put these?"

"You don't want to talk about what Molly said? Does she still think so?"

"I don't know."

"And is that by choice, not knowing? And whose choice?"

"I want to do what she wants me to do."

"But it's hard to do that, in a spacesuit, right?"

"I don't know what she wants me to do. I don't know if she does, either."

"Prin, I know you're not comfortable with this language, and I respect that, but acknowledging that you share PTSD with Molly, whether or not you have it, would be helpful."

"Are you saying I gave Molly PTSD?"

"I don't like how that sounds, either. But maybe the situation has given it to her. Wouldn't that explain a lot? What do you think?"

"Like I have said to you, before, I'm convinced that thinking too much, and talking too much, and also, in a way, praying too much, is what got me here."

"Yes. That's good. That's very good. And where is here, for you?"

"It's here. It's holding troll dolls, talking to Dr. Lisa."

"Good, Prin. Yes, you're in the moment. Right here, right now. Not orbiting away from it, like maybe sometimes happens at home?"

"Where should I put these?"

"Very good! Prin, that's the kind of question you should be asking. Well done. Good. Really good. Really, really good. I know it can feel kind of dark and bottomless in these places, but I think we're making some genuine progress here."

My last session with the therapist.

5

"CAN I JUST explain?" said Kyle.

He was standing in front of me on the sidewalk. His eyes were small and black and shining. His phone rang and he answered it and then held out his hand for me to wait a moment. I turned around and joined the jostling city.

Kyle was in front of me again, now walking backwards.

"Please, just hold up, okay? Please! I have someone on the phone who can vouch for me. We both came all this way. Just talk to her. Take my phone. Take it!"

I stepped to the side, to the entrance of a hotel. Kyle blocked me again and held the phone up between us.

"Kyle? Are you still there? Who are you with? Who is this? Who are you? Identify yourself immediately! Who do you think you are, mister? This is Lucille Newton. Who are you? What are you doing with my son in New York City? Did you meet him online? You did, didn't you! Dirty man! You dirty, dirty man!" she said.

"MOM!" said Kyle.

I went into the hotel and found a free wingback in the lobby. Someone was playing Wham!'s "Last Christmas" on a grand piano. Kyle came in and found me and pleaded with the older woman in the chair beside mine.

"Young man, you want me to give up my seat? For you? And, may I ask, are you even staying at this hotel?"

"I'm sorry, he's trying to speak with me. Please don't get up. I will," I said.

She checked for her clutch and left.

Kyle sat down.

I stood up.

Kyle stood up.

"This is ridiculous. Please, leave me alone."

"She still wants to talk to you."

"You mean, your mother?"

"She won't stop. She will find you. She will hunt you down if you don't talk to her. Believe me on this one."

I took the phone.

"Don't you do that again, mister. Kyle told me that you're a professor and that he invited you to meet and discuss another of his latest businesses. Is that correct?"

"Yes."

"Well at least you sound ashamed! I want him home. He's never been outside of Indiana before."

"Indiana?"

We went to a Starbucks. Coffee for me, and a Billy Porter New Year's Eve Ball Frappuccino for Kyle.

"You didn't go to Princeton," I said.

"I took a MOOC there and VPN-tunnelled to New Jersey for the first class."

"And you don't live in Brooklyn."

"I do," said Kyle.

"But your mother wants you to come home, to Indiana."

"She's correct."

"Your mother also said you've never been outside of Indiana," I said.

He nodded.

"I have an appointment in about an hour and I promised your mother I'd at least get you to the bus station to go back ... where?"

Kyle sat up straight with his shoulders back.

"Okay. I am going to be precise in my speech. I am from Brooklyn, Indiana. It's about an hour east of Terre-Haute and less than that north of Bloomington. I grew up there. My mom is a homemaker, and my dad works in a packaging factory in Terre-Haute." said Kyle.

"So what are you doing in New York, proposing to be my agent?" I said.

"Well, you're the first person who ever called me back."

I stared into my coffee. Little bubbles clung to each other around the inner rim. They merged and split into nothing. In the corner of the Starbucks, winter-hatted music students were playing Wham!'s "Last Christmas" on guitar and upright bass and cello.

"Kyle, how old are you?" I said.

"Listen, I paid almost $200 for this gym bag so that I could walk into Equinox and then walk out to meet you and look like the kind of guy who walks out of Equinox to meet you. Will you just let me say what I have to say? And if you're not inter-ested, then I do sincerely apologize for wasting your time. But you came all this way. I've done the work. I have."

"Fine. Tell me your proposal, Kyle."

"Thank you! Okay. Here goes. You ready? You're not going to go all Rain Man on me again? No? Okay. Here goes. Prin, in light of your professional and personal experiences, based on what's publicly available, I can tell you that there are three current opportunities for you to consider ... through my services."

I sipped the coffee.

"So, continue? Okay. Okay! Option one ... a private security and education company with branches in France and Montana is looking for teachers willing to live and work with re-transition-ing radicals ... Two ... a firm from Ottawa, Canada that recruits values-candidates for elections ... in Canada, just to be clear ... Three ... there's an amusement park village in Sri Lanka look-ing for a Greater Toronto Area global brand ambassador ...

"Kyle, finish your drink. It's time to leave."

"You're not taking me seriously."

"That's right. I'm not. I did. I flew down here to meet you, didn't I? And that was a mistake and that's on me. But I am a man with responsibilities. I have a family and I am in a situation where I need to earn some money and I thought you might be able to help me do that because that's what you've been saying on my voicemail for over a year now. But what you're describ-ing is unrealistic and embarrassing for both of us."

"What were you expecting?" said Kyle.

We walked to the Port Authority in silence. Kyle almost said something at every corner but kept looking away. I pointed to the building and left.

"Prin, wait! I have one more idea! Prin!"

My day in New York was made possible by the modest fund I was given as part of my settlement, which let me continue to research representations of sea life in Canadian literature. I could make another such trip in four years. As it happened, just when I was going to meet Kyle, a feminist theatre collective was staging an anti-Disney intervention in an old tropical fish store in Brooklyn. I wanted to investigate whether the play—*The Mermaid's Tale*—was an homage to Margaret Atwood.

By intermission, Kyle had phoned three times and sent seven texts.

What if he actually had an idea?

No. He didn't.

What was I expecting in coming here?

What dignity was I defending, in ignoring him?

And what was wrong with giving someone one more chance?

I looked around the dark lobby—skinny people in floppy hats and jackboots; a grandmother comforting two sobbing little girls. I found a free space beside the counter where people were supposed to check their privilege. But the music—a girl-band speed-metal version of Wham!'s "Last Christmas"—made it impossible to talk on the phone. I stepped away from the smell of krill and the greenish aquarium light into Brooklyn's carbureted cold and called him.

"Hi Kyle."

"Fine. You want to make money? Fine. There's a program that I can apply to, back home. It's a speaker series. And because you gave that TED talky talk about Frank Capra and Ant Man over in the Middle East last year—"

"It was a public lecture on Kafka's *Metamorphosis*."

"Tomato and ketchup. The point is, I can say you're qualified. The topic has to have something to do with the writer Dante and making yourself or the world a better place or something. Ten talks in two days, in a few towns around Terre-Haute, and after expenses and my fees, you'd clear $5,000. Canadian. Are you interested?"

"Yes. If this is real, then yes. Is this real?" I said.

"It's for real. It's boring and small town and it's for real. Let me put you on speaker."

"I don't need to talk to your mother again."

"I hear that! No, I'm just trying to read from the Facebook post. Okay. So, you'd have to give me a paragraph description of your talk and also your resumé. Someone will probably call to confirm you're a real person. As if my word's not good enough."

"Why didn't you mention this earlier?"

"Because, like I said, it's small town and it's boring. That's not what I'm about. That's not the brand I'm building, the influencing I'm looking to influence as an influencer."

"Kyle, I am interested, but I need to know it won't be just another situation like today, where I'm going to show up in Indiana and there's nothing there."

"It's Indiana. There's nothing there. That's why I'm here. That's why I'm trying to—"

"Could I speak to someone other than you about it? And other than your mother?"

"Hold up there. One joke about my mom is fine. I get it. Two's approaching the red line in the sand."

"Understood."

"Anyway, the company my dad works for is the sponsor. Okay? Happy now? Check your email."

The door to the theatre banged open.

"The second act is beginning!"

I left to find a bookstore.

6

TWO DAYS BEFORE going to Milwaukee for Christmas, I flew to Indianapolis. Kyle picked me up in a Tesla. I skipped the pill before the flight. I wasn't dreaming. We drove to the low-rise apartment complex on the outskirts of the city where he'd rented the car that morning. The owner met us at his front stoop, which was covered in bushy tinsel caterpillars. He agreed to give Kyle nearly a full refund because he'd forgotten to take his daughter's car seat out of the Tesla before renting it, and the little girl's mother had been close to killing him.

Kyle warned me, he warned me, but I insisted, and so we took his car instead. The Grand Marquis needed a boost. I turned back and asked for help. The Tesla guy laughed. Kyle's car also needed gas. Still laughing, the Tesla guy made for his own car carrying a camouflage diaper bag and a hard-juking young German Shepherd on a short leash.

Eventually other smokers appeared in the parking lot. They all had jumper cables and jerrycans in their trunks.

"Did you paint the car yourself?" I said, to break the silence.

"A friend helped me. Matte black," said Kyle.

"That's his name?" I said.

"No. His name's Greg."

"Okay. The wheels are very silver," I said.

"Mercury mag wheels. Thanks."

"Kyle, I think we need to keep our costs reasonable, okay? At least, that's my reading of the agreement you signed on my behalf. And because of what you were able to negotiate as a fee, before we even started, which was really good, by the way, and looking at the kinds of places we're going, I don't think it would have gone over well if we'd showed up in a Tesla."

"You're the talent."

Kyle sulked and I went over my notes and the engine sang like Eddie Vedder as we travelled along the highway until we reached the public library in Greencastle. Set back from the street by broad stairs, it was built of red brick and bleached concrete. Four great pillars held up a blank frieze and a pediment, which was also blank save for a dusty round window. The roof was made of orange terracotta tiles. A spiky-headed black iron lamp on a long heavy chain hung in front of a pert burgundy canopy.

Wet snow was falling, the fat flakes splatting like little water balloons on the roof and windshield.

"Perfect," said Kyle.

"Meaning?"

"The starter goes when it rains. Unless we can push the car into a covered spot, we'll have to wait until it dries out."

"There's nothing we can do?"

"Of course there is. Remember?" said Kyle.

"Is there anything we can do other than renting a Tesla, Kyle?"

"Fine."

He got out of the car and slammed the door and took a black tarp out of the trunk and spread it over the hood. He leaned down beside each front tire and secured the corners of the tarp and returned to the car, slamming the door again. He flicked wet snow onto the dashboard.

"Do you want to wait in the car?" I said.

"Who are you, my prom date?"

"There has to be someone in there who's a little more grown-up and a little less whatever you were trying to be in New York—"

"I was just trying to be New York, in New York. Here, who cares what I am?"

"We both have to be at our best for this to work," I said.

"First time in West Central Indiana, I see," said Kyle.

I opened the car door and shielded my notes from the smacking snow. Kyle ran up beside me just as I walked up the library steps, and then he was in front of me, pushing through the front door and greeting everyone like a beaming Jack Nicholson breaking into a bathroom. The librarian was "just so excited to be part of this" but also—and this would prove a recurring theme during my two days of Dante lectures in West Central Indiana—apologetic.

"You know, with the busyness of the holidays and all, it's just so hard to get people out for events," she said.

Seven people listened to me talk about Dante at the Greencastle Public Library, nine at First Christian in Martinsville, almost three hundred students at Cloverdale High School—writhing, texting, sleeping—and again seven, or nine if you count the caregivers, at Miller's Merry Manor in Monrovia. No one came to my final lecture of the first day, in the community café at the Kroger in Paragon, other than Kyle and the in-store nutritionist.

"I mean, this is really interesting, but what is it? And what are you doing here? I guess my question really is, why are you talking about this stuff here, in the Kroger?" she said.

"Are these the same questions you get every day?"

She laughed and nodded and shook her finger at me.

"But really," she said.

"Kyle, do you want to address these questions? Kyle? Kyle!" I said.

"Do you sell avocado toast?"

"Perhaps I can address your questions," I said. "As I understand it, a company from right here in Indiana is sponsoring a lecture series through its charitable division that provides people from all over the state with the opportunity to learn about an important writer from a long time ago whose work continues to be relevant to our lives, today. Dante's journey, as I've been suggesting to all of you, to both of you, well, to you, this afternoon, has a lot to do with learning from others' examples, whether those examples discourage vices or encourage virtues," I said.

"So it's all about making healthy choices?" said the nutritionist.

"You could put it that way."

"Well, I guess your friend Dante and me are doing the same kind of thing for folks!"

We left the Kroger with healthy eating guides and Sloppy Janes. The wet snow had given way to an ambient mist as we drove to the hotel in Bloomington.

"This isn't a hotel," I said.

"You're a professor, aren't you?" said Kyle.

Kyle had sublet a two-person room in a dormitory at Indiana University. The occupants had returned to Beijing for the holidays.

"Look at your face! Prin, I'm not staying here with you. There's a Garth Brooks karaoke party happening in the basement lounge. I'm going to check that out," said Kyle.

"And then?" I said.

"And then? Well, you never know. But I'll find a place to sleep. Trust me. I'll have pictures in the morning."

"Please don't."

"For sure. See you tomorrow," said Kyle.

He lingered on the threshold, checking his phone and generally nodding.

"Kyle, would you like to eat your sandwich in here?"

"Did you want some company? Okay."

We ate in friendly silence at the corner of a glossy white built-in desk. Afterwards, Kyle took the electric kettle and filled it at the kitchenette down the hall. I found teabags and Vitamin-C packets in a wicker steam basket beside two Confucius Institute mugs.

"So," said Kyle.

"So."

"So, what do you think?"

"So far, so good?' I said.

"Sure. But did you mean what you said to the lunch lady at the Kroger?"

"What did I say to her?"

"Well, you were all enthusiastic about what she thought reading Dante meant. That it's all about healthy choices," said Kyle.

"I think it's a way of making sense of the poem that's basically right, yes."

"But you said the same thing to that choir director in the church in Martinsville. He was like, Dante's really all about hell being people out of harmony and heaven being people in harmony. Then same thing, with the director of the old-age home in Monrovia who said Dante's about how doing the same thing every day is a way of punishing yourself versus changing your routine a little bit to get to a better place. And then you did it again with that careers counsellor at Cloverdale High who asked if Dante's about knowing how to be honest about your strengths and your weaknesses in an interview..."

"I thought you were wearing earbuds, the whole time," I said.

"I was. So?"

"Okay."

"So? So what's the deal?"

"To all the people who asked these questions, yes, I was explaining that each question led to another way of making sense of the poem."

"Right. So everybody's basically right—"

"Dante's telling a universal story, Kyle, and the way that universal stories work, when they are great stories, is that everyone can find their—"

"Here we go with the pronouns—"

"We can all find our experiences in these stories, Kyle. I think we saw that, today."

Kyle meditatively stirred his hot Vitamin-C drink with his pinky.

"It looks like you want to say something else," I said.

"I get it that what we, what maybe I was trying to do in New York, didn't make a lot of sense, at least to you. I apologize for what I said about you being out of work and needing cash."

"You didn't say that, exactly. And to be honest, you weren't entirely wrong."

"Story of my life. Anyway, what we're doing doesn't really make sense."

"Meaning?"

"Meaning, you're getting paid $500 ten times over; we're getting paid that much, less my fee, for you to go around Indiana talking about some poetry-writing Italian stalker who died seven hundred years ago. Maybe Dad's right."

"About?"

"He thinks this is a scam. Not what we're doing, but what they're doing while everyone thinks what they're doing is what we're doing."

"Who's the they, Kyle? Do you mean the people behind

the charity that hired us? I spoke to a lawyer from Indianapolis whose firm works for the packaging company and that, oh, I see, that's the company that your dad works for, too. Is that what this is about?"

"He sits around the break room with his buddies and they come up with all kinds of stuff. You know, 'What about the American Worker?' and Huawei phones make guys pee sitting down and Tom Brady gets CRSPR and quinoa makes guys pee sitting down. Perdue Chicken and Purdue Pharma and Purdue University are all the same company. That kind of thing."

"Right, but what are they saying about what we're doing?"

"They're saying that the company's founder is really into Dante, and, whatever, my dad's into tropical fish and Dale collects baffles, but paying you and me all this money to go around talking to not a lot people has to be about something else. The old man's retired and doing something big over at the basketball arenas in town. Lot of new construction jobs, lots of guys driving to work from out-of-state, and lots and lots and lots of rumours about what's going in—luxury golf, Amazon, drone testing, housing for illegals, MMA, Monster Trucks, martial law prepping warehouse, end-times prepping warehouse, NFL winter combine, film studios, fan experiences—*Walking Dead* in one building and *Harry Potter* in the other. I mean, I'd probably go to both. Anyway, none of us really knows what the connections are with all of this. But Dad and his crewmate Dale think something's going on. They don't like the old man's son. They think he's trying to keep the old man busy while he tries to do something with the company, now that he's in charge. Have you met him yet? Hugh? He tells everyone to call him Hugh."

"I haven't met him and I don't really have an opinion about what the company is doing or not doing. But tomorrow morning we start again with the next five lectures. Alright?"

"Okay. I'm on it. Speaking of which, I got friends in low places."

"I don't think anything's going on like that, Kyle, with the company."

"Going on like what? I'm talking Garth Brooks karaoke! Can't you hear what that pretty little thing just started singing downstairs? I think I want to be her friend!"

He left and I called to say goodnight to the girls.

"Dad! When you get here, we're all going for breakfast at the new pancake house! And then ..."

"Dad! We're all going sledding! And then ..."

"Dad! We're going to have a hot chocolate lunch! A lunch that's all hot chocolate! And then ..."

"Dad! Don't worry, we'll have carrot sticks too. Then we'll go skating downtown! And then ... and then ... Mom, take the phone. Please? *Please!*"

"Hi Molly," I said.

"Hi. Kids, go get ready for bed. Go!"

"Sounds like the kids are planning a lot for us when I arrive."

"You'll be here in time for their choir concert, right?" she said.

"I'll need a ride from the airport, unless you want me to rent a car or something," I said.

"Why would I want you to do that?"

"I don't know."

"Everything going okay with your ... lectures?"

"Fine, thanks."

"Do you want to tell me about them?"

"Do you want to hear about them?"

"Alright."

"Alright, as in yes, you want to hear about them?"

"It's getting late, Prin."

"Yeah."

I went to bed with a jagged-feeling heart. Karaoke bellowing below me. On the ceiling above the bed was a galaxy of pinups—Jack Ma and Chinese starlets in crêpe dresses. You could still see them in the phosphorous white light coming from the parking lot. I didn't fall asleep for a long time. I could have taken half a pill but I wanted to be fresh for the morning. And if I arrived in Milwaukee after a sleepless night and a long day of work, all for them—well that would be alright, too.

After midnight, two guitars smashed together downstairs. A few minutes later, there was a knock on the door.

Kyle took the lower bunk.

Jonesville, Taylorsville, Mooresville, Danville: I delivered four of my five Dante lectures the next day. The fifth, a Zoom session hosted by the Young Adult Fellowship at Coatesville United Methodist, was cancelled because of "Internet." Now I could catch an earlier flight to Milwaukee, and I was going to, until I was asked to meet with representatives from the company sponsoring the lectures before going to the airport.

A morally invincible text message.

But she didn't reply.

We drove into Indianapolis and went to an office on the sixth floor of a stumpy tower. The whole place was about to burst into a Christmas party.

"Excuse me, professor, but Hugh's ready for you now. Would you please follow me?" said an older woman in rimless glasses.

"Just me? Okay. Kyle, do you mind waiting—"

But Kyle was already bouncing towards the party room. He was wearing a tinsel boa and carrying a tray of champagne flutes filled with cheesecake and whipped cream.

I was walked down a long hallway decorated in oil paintings and bronze statues—Indiana landscapes, farm-boys and Indians. I entered a room through a panelled door. A man was waiting in there for me.

He was tall, gangly, pink-skinned, and bald. His eyes were popped, and his lips were thin and pink and pursed. He had crammed himself in a corner window. Behind him, the city spread out—muddled, late-afternoon skies were blocked here and there by modest glass-walled buildings. Downtown Indianapolis made me think of TV shows about lawyers.

"Prin, right?" he said.

"Yes. Nice to meet you …"

"Call me Hugh. I'm Charlie Tracker's son. Charlie?"

"The Dante guy?" I said.

Hugh un-boxed himself from the window and went to a table with a pitcher of water and no glasses. I sat down across from him.

"That's a way of putting it, sure. 'The Dante guy.' He'd probably like it, actually. Gourmet salt of the earth. That's my dad."

"I assume you wanted to meet to discuss these Dante talks I've been giving."

"Correct."

He studied me.

"I'm not sure how much you've been told, but I know the attendance at the first set wasn't what anyone hoped for. But it's almost Christmas and, and—"

Hugh held up a hand that looked like it could cover my whole face. My phone started beeping. It was the emergency signal the family had started using after Dragomans.

"Excuse me for a moment," I said.

It was a text from my mother. The only one who actually used the emergency signal.

I thought you were in Milwaukee with Molly and the girls. Why are you in Indiana with this idiot? And do you have your pills?

Under her uncordial text was a screenshot of selfie Kyle, many-times filtered, standing in front of the Christmas party crowd down the hall. "Celebrating my brilliant client Professor Prin lighting up Indiana with inspiring talks about Dante! He's also from Toronto @drake! DM me about doing something together! #Illgiveittosomeonespecial"

I shut off my phone.

"Sorry, Hugh. You were saying? Or, actually, I think I was saying …"

"Look, we're happy with what you've been doing. I wanted to see if you're interested in doing something else."

"Yes. More lectures?" I said.

"No. I said something else."

"Yes."

"But you don't want to hear the details, first?"

Fuck buts.

"Of course. Go ahead."

"So, you're not exactly a Dante scholar. Is that fair to say? I had one of our people look up your research, and it's not in this area. And they also noted you came out of a pretty messy situation in the Middle East a little while back, though the business angle made sense from what I could tell. Everything alright now?"

"Fine. And anyway, obviously I'm not a Dante scholar, but I think I've read enough Dante to give more of these talks to, to—"

"Dumb Americans?"

"I wouldn't put it that way."

"Good. If he catches even a whiff of that kind of thing, you're out. It's already happened. You're not our first interviewee."

51

"You mean your father."

"Correct."

"Kyle, my, Kyle, the one who arranged this, told me your dad is involved with a construction project in Terre-Haute."

"There's a whole team of consultants and domain specialists doing the heavy-lifting."

"And what's his involvement?"

"It was his idea. Charlie—my father—see, he loves Dante. He's loved him since Vietnam. Which sounds weird, I know. There's a story. It's more than a hobby for him. Anyway, I grew up hearing it, reading the comics, then reading him, then going to Florence to see Dante's house—I've promised to take him over there again, actually, this spring, when things at work slow down. I'm probably the only person in the Indiana National Guard who can tell the difference between Malebolge and Malebranche. Which obviously explains my rapid rise through the ranks."

Hugh barked a laugh.

"Anyhow, now he's retired from the company and I've taken over and succeeded him. Part of his agreeing to leave was getting to work on this retirement project of his, which he thinks is going to save our town. Actually, what *I'm* doing is going to save our town."

"What are you doing?"

"Making our company relevant for twenty-first-century America. You don't really need to know more than that about my piece. What you do need to know is that I need my dad focused on his work so that I can focus on mine. That's where you come into the picture."

"Dante, a construction project ..."

Hugh leaned across the table.

"Dad's retirement project is to be the public face of a multimillion-dollar sequenced investment in our town and our company. But he needs to think he's in charge, and he needs someone he can tell his Dante stories to, and he needs someone to send into meetings with the others."

"The others?"

"The others I've let him hire for this. People who worked for him when he ran the company."

"And do they know?"

"Meaning, do I talk to them about Dad, the way I'm talking to you about him?"

"That's right."

"No. They're his people, and they're loyal. They probably have some questions, but they need the work too, so they don't ask."

"And I'd be working with your father and with them? Doing what, exactly?"

"For a while now, there's been this professor working on the project with two of his professor buddies. This is a guy Dad hired years ago to build him a library, and it's really, really not working out with him and now Dad's calling me all the time to complain, and just like that he's asking me what's going on with the company. Which I can't deal with right now."

"So you want to replace the professors with me?"

"No. We're stuck with them. Kind of a package deal, related to the overall plan. Dad can explain if you get that far with him."

"So he's hiring me, or you're hiring me?"

"What do you think?"

"You."

"And what do you think he thinks?"

"Him.

"Can you manage that?"

"Yes."

"Alright. Now, don't sue me, but are you Christian?"

"Catholic."

"Close enough these days. Are you a family man?"

"I am."

"And your wife and kids would be okay with moving to Terre-Haute for a year?"

I waited for the next question.

"Okay. Now, if your interview goes well—meaning, if you can humour him for more than five minutes, unlike the other professors we've interviewed—and you're offered the position, you'd be working *with* my father, and *for* him, as far as he knows, but you'd be working *for* me. We need to have that understanding from the beginning."

"We already do."

"Excellent. Then we'll set up the interview with Dad down in Terre-Haute for after Christmas. Enjoy the rest of your time in Indianapolis."

He laughed and ate almonds from his pocket as he walked me to the door.

7

"PRIN! IT'S YOU! In the flesh! The real Prin! Hi Prin!"

I looked around the airport. Drug-sniffing beagles in tufted vests. I had a prescription.

Things were cotton-swabbed—my eyes, my ears, my tongue. My fingers were playing piano on top of each other. I didn't take it every day, certainly not twice every day, but I wanted it before going to Milwaukee. Not because I was going to Milwaukee, but because I'd had a balloon glass of red wine with Kyle after my meeting with Hugh. He asked that I please keep him part of this.

Whatever this was.

We hugged it out and I left Indianapolis.

I'd sort of fallen asleep in Chicago while waiting for my connection. I was the last passenger to board the flight to Milwaukee. I went back to sleep, immediately, and a flight attendant woke me, and I was the last to leave the plane. Walking happened. Now I was standing inside sliding doors that kept opening and closing, sending in air-sucking blasts of exhaust and cold. But so far as I could tell, and I squeezed my eyes and looked around to make sure, no one was leaving. I stepped back and to the side, and then the doors stayed shut.

I checked my phone. No messages from Molly. The children's Christmas concert started in an hour. If I sat down and napped against the terminal window, would she see me from the curb and wake me? How would she wake me? With a hug? With a hug and a kiss? A kiss? Do I tell her about the pool now, for Christmas? And the Indiana job? Job and a pool? For me, for her? From me. For her.

"Hey! Hi! You're Prin, right? You have to be! Hey! Hi! I'm Wyatt! Molly sent me!" said a very tall man.

"Who?"

"Molly! Your wife!"

"No. No. Who are you?"

"We can talk on the way to the concert. Alright! Let's go!"

Now I was awake.

Wyatt drove a burgundy Mercedes Sprinter. He had five sons. He was really happy to meet me at last. He'd heard so much about me.

Molly was helping backstage at the concert that their home-schooling group was putting on, and so Wyatt had volunteered to pick me up from the airport.

"Oh gosh, look at this traffic. This isn't too great, huh? Nerts! I hope we're not late for the concert because of rush hour. Man, rush hour is just getting worse and worse these days. Do they have a pretty bad rush hour in Toronto?"

" ... "

"The kids are very excited. They've been working so hard. This is going to be awesome. Your girls are really excited you're coming, by the way," he said.

" ... "

In my head, a giant Ken doll in a Christmas sweater was lying on a cookie sheet in an oven, melting in place.

"Okay. Let's see if our friend Mr. Garmin can find us a shortcut to the church," he said.

56

The traffic looked at me like thousands of blinking red eyes.

We were about the same age. Beyond that, there was nothing between us. Nothing. No one. Wyatt was six-feet tall with lit-up blue eyes set deep in a round, *almost* pudgy face. He smiled—he seemed capable only of smiling—and his smile was also lit up, his teeth white and close and a little sharp.

"Care for a little warm-up?"

He pointed to a thermos.

I took a sip.

"Oh, this is, is this just hot water?" I said.

"Mormons aren't big coffee drinkers. Pureness of body and all. Sorry!"

"You're a Mormon?"

"Not sure, I guess, how much Molly's already told you. I mean, about me."

"Sure."

"Did she also mention the whole Mormon-no-Catholic-girlfriend thing, because of the Apostasy and stuff?"

"I'm Catholic," I said.

"Well obviously! You're the lucky guy who married Molly!"

"How much longer until we get there?"

"Mr. Garmin here is saying we're probably about thirty minutes away, which gives us some time to talk! I already texted Molly we're going to be late."

I turned on the broiler.

"Why don't you tell me about *your* wife?" I said.

"Tabitha. Tabby for short, which is funny, because she's almost as tall as I am. She's great. We met at BYU and got married in medical school and moved to Milwaukee and, well, five great little guys later, here we are!"

There we were, stuck at the butt-end of Milwaukee rush-hour traffic. Wyatt kept asking me questions—about Toronto, about Sri Lanka, about what the big deal was with *The*

English Patient, about the food in Indianapolis, the weather in Indianapolis, the driving in Indianapolis. He agreed with each of my answers (which were "Yes" and "No") then laughed in a clear and controlled way before proceeding to the next question.

"Look, Prin, I'm usually a lot more talkative than this. I'm sorry. But, well, I should probably tell you, I've been kind of nervous about meeting you. Actually, I volunteered to pick you up, just so we could have a little chat about things."

"What things?"

"Not sure how else to put it. But anyhow, you probably know that Molly and I reconnected while you were stuck in that awful situation over in the Middle East."

I closed my eyes and watched a troll doll pitchfork a Ken doll.

"Yes. I know Molly's on Facebook," I said.

"Right. You are a fortunate man, let me say. Molly sent out this giant prayer request and somehow it got to me and by then, you know, Facebook was saying you'd been killed."

"Yes, even after I was back in Toronto—"

"Exactly! Oh, sorry, I cut you off. What were you going to say?"

"Nothing."

"Okay. Don't take this the wrong way, but are you familiar with Corinthians 15:29?"

"Not off the top of my head, Wyatt."

"'Else what shall they do which are baptized for the dead, if the dead rise not at all?'"

"I'll take your word for it," I said.

"That's really great, thanks. Trust is important. Anyhow, well, when I saw the news on Facebook about you, I mean the update that you'd been killed, and figuring that of course after we broke up in high school Molly would only marry a fellow Catholic, I prayed for you."

"What's Garmin say? How much longer?"

"It's recalculating. Now we're at, oh boy, now we're at thirty-five minutes! We should still make it. Anyway, I just wanted to let you know that I arranged a kind of special prayer for you, thinking you were dead, like I said," said Wyatt.

"What kind?"

"Oh sure. I'm guessing you're also not familiar with Mormon prayers for the dead, specifically what we call the Baptism for the Dead," said Wyatt.

"Correct."

"Okay, one of the things is, well, it's hard for any of us to know everything about what's going on around us today, but we believe, as Mormons, that, well, we have a pretty good idea of the future, a kind of holy far-sight, you could say, because God gives us that much light. And it's by that light that we have the chance to pray for others, specifically those who have died without being given the gift of faith."

"Your faith."

"Yes. Faith."

"Yours."

"Well, ours, now!"

"Yours."

"Ours."

"Yours. Yours."

"Sorry, I know, this is awkward. You could say it's all about going to heaven, that we're all going to heaven. But when it comes to you, Prin, here's the thing: you're already in heaven."

"I'm sitting beside my wife's Mormon ex-boyfriend in traffic," I said.

"Yeah, that's what makes this so awkward. That's why I wanted to talk before we got to the concert. The day Facebook said you died, I contacted my Temple and volunteered to be baptised for you, that's what we call being a proxy on earth, to get someone into heaven. Anyway, there were a few steps involved, but in the end it all came together. And so, in a manner of speaking, now you're in heaven."

"I'm in Mormon heaven?"

"Just heaven. And just ex-boyfriend."

"How do I get out of Mormon heaven?"

"Well, I mean, that's not something that's part of the dispensation. I mean, who would want to get out of heaven?"

"I'm in Mormon heaven?"

"Just heaven."

"How much longer?"

The concert had already started. Molly must have been backstage. The church basement was packed. Wyatt had saved me a front-row seat, beside him and his father, a squinting, cuddly old man. Like a cross between Charlton Heston and a Care Bear.

We'd arrived near the end of the children's reading of *A Christmas Carol*.

"'He recoiled in terror, for the scene had changed, and now he almost touched a bed: a bare, uncurtained bed: on which, beneath a ragged sheet, there lay something covered up, which, though it was dumb, announced itself in awful language…'"

I went to the bathroom. My shaving kit was in Wyatt's trunk. I washed my face with cold water. The taps were old and the water smelled like flat Coke. I pressed my hands into my face.

Proxy on earth.

Proxy heaven.

Who was Wyatt?

Who was Wyatt, right now?

How to ask?

When?

Why hadn't she mentioned him to me, all these months?

A rat died in our basement ceiling, one winter. Electric floorboard heat.

"It smells like bacon soup down here," said one of the girls.

It made your eyes water, it was so strong.

I never told Molly, and never made it a kid's party bit, but eventually I tried confessing that some part of me liked it. I liked the smell down there. The priest rejected it. He said I wasn't sinning, I just needed to call an exterminator. I told him I was worried that my heart was down there, in the basement, with the rot. He said, when in doubt, pray the *Sursum corda*.

Lift up my heart, Lord.

Sursum corda.

I stayed in the bathroom half-talking and half-praying until I heard applause. Other men came into the bathroom, one of them two-handing a writhing, raging toddler. I left.

"Our next song is sure to wash away those heavy holiday blues," said an older boy at the podium.

He passed the paper to the girl beside him. She stepped in front of the microphone, giggled and apologized, and he leaned over and pointed. They both giggled. The crowd giggled.

"And leave you feeling pure and light and ready to join the shepherds in searching the skies for the Christmas star!" she said.

I found a seat near the back. The singing was loud and off-key, on- and off-beat, and the loudest voices didn't know the words.

Pippa and Maisie, six and eight, my two younger daughters, were in the front row.

It skipped a beat. It came back faster. It lifted up, a little.

They weren't just singing. They were scanning the crowd.

Looking for me.

But even floating on their tiptoes they couldn't see that I was waving. Their mouths were sweet little O's. Earrings caught the spotlights. Their hair was in lily pads, ribbon-tied. Their ribcages, their ribcages, I could see them working hard at their hosannas through their close-fitting dresses, ruby red and emerald green.

Little singing jewels.

My children looked cold in this metal-poled church basement, trying to find me and trying to be heard above the older boys in the back row. Wyatt's sons. Child-giants in khakis and black ties and white short-sleeved dress shirts. One of them wore a hunting horn. Dante came to me. The three giants stuck in deep hell, bellowing *"Raphel mai amecche ʒabi almi"* while my dazzling little girls sang "Hark, now hear the angels sing …"

How many times before you answer me, Lord?

Sursum corda!

Two days later, on Christmas Eve, my older daughters, Philomena and Chiara, called me to a private conference in their double-bunked bedroom in Molly's sister's house. Everyone else was downstairs, eating breakfast. The house sounded and smelled like a waffle factory under attack. A Gregorian Christmas chant was streaming. Pippa and Maisie were outside with the other little cousins and with Florian, the family Dalmadoodle. Whenever my younger daughters couldn't think of anything else to talk about with me, they'd ask if we could get a dog when we all moved back to Toronto.

I never actually said no.

When we all moved back.

The days since the concert had been busy, very busy—almost busy enough. A human-resources officer from Hugh's company called to set up the interview with his father in Terre-Haute for early January, and since then I had been reading Dante in the Great Room. In fact, this was like any other family Christmas, almost. My in-laws treated me perfectly well. Actually, they treated me perfectly, even professionally. I had no idea what they knew about our situation. But they knew something. Did they know more than me? One morning I found a brochure tucked into my Dante: it had a wilted rose on the front cover; it was for a marriage-renewal weekend in Minnesota.

I was staying with Molly in the sewing room, where she'd been sleeping since July.

"Molly? Molly."

Both nights, she went to sleep with her back turned away.

Both mornings she was already at spin class when I woke up. She must have lost twenty, even thirty pounds, since moving to Milwaukee. Where she'd always been full and round, now she was full and firm. She came back from spin class in yoga pants and a light jacket over a tank top. She drank water with lemon and salt. Her face was flushed and her clavicle and shoulder blades and cheekbones were sharp, hollow, Quattrocento.

At night, I wanted to tell her. I would have, if she just turned around. From my sleeping bag on the carpet beside the bed, I wanted to reach up and touch her shoulder.

"Molly? Molly."

I also wanted to ask her why, all of these months, no mention.

Because there was nothing to mention? Because there was something to mention?

"Dad. Dad! Are you listening? Seriously. Did you hear what Philomena just said?" said Chiara during our private conference on Christmas Eve.

"Dad, what are you getting Mom for Christmas?" said Philomena.

"Dad. Dad! Seriously. What are you getting her?" said Chiara.

"You need to call Dr. Wyatt, Dad," said Philomena.

"Dad. Dad! Seriously!" said Chiara.

"I am not calling someone else to get ideas for Mom's Christmas gift. He's a doctor?"

"Dad, look at me," said Philomena.

"Dad, look at her," said Chiara.

I looked.

She had popsicle-stick scars under her nose. Since when did I have a daughter who waxed her upper lip?

"Dad! Dr. Wyatt is buying something for his wife, Dr. Tabby. Rod told me. He's the oldest," said Philomena.

She waited a moment. This was fatal.

"YOU LIKE ROD!" said Chiara.

"Gross," said Philomena.

"YOU DO!" said Chiara.

"He's Mormon," said Philomena.

"Good girl."

They both looked at me.

"Also, you don't have to call these people doctor. Do I ask people to call me professor? Also, you're looking very pretty these days, Philomena," I said.

She rolled her eyes but smiled, just a little.

"Anyway, Rod didn't know what it's called, but it's some kind of exercise bike that lets you go online and ride with other people, from all over the place. He's buying two. He's such a cheugy," said Philomena.

"He's buying bikes for both of them? He's buying his own Christmas gift? Do Mormons even celebrate Christmas?"

"Dad. Dad! This isn't a Catholic-Mormon thing. Seriously!" said Chiara.

"Dad. Dad! Mom goes to spin class with Dr. Tabby," said Philomena.

"And?" I said.

"And? Really?"

"And the other bike's not for himself. It's for ..."

"Oh," I said.

"FINALLY!" said Chiara.

Philomena held my eye. She really held it, and nodded.

"Prin, my goodness, how can we afford this?" said Molly, late Christmas morning.

"You look great, Molly. Like a Qua—"

"These online exercise bikes are so expensive. It makes a new pair of Blundstones seem a little meagre."

"Well, I see how early you have to leave to get to the gym because of homeschooling, so now you can work out right here. You don't have to go anywhere else. With the app and the screen you can bike with people from all over the place. It's supposed to be delivered by the first week of January," I said.

"Wyatt bought one of these for Tabby."

"Yes. Wyatt. The girls mentioned his plan. Chiara said that Philomena liked Tod—"

"Rod."

"And Philomena said *Ew, gross, he's Mormon* or something like that."

"I'll talk to her about that."

"I don't see the need."

"Okay."

"Okay."

"But with all the work on the house, can we afford this?"

"Well, that's the whole point of this interview I have in Terre-Haute, Molly."

"Dante isn't exactly your field, Prin."

"That's part of the reason I'm being recruited, actually. I'd be working closely with the CEO of a company based there. Anyway, I'll know more after the interview. I plan to take the job if it's offered. I can do it without breaking the rules of the settlement with the college. It means moving to Terre-Haute. I'll go back to Toronto when I have to, if there's something with the house. Also, I'll be closer to Milwaukee. I can visit."

"Okay. You're not inviting us to come stay in Terre-Haute?"

"Do you want to?"

"I want to be invited."

"Then you're invited."

"Okay."

"So you're coming?"

She shook her head.

"It's been more than six months, Molly."

"I don't want to do this on Christmas, Prin."

I ran my fingers across my forehead. I played with the fancy butcher paper that had swaddled my Christmas boots. Molly flipped through my copy of the *Divine Comedy*.

"Did you know about Mormon Heaven?" I said.

"What?"

"Mormon Heaven. Did you know that, thanks to your friend Wyatt, your Mormon ex-boyfriend Wyatt, I'm in Mormon Heaven? And that he thinks he's my proxy on Earth?"

"You're not in Mormon Heaven, Prin. You're standing in front of me, on Christmas Day, in my sister's sewing room."

"We know that. And God knows that. *God* God, not Upstate New York God."

"There's no reason to be nasty to Wyatt. He meant well. He means well."

"Present tense."

"Thank *God* God I'm married to an English professor."

"Wrong."

"What?"

We looked at each other. She was trembling at the shoulders. My arms felt so heavy.

"You're married to a *former* English professor. Why have you never mentioned Wyatt?"

"I have. I did."

"When?"

"Years ago. When we first started dating. You told me about breaking up with her. Wende."

"Yes, I remember telling you about that. About her."

"Her. And I told you about breaking up with him."

"Okay. And years later, when I met her again and we had to work together—"

"Had to."

"Really, Molly? You want to do this now, on Christmas?"

"No! I want to go back downstairs. Just stop, please. I don't want to. Stop."

"Why have you never mentioned Wyatt?"

"After the attacks, when everyone thought you were dead and it was all over Facebook for so long, even after you came back, he saw something and somehow made the connection and messaged me to say he was praying for you," she said.

"And you became what, Facebook friends? And now you exercise with his wife?"

"She also homeschools. He made the connection when we moved here."

"How did he know you'd move here? Did you tell him?"

"Facebook."

"So he made the connection between his wife and his ex-girlfriend. He got the two of you together."

"I don't understand why you're spelling this out."

"He's Mormon, Molly."

"Really, Prin?"

She handed me my Dante and walked out of the spare room.

Not lifted up. Zinging and crashing, my heart. I took a deep breath before going back down to Christmas.

But bacon soup.

8

KYLE PICKED ME up from the Indianapolis airport in early January and drove me to Terre-Haute in his father's twenty-year-old Cadillac DeVille. We stopped at a Wal-Mart, where I shed that early morning feeling with Dixie-cup espresso shots. Kyle shotgunned an energy drink.

We turned into a neighbourhood where the streets were named for presidents and generals and Wagner and historic German-Americans. Houses appeared only here and there, all of them set back on massive flat lots walled off by tall trees and well-barbered hedges of evergreen. Eventually we reached a cul-de-sac with one driveway.

"So, are you nervous?" said Kyle.

"No," I said.

"Excited?"

"No."

"Just ... focused? In the zone? In the Dante zone?"

"Right."

"You know, just in case you need me in there, I read some Dante over Christmas."

"Really? And?"

Kyle stopped the car before the driveway. He began squinting. He took a folded paperback copy of *Inferno* out of his jacket pocket, mussed up his longish, spiked hair, and sighed. He began reading. He stopped and hit the steering-wheel with the book. He checked his father's steering-wheel for marks. Then he hit it again.

"Fuckin' Dante ... poetry-writing fa—"

"You read Dante by watching *Seven?*"

"Hey Prin, I'm just trying to lighten the mood a little before you go in there."

"Alright."

"No. Seriously. Are you feeling alright? You need to be up for this."

I had left Milwaukee before New Year's. The stated reason was to get ready for the interview—all the books I needed were in the condo's second-floor hallway. I promised the children I would come back soon, or that they would visit me somewhere really interesting in January. The night before I left for the airport the younger girls barricaded the front door with green-and-gold volumes of the Catholic Encyclopedia and red-and-black volumes of Funk & Wagnalls. Beside the stacks, a crayoned sign: "All the books you need are here, Dad." I took the sign with me.

The older girls were brittle about my leaving earlier than planned. They told me they understood. But they hadn't heard my Christmas Day conversation with Molly. What they *had* heard—passing back and forth in the hallway, pretending to check their phones—was absolutely no conversation between us since Christmas Day.

I waved goodbye from a cab in front of the quiet house, at first light on a cold morning. My children's faces were in the windows, lit up by window-ledge Christmas candles. Blank, sad, knowing without understanding. I wanted to take a picture and send it to Molly.

Post that on Mormon Facebook.

"Let's go, Kyle. We don't want to keep Mr. Tracker waiting."

His house was made of fieldstone and red brick and had a lot of snowy land around it. There was a two-storey quad-car garage off to the side, almost as large as the house itself, with an elaborate heating system bolted to it. The driveway was dry.

"That means it's heated. And did you see how far it goes? Do you have any idea what that would cost? I mean, we're not in Brooklyn anymore."

Kyle got out of the car and went over to my side and opened the door for me. He turned and stiffened and nodded at the older man in a red-plaid hunting jacket now standing at the front door. Kyle leaned one way and then another, trying to see into the house.

"Kyle. I think we're good."

He nodded at me and went back to the driver's side.

"Hold on there, friend. Are you Dan Newton's son?" said the old man.

"Sir, I am, sir. Yes, Kyle Newton. I won the Larry Bird basketball at the company picnic in 2015. I'm also the one who helped arrange Professor Prin's Dante lectures last month, sir."

"Is that a 2003?"

"Sir, it is! Did you, do you want to take it for a test drive?"

"Tell your dad he has good taste in Cadillacs. And tell him that buddy of his, Dale, isn't right about everything."

"Will do! Sir!"

"Okay then."

I followed the old man inside.

We went to a sitting room with floor-to-ceiling windows looking out at a big, flat snowy field that ended at a thick stand of evergreens. There were neatly stacked copies of *National Review* and *Time* on the coffee table. The mantel above the gas fireplace had photographs in black frames—a bride and groom on the front steps of a small-town church; a little boy with big lips in a two-piece velveteen suit and knee socks; two young men in army fatigues, arms around in each other, smiling and smoking and squinting in tropical sunlight; a younger old man surrounded by workers, everyone in light-coloured jeans and company T-shirts cutting a giant cake shaped like a clamshell and decorated with spaceships and laser beams.

"You have a very nice house," I said.

"Thank you, Prin. It's new. Truth be told, I had it built after my wife died a couple of years ago. The old place, over in town, where we raised Hugh, whom I know you met in Indianapolis, was just too big for one man. I would have been rattling around in there. Can I get you anything? Keurig? Diet Coke?"

"I'm fine, thanks."

"Take a seat. So, I understand you're a professor. I actually read something of yours, about seahorses and male anatomy in Canadian literature, I think. Pretty specialized stuff, I have to say. It was published in …"

"*PMLA*."

"Which stands for?"

"*Papers in Marine Literature and Art*."

"Right. And I also know about your situation in the Middle East and that you were involved in an educational business venture there that didn't work out."

"Yes."

"At least, I know what can be known about it."

"I had to sign something."

"I'm not looking for details. But I do commend you for going over in the first place. Whatever you did to get out of there, well, it's none of my business, but congratulations. I know getting out of hell's a lot harder than getting into it. Vietnam."

"Hugh mentioned you were a veteran."

"He's a National Guardsman."

"Yes. He mentioned that as well."

"Trying to impress you! With that!"

"I actually delivered a public lecture on Kafka while I was there, kind of like the Dante talks I gave last month. That's when I met your son."

"I saw the emails about it. Also, you're Catholic, and a family man, correct?"

"Yes."

"Did Hugh say that's what I would ask?"

"He did."

He leaned across the coffee table.

"What else did he say?"

"He said that I would have to move to Terre-Haute, and that the position involves a Dante-related construction project, and that I'd be working closely with you."

"Working with me, or working for me? Which one?"

"Working for you."

"Because I don't need a babysitter with a PhD."

He stood up.

Was the interview over?

"Is the interview over?"

"Follow me."

We walked to the garage. Inside, behind two old Cadillacs in pristine condition, was a staircase to the second floor. Above a solid-wood door was a woodworked sign, the letters burned in florid Germanic script. *Mantua Cave.*

"Up there, behind that door, my friend, is the finest private collection of Dante editions and Dante memorabilia in the entire Midwest. Would you like to take a look?" said Charlie.

"Sure," I said.

"That didn't sound as enthusiastic as I was expecting, Prin. You know, I used to get requests from all over the

73

place—England, Germany, even from the East Coast schools."

"Mr. Tracker, I think I'd be more enthusiastic if I had a sense of what this is all about."

"Fair ball. And look, if this is going to work out, just call me Mr. Tracker in front of my people from the plant—not for me, for them. But otherwise, it's Charlie."

"Understood, Charlie."

"Good. Why don't we go for a drive and you can see for yourself what this is all about? If you're not interested, you can call Dan Newton's son to come pick you up. If you are interested, and I think you're going to be interested, Prin, I really do, then we can come back here and talk, and I can show you my Dantes."

We drove into Terre-Haute. The day was cold and bright and blue. Chimney stacks, exhaust pipes, mouths steaming and smoking. Charlie told me his company was America's largest family-owned packaging company still operating west of Pittsburgh. He founded Tracker Packaging after Vietnam. He'd started with a few employees, and now five hundred people worked for him. Worked for Hugh, he corrected. There had been plenty of offers over the years to move to Arizona and that kind of thing, and the unions had tried to get in there, and multinationals and pension funds from Connecticut and Spain were always trying to buy them, but Charlie and his people had stuck it out in Terre-Haute. Most of the other manufacturing around town—Coke bottles, CDs, DVDs, ICBMs—had either moved or shut down. All the new business was in treatment centres, retirement homes, prisons, and retraining programs. The people were still the same.

"That's what I call the American contrapasso," said Charlie.

"Because in Dante, in hell, you suffer the exact opposite of what you did in life," I said.

"Pretty good for a Canadian seahorse scholar!"

"What do you make packages for?" I said.

"Prin, that's the big question these days. When it comes to clear packaging, and a company our size, the machines can really only handle a few moulds at the scale the client's looking for, and if you pick the wrong one, you're in trouble. Years ago, we almost went all-in on jewel cases for CDs—it made a lot of sense. CDs were just coming out, and there was a major record manufacturer in town. We could have qualified for State and County tax credits, and it's a good story to tell at the Rotary dinners and all. I mean, I was tempted. I was really tempted. The CDs for 'Born in the USA' were stamped right here in Terre-Haute. But those products require a heavy-gauge plastic and the carrying cost on the raw-materials side was just too much for us. And how long until CDs went the way of eight-tracks?, I thought. I mean, I love Springsteen, and we had front-row seats when he played at the old arena, but I didn't think the album was going to sell like they were saying. But they were right, and they found a company in New Jersey, home-team advantage, and after that they weren't interested in having us make cases for their other discs. And thank God! They're almost gone now, and we're still here. Anyway, to answer your question: before they went completely offshore, we used to work with toy companies a lot—action figures, baby dolls, toy guns, miniature tea sets. Turn of the century, we won the sole US clamshell contract for the new Star Wars line. We've held our own against South Korea, then Taiwan, and now China. But that Jar-Jar Binks almost killed us!"

"I see."

"But we survived. And these days, it's mostly clamshells and tubes for ladies' cosmetics. Rigids are an option, more masstige cosmetics is another."

"Massage cosmetics?"

"Masstige. Industry term. Mass market prestige. Actually,

keep that term handy. Anyway, we could even go into confection if we found someone who understands current American eating: we'd want something luxurious, but portion controlled. But never mind my ideas. Hugh has ideas, I know. He has plans. He really wants us to go into medical. Not just medical. He wants us to go into pharmaceutical."

"Pills?"

"Pills."

A man and a woman were walking along the avenue just ahead of us, where the downtown seemed to start—auto-parts stores and Walgreens and Wendy's were giving way to bail bonds and pawnshops and liquor stores and lime-washed bunker bars, their Budweiser signs glowing red against dim, narrow windows trailing scraggy old tinsel. The man was carrying a black garbage bag that bulged with dirty laundry and the woman was pushing a stroller. They were wearing ski jackets over pajama bottoms, plaid and pink. Both had long hair that looked like overcooked pasta, and they walked with a languid-to-rickety bounce, as if their bodies were built of clattering coat hangers. When Charlie drove past, I turned and saw their bony and pocked faces, the deep wells around their vacant eyes. Their mouths were moving like they were chewing gum and chatting, but they were doing neither. They were neither young nor old. Two little kids in washed-out snowsuits sat in the stroller. The older one had her arms around the younger one, who was sitting in her lap holding a Spider-Man.

"Pills," said Charlie.

We continued on through Terre-Haute's little downtown—rows of big-little brick buildings chipped and discoloured and broken up here and there by vacant lots. Downtown Terre-Haute looked like the mouth of a retired hockey player. A few blocks further on was the Wabash River, the cold January air raising steam from its still waters. "I'd quote Dante on the Arno to you, but the people he connects to his river he also puts in hell. I'm long out, thank God!" said Charlie.

"Which puts you where, now?" I said.

"I like that. No one asks me questions like that, Prin. They just humour me because I'm the boss. But your question raises maybe another issue we'll have to discuss if this works out."

"You're either in Purgatory or Paradise, to think in Dante's terms."

"What I think isn't what I believe though, friend. I'm a Christian. I'm not a Catholic."

"No Purgatory."

"For a couple of reasons. But what about you?"

"I'm Catholic."

"So you get to think in Dante and believe in what you think. That situation in the Middle East, I take it that was your inferno?"

"You could say that."

"And now you're in Terre-Haute and you're looking at a job that might keep you here for a year. What about your wife and kids?"

"They're living in Milwaukee while some work's being done on our house in Toronto."

"I'm sure we could find a family-sized place here for all of you."

"I don't expect they'd move."

"Don't want to pull them out of their dance classes and all?"

"Right."

"Sure."

He kept driving. Past a hospital complex we came to a great paved plaza. It led to two basketball arenas. One was old. One was new. A few cars were parked near the entrances. A traffic-attendant booth was set up between the arenas. A chubby man stepped out and waved.

"Here we are, pilgrim. Welcome to Dante's Indiana."

9

"CHARLIE, WHAT'S A Dante theme park?"

"Well sure, everybody has that question."

"And you're the guy to answer it, right?"

He smiled and shifted around in his seat.

"A lot more than the consultants and the professors, I'll tell you."

"So?"

"You ready? You want to hear this? When you do, Prin, you're in for the whole thing."

"Let's hear it."

"Well, you know about Disney World."

"Of course."

"And you know about Genesis Extreme."

"Genesis Extreme? No."

"Doesn't your family watch *America's Got Jesus?*"

"I've heard of it. Something about a boycott, last year.'

"They won't even let us have a TV show anymore."

"I'm guessing you have something in mind that's somewhere between Disney World and a Biblical talent show?"

"More like, a cross between Disney World and a Biblical theme park."

"Okay."

"I don't know how much Hugh told you, or how he put it. How'd he put it?"

"He said this was your retirement project."

Charlie snorted.

"Makes it sound like I'm painting a sailboat or something. Anyway, I know he wants to keep me busy and away from the company. But I'm also looking at this as a businessman, Prin. As a way to help out a town and a lot of folks in need. Because, if we get this right, well, I think there's a lot in Dante that would appeal to a whole lot of people. Different types of people."

"Masstige."

He tapped his nose.

"Can I clear?" said a young Hispanic woman.

She was wearing a black-and-ketchup apron over a white shirt and black bowtie. Charlie thanked her. We were having lunch in an empty Steak 'n Shake. We hadn't gone into either arena. I'd wanted to, but Charlie said it was premature and that we would startle the horses. I asked what horses, and Charlie had suggested burgers.

"People like her, Prin. She can't take her kids to Disney World on Steak 'n Shake money, but she can take them down the street, to a real American theme park. Couple of rides, some games, maybe learn a little, too. And she's not alone, trust me."

I nodded and sipped my malt. Charlie's eyes were bright, his pale cheeks red. Sitting against the hardback booth in his red-plaid hunting shirt, his face so flushed, it looked like the restaurant's deep-red walls were bleeding into him.

How convincing was I, so far?

"Prin, we should play poker sometime. I can see it all over your face. But hear me out. A couple of years ago, when I was getting ready to leave the company, I signed a lease for our town's two empty basketball arenas, a dollar-a-year for fifty years. Hugh and I talked it over, went back and forth, back and forth, you know. Anyway, eventually we landed on a plan. To Hugh's credit, he found some outside investors, and we interviewed a few firms before deciding on Turnstyle Solutions. They've consulted, start-to-finish, on parks and attractions over in China, in Dubai malls, in Texas—and they delivered a full green-light feasibility report for this. I sent copies to city hall. Now, those folks were probably all just happy we cleared out the addicts from the arenas after they built the new one to attract a WNBA team. Which, news flash, didn't work out. What I'm doing isn't some crazy old man idea. Or just a retirement project."

"Of course. Hugh didn't just say this was your retirement project, Charlie. He told me this was serious. A big deal."

"Did he say that too?"

"Absolutely."

"Glad to hear. Not the kind of thing he'd say directly to me, of course. No fault there. Fathers and sons."

"Yes."

"And believe me, I'd love to learn a little more about you. But first, business. Just think about this like I do, for a minute. Basically, the value proposition is this: anybody in Middle America who'd go to both Disney and Genesis Extreme can cut the difference and save money by coming to Dante's Indiana, instead. Did you know, Prin, that something like half of all Americans who call themselves middle-class—and by way the way, *all* Americans call themselves middle-class—live within a day's drive of right here, Terre-Haute, the middle of the middle of the middle of America? That's the main market. And then there's homeschoolers and private-academy types, wanting to bring their kids to something entertaining and educational, and then there's your unicorn-blood types who think *Inferno*'s the only thing he ever wrote, and general amusement-park people, who'll go anywhere, and then the regular people from around here who're looking to go somewhere safe and clean. There used to be lots of good places you could drive to and get home the same day, but now there's only one left. It's outside town. I used to take Hugh there in the summers. These days, I wouldn't ever take my grandkids. You'd never take your kids. No one takes their kids there anymore. Did Hugh really say that?"

"Say what?"

"That this was serious? A really big deal?"

"A sequenced investment in the town and company."

Charlie gave me a funny look.

"That's the way he put it?"

"Something like that, yes."

He nodded.

"Charlie, I'm still having trouble imagining what this is."

He half stood up and stretched out his arms.

"Picture a Great American Heaven and Hell!"

I looked around the empty restaurant.

"Everything will be based on something in Dante but also make sense for your everyday American. Masstige, remember? So there's going to be rides, floor-shows, I don't know, acrobats, sorcerers, spaceships, choirs. People walking around dressed like angels, devils, demons, fireworks, light shows, ice capades. We'll get some iPads set up so you can learn more about Dante, serve some devil dogs, angel-food cake. I'd like to donate my collection and have a dedicated room for it—"

"Your Dante stuff, from above the garage?"

"Not stuff, Prin. Believe me, not just stuff."

"Sorry."

"I want to do it, and he won't let me. Says it's too valuable to let the public see."

"Hugh?"

"No. Somebody else you'd be working with."

He crossed his arms.

"Anyway, the consultants pitched staying on all the way through—the turnkey model, and I was tempted, and obviously

Hugh wanted me to do that. He grills with gas. But I like going with my own people. So we compromised."

"Which means?"

"They retrofitted both arenas for indoor-theme-park use. To qualify for the State credits, they had to hire 50 percent local labour, and Prin, they hired 50.1 percent. But still, those were good jobs, and there's more to come. The next step is to fit out the arenas with rides and concessions, and then hire the service staff and park performers. Turnstyle Solutions gave us a whole list of options for attractions and positions, and they have a team of designers and fabricators to do the finish work, the major ride installations, that kind of thing. But we're behind schedule. We've already missed the summer market and so now we're pegged for the fall. Inferno will open on Halloween, and Paradiso twenty-four hours later."

"What about Purgatory?"

"Fair ball. Look, there were only two vacant arenas, and, well, everybody gets heaven and hell, Prin, and no offence, but Purgatory is more of a, well, you know."

"Yes."

I looked around the empty restaurant, the smudged daylight, the listless streets outside.

How long was I going to be in this place?

"Anyway, at the current pace, that's not going to happen either. But before I call in the consultants to take over, I want to try one more approach. Hugh agrees. I need to add someone to my team. Make a change."

"You want me to replace one of your own people?"

He made a sour face.

"Not exactly one of my own. The guys and the young lady are fine. More than fine. Good people. The problem is, when this all started, we found out that we'd also qualify for a stack of tax breaks if the project could be designated as educational.

It made good sense, business-wise, and so I asked the fellow who helped me put together my Dante collection to sign on as the academic resource. He said yes right away. Maybe too fast. But I can't blame him. As usual, he was between teaching jobs, and the private-rare-books-library-building business isn't booming these days, and it turns out we don't even have to pay him. He qualified for a State retraining program and asked me if he could bring along a couple of his friends. I said sure. Didn't touch our bottom line and we could list them and their PhDs on our reports. Everybody's happy. But then things went sideways."

"How?"

"You ever watch mob shows, Prin?"

"A few."

"So you know what a no-show job is?"

"Yes, I know about no-show jobs."

"Well, tell them then! They show up, every day, and they think they owe it to the tax-payers of Indiana to make sure that every part of our park is educational and based in Dante. They keep saying this is their 'stated academic duty to the project.' Must be in the fine print somewhere. And guess what? There's a problem with every idea! Nothing from the consultants is educational enough or faithful enough to Dante!"

"And you don't want to be arguing with them, yourself."

"Me, in the same room with them? Telling old stories and bringing the donuts? Now *that* would be a retirement project."

"But you can't get rid of them without losing your tax credits."

"Exactly! See? You get it. I wish we'd found you earlier."

"Thanks, Charlie."

"That's right, Prin. You should sit up a little more. I'm interested because you have some educational business experience, and also you're a family man and a professor, but like those talks you gave last month proved, not *that much* of a professor."

"Thanks."

"Don't start slouching again! Take that as a compliment! It is, where I'm sitting. Listen, the kind of people who'll visit Dante's Indiana want to go for a drive while they can still buy gas and have a little fun and see something good and eat something good and sure, maybe learn something, too. But they're not stupid about their money or their time. And from what I can tell about those talks you gave before Christmas, you know how to speak to these kind of folks, unlike some of the others who gave lectures, and you know what Dante was really doing, why he was doing it."

"So it's a good thing I'm not a Dante scholar? I mean, I'm no expert."

"Which is the last thing we need in this country! Look, you're a believer but you don't swing your rosary around, and you can read a footnote without sounding like a footnote. A Catholic professor but not too much of a Catholic professor. Am I right?"

Pool. House.

I nodded.

"This whole thing probably involves millions of dollars."

He nodded and sipped his malt.

Maybe a pool house between the pool and the house?

"You want to know about a sequenced investment? Sixty million is the build and year-one budget for what we're doing here—in industry terms, we're doing a regional-scale, two-venue interconnected indoor theme park. We're already halfway through our funds with those retrofits, which is where we want to be, budget-wise. But our project manager tells me we're not spending like we need to at this point, if we want to open by Halloween, and I believe her. She's fantastic. She grew up in Terre-Haute and her father's been with Tracker Packaging since high school, and she went to Harvard Business School, and I don't care what they say on Fox, she didn't get in because of affirmative action. Or maybe she did, but she would have anyway, and if she didn't, then Charlie Tracker's all for affirmative action. You heard it here first. She's just fantastic. And a delight. Any problem working with an impressive young African-American woman? I mean, any problem I need to know about, right now?"

"No. That won't be a problem."

"Good. Now what she needs, and what I need, what everybody needs, is a go-between. A translator. Someone who can hear things in one kind of language and say the same things in another kind of language. Maybe cut out a few words or add a few, now and then. Not too stuck on one thing versus another, but able to understand why others are, humour them just enough, and go on to the next thing. My private library guy can't do that, God bless him, and damn it, he won't just no-show on the State dime, either."

"So I wouldn't be replacing him."

"No. Like I said, I've read some of your scholarly stuff. We definitely still need him and his buddies on the paperwork to say what we're doing with Dante is educational. And anyway, they're on someone else's payroll. I can't fire them."

"So you want me to convince them to stop showing up for work?"

"Tell them they have to grade papers now. Just kidding. I don't even want to fire them, really. Look around. My rare books guy's done good work for me in the past, with the collection, and I'm loyal. But if they insist on showing up, all they should be doing is, you know, kicking the tires a little. Not puncturing them and then lying down in the middle of the intersection. Like with the boats."

"The boats?"

"You'll see. If you get the job."

I didn't have the job yet.

"So I'd be working with the other professors?"

"More as part of the main team. You'd be working with the project manager and the other team leaders already working with her—in operations and procurement—and you'd check in with me once a week or so, and also, I guess, with Hugh, whenever. I'm looking for a one-year commitment. Six thousand a month, and all the help you need with taxes and immigration. We'll give you an apartment and a car and a travel allowance to see your family or bring them here. That's up to you. There's also a budget for research," said Charlie.

Seventy-two thousand dollars for a year. American. Most of that I could bank. I'd live on jerky and water. They'd come home to a new house, a new pool, new life savings.

"Prin?"

"Sorry. You said a budget for research? You mean books?"

He snorted and jerked his thumb at the restaurant window.

"I have all the books you need."

"Then what?"

"Well, if you want to visit Disney or Genesis Extreme to get some ideas."

"Wasn't Dante from Florence?"

"Good one. I once dragged a teenaged Hugh there with me. Maybe I've had my Purgatory already, right?"

"He mentioned the two of you were going back this spring," I said.

"He said that, huh? Who knows? Maybe it'll actually happen. You travel a lot with your kids?"

"Not lately. As I mentioned, they're in Milwaukee."

"With?"

"With their mother. My wife. That's right. I mentioned this to Hugh as well."

"None of our business, of course. And Hugh's one to talk about family life."

"So what now?" I said.

"Well, it's four o'clock and we've finished our malts and the Sycamores are playing Valpo tonight and I want to vacuum the car before tip-off. Or I can TiVo it and tell you why, I mean really why, I'm doing this. Decision time. What's it going to be, Prin?"

"Show me your Dantes."

10

"I went to Vietnam in 1971. My father was at Normandy. My grandfather fought in the Argonne Forest, under Black Jack Pershing himself. You can find Tracker tombstones in Union and Confederate cemeteries. Military service is something we take seriously, and always have. Hugh could have gone to Afghanistan, even Iraq. He gave out sandwiches at the Superdome during Katrina. Which is neither here nor there, I know. Anyway, I'm telling you this so you'll know that when I went to Vietnam I was a different kind of cherry. I was ready to do what was needed, like my father, and his father, and his fathers, but what a mess. By 1971, nobody who wasn't a career officer could say what was needed in Vietnam, except more drugs and don't be the last man to die for no good reason. And the career officers just said shoot more of them. I won't use the term. I always hated it. I didn't like that shoot-first, shoot-always attitude any more than I liked the lack of discipline with the other grunts. So I was kind of in no man's land.

"Two weeks after I arrived—picture a tailgate party in the jungle, but you were always waiting for somebody to shoot you—our firebase was attacked in the middle of the night by fifty little guys in swim shorts and grease. We were supposed to hand over the base to the South Vietnamese at the end of the month, and they already had a small detachment with us. They weren't touched. Zero casualties, and zero shots fired from their position. Eighty of us were killed. Bodies burned all over the place. To this day, Prin, I cannot be anywhere near a pig roast. It was suffering and burning hell and nobody, not even Dante, *not even Dante*, has anything on the real thing. I know they say he saw men being burned alive in Florence, and that he would have been sentenced to the same thing if he ever came home, but in the poem—in your *Purgatorio*—the most he says is that he remembers the sight of it, not the smell. I don't think anyone can say what it smells like. I don't think anyone should. Anyway, while the brass were planning investigations and who to relieve of duty and that kind of thing, the ARVN guys, the South Vietnamese, wanted to prove their innocence. They wanted to prove they were on our side. Remember, the VC didn't go anywhere near their part of the base, and during the attack they didn't defend. They had a big howitzer mounted, and no shots fired.

"A while after the attack, I don't remember how many days anymore, two Arvins came up to me and another cherry, an Italian fellow from Brooklyn. I didn't really know him at the time. I never did, really. Other guys called him Kelly Blue Book because he obviously wasn't Irish and he was always reading this little blue book. The joke was—he was Italian, and probably a greaser, a mechanic, so what else would he be reading? All I knew was that whatever he was always reading wasn't the Kelly Blue Book and it wasn't the Bible. Anyway, the Arvins wanted to show us something in the village down the road, but there was no way we were leaving the base, or what was left of the base. They kept saying we should come with them. We said no. They went hooch to hooch. Nobody budged. You could tell this was driving them a little crazy. They stopped asking for a couple of days but then started all over again, this time just to come to *their* part of our base. The Italian from Brooklyn puts his book in his pocket and says to me, 'Let's go see.' I said we might be killed, captured, or court-martialled. He said we were already sitting ducks for all three options. He said he was going. Don't ask me why—maybe I was feeling bad I didn't do much of anything except save my own life in the attack, maybe I was thinking about what my father and my grandfather would have done—but I was twenty years old and pretty sure I wasn't going to see twenty-one. So I went."

"And?" I said.

We were sitting in leather chairs in Charlie's private library above his four-car garage. The place hummed with a humidity-optimization system and was lit by warm yellow library lights. The walls were lined in bookcases that shone like dark molasses. It felt like we were sitting in a honeycomb.

The bookcases were filled with editions and commentaries and divided by blown-up photographs of Charlie with Robert Hollander, Roberto Benigni, Tom Hanks. One wall had four clocks, showing the times in Jerusalem, India, Spain, and Indiana. Another wall displayed honorary degrees from Wheaton, Baylor, Grove City, and Dordt, and also elaborate, fat wax citations from the Dante Society of America and Casa Dante, Firenze. In between the bookcases and the leather chairs were tabletop vitrines. They held large, very old books, their covers red and black and dented along the edges, the titles embossed in flaky gold letters, the inside pages frittered here and there. In two other vitrines, long, yellowy sheets rested on pillowy white fabric: dense writing, in black ink, with tendril- and talon-wrapped giant first letters facing drawings of dark woods, lost faces, roiling and torqued bodies.

"So we go, and there's a bunch of them standing around a hut. Inside, all you can hear is a man, and he's crying. Sobbing. Just heaving and crying. Crying and crying. We figure out that they've taken someone from the village that they say knows who attacked us, where they are now, that kind of thing. They're keeping him in the hut until he tells them, so they can prove it wasn't them. What they did in that hut, they did for us. They did *that*, for us."

His voice broke, and he pulled out a handkerchief and blew his nose. His cheeks, so red at lunch, were bone white.

He looked away, nodded to himself, smiled at me, and took a deep breath.

"You alright? Do want to take a moment?"

"Thanks. Happens every time I tell this part. What we did to them, during the war, I mean, you've probably seen pictures. It was awful. What they did to us, same. Same. But what they did to each other during the war … the things you heard about. Back then, I thought they were just trying to scare the new grunts with stories of burying people alive and cutting off men's heads in front of wives and children and that kind of thing. Plus half the guys telling the stories were drunk. The other half were drunk and high. So I just thought they were trying to shake us fresh cherries from the tree. That's what I thought. But then there we were, at the Arvin part of the base, and the man in the hut was crying and it was a weird crying, a bad crying. Two of the Arvins yelled into the hut and the man kept crying as if he didn't hear them or didn't care, and they opened the door and yelled again, kind of like for him to come out. He didn't. They told us to come closer. We didn't. Now these Arvins are getting nervous and twitchy and we weren't given sidearms or anything, and I'm thinking maybe we should go back, but then Kelly Blue Book from Brooklyn says to me 'Keep an eye,' and he goes up to the hut and he thinks about it, and then he looks inside. 'Jesus! NO!' he says, and flies out of there and bangs into me and holds me at the shoulders like he's drunk, and he heads back to his hooch. He stopped and threw up. Threw up again. I watched him go. Then I looked back at the hut. The crying hadn't stopped. The Arvins are telling me to look, too. They're calling me to come and see."

"Did you go? Did you look inside?"

"Two boys and a girl. His kids. His children. They put his children in there with him and starved them to death right in front of him so he would tell who did it, where they were, whatever. Little kids. He probably didn't know anything about the attack. Or he knew everything, but the cause mattered that much. Which is bull. Three little kids, right in front of you? Your own little kids? No cause matters that much. He didn't know anything about the attack and those kids didn't know anything, but they wanted us to see, the Arvins, they wanted us to see they didn't know anything about it, either. This was their way of showing us.

"I went back to find the guy from Brooklyn and he was sitting in his hooch with that blue book on his lap. He wasn't reading. He was just looking down at it, kind of catatonic. It was this blue book, right here," said Charlie.

He handed me a clear plastic bag. Inside was a piece of very soft, butter-yellow leather, wrapped around a small royal-blue book. There was maybe a bird embossed on the front cover; it was hard to make out through the fading and mould. The spine was broken and the cover boards were held in place with a rubber band. You could see some of the loose papers between the boards: Italian on one side, English on the other.

"He was reading Dante in Vietnam," I said.

"Not just reading it, Prin. He was seeing it all around him. He saw Dante in there, in that hut," said Charlie.

"Ugolino."

"Ugolino."

"But the village man, he didn't, he didn't—"

"No. He didn't eat his children like Ugolino in the tower. He just watched them starve to death."

93

"Why do you have his book, Charlie? Is that how you started collecting?"

"Look. I mean, really, look. Over there. In that middle case, I have a 1529 Venetian edition, Prin. Jacopo Da Borgofranco, at the request of the great Lucantonio Giunta. The only other copy in all of America's up the road, at Notre Dame. And a few more editions as good as that. But that little book in your hands, that falling-apart 1958 reprint of the seventeenth edition of J.M. Dent and Sons. Temple Classics. Wheeler translation. Probably sells for pennies over on Amazon. That book matters more to me than anything else in this room."

"Because of who read it before you?"

"Good. You're really listening. The next morning, I woke up and there it was, the book, on the ground beside my cot. He must have left it there before he, well, all we know is that he walked off the base in the middle of the night and even with all the extra watches and the new tripwires after the attack, nobody noticed. I like to think he's still alive out there, somewhere. Maybe I'll run into him at a car show some summer. I mean, if he knew Ugolino's story, he knew the rest of *Inferno* well enough to know what happens to suicides in the next world."

Neither of us spoke for a while.

Money for the house. The pool. Bring them home.

But what was he asking for?

"Still with me, friend?"

"Yes. Yes, I am."

"I thought so. That look."

"What look?"

"The look a man gets when there's more to something than he thought. Am I right?"

"Go on, Charlie."

"Yes. I thought so. I did, Prin. Now, if this works out, about this thing between us: whatever Hugh says about it, whatever goes on outside this room, it needs to be about more than just you getting the job. None of the other professors I've interviewed have gotten this far. Have made me want to get this far. Go this far. Sure, I've built this room and still read a canto a day every day and I've visited Florence and taken the tours and all. But for me, I started reading Dante in country, and I didn't understand a damned thing except that a man could live or die from reading it, which I'd thought was only true of the Bible. But I wanted to read it, to live. So forget the PhD. Have you ever felt like that, Prin, just from reading a book?"

"Yes."

"From Dante? The Bible?"

"No. It was from *A Christmas Carol*, a couple of weeks ago."

"Come again?"

"My kids were in a pageant. I hadn't seen them in a while."

"I see."

"And ... before that, from reading the reheating instructions for the microwave."

"Same problem?"

I put aside his blue book and rubbed the scars on my forehead. Knuckled my eyes. A pulling had started.

"Prin? You with me?"

"I am, Charlie. I am. *I am*. Okay? But what else do you want me to say at this point?"

That I want them back? That I want half a pill? Both?

"What do you *want* to say, Prin? I mean, what do you really want to say?"

"When do I start? I want to start."

"Is that all, Prin? Really? Or is it that you can't because you had to sign something?"

"No. It's not that, Charlie."

A pulling in my chest.

Sursum corda? Here? Now?

"What is it, then, Prin?"

"Something else."

"Someone else?"

"Yes. More than one. I want this job so I can bring them home. So I can go home."

"Good. You've already started. See you next week."

11

I TOLD MOLLY and Lizzie and Kingsley that I was moving to Terre-Haute to work for a wealthy Christian businessman who was building a Dante theme park.

"Okay Prin," said Molly.

"Okay Prin," said Lizzie.

"Okay Prin," said Kingsley.

I didn't tell them about my understanding with Hugh. Their responses would have been

"Okay Prin,"

"Okay Prin,"

"Okay Prin."

I also didn't tell them about my talk with Charlie. I didn't pray about it, either. Whatever was there, was there. Was put there, to get us somewhere else.

I arrived in Terre-Haute in mid-January and reported to Human Resources at Tracker Packaging. I waited in a bright, clean lobby that had healthy plants and fresh copies of *Sports Illustrated* and *USA Today*. Muted television screens showed *The Today Show* and a commercial-free recording of a basketball game. There were other people in the lobby, men and women both older and younger than me. They had tattoos on their forearms and necks.

"Excuse me. Can we ask you something?"

"Sure," I said.

"Do you work for Mr. Tracker?" one of them said.

"I don't work for Tracker Packaging, if that's what you're wondering," I said.

"So then, are you one of these consultants from Chicago or Merck or wherever?"

"No. I'm a professor, and I'm doing some work with Mr. Tracker, Mr. Charlie Tracker."

They left me alone until my number was called.

I was given keys to a company car and to an efficiency apartment twenty minutes from Tracker Packaging and about ten minutes from the arenas. It was located in-between a gas station and rib restaurant on Highway 41, north of town. I found a fast Sunday Mass downtown—widows and winos—bought groceries and unpacked into two bare rooms overlooking eight lanes of sparse traffic. For dinner, I had a single-serve kale Caesar salad after deciding against the sous-vide chicken breast I'd bought at Wal-Mart. It looked like an autopsy sample. Kyle texted and texted. I put photo magnets of the girls on the small, rust-flecked fridge in the kitchenette and put a crucifix and picture of the family on the bedside table, along with my night-time reading—some Cheever stories. Not that anyone noticed. I left my Dante books and computer on the oblong table bolted against the wall between the couch and kitchen counter.

I went over to the couch and sank down and opened the *Divine Comedy* to the fourth canto of *Inferno*. Limbo. A place with no tears, no pain, just an eternal life of hopeless longing.

Tomorrow was my first day. It would begin with four phone calls—Hugh and then Charlie, and then Hugh calling to find out what Charlie had said, and Charlie calling to find out what Hugh had said. After speaking with each Tracker about the other Trackers, I would meet with the project manager and the other members of Charlie's team.

There was still the rest of Sunday ahead.

I could credibly go to sleep in three hours.

I could probably read Dante for about two hours.

I would talk to the girls for five minutes, and then Molly, probably. But what about the other one hundred minutes? I flipped channels—sports, shouty news programs, a piano-filled Christian movie about a guy who works in an office and wants to be more like his black friend.

I turned off the television and went to the window. Terre-Haute's outskirts were a whiter shade of grey. The only places I could walk to from my apartment building were the rib restaurant and the gas station. The rib restaurant offered discounts for veterans and seniors and also had big-rig parking. I looked back at the gas station and saw a large brown-and-gold leonine flag pressed against the window near the cash register, its edges folded over faded placards advertising the state lottery and deer feed. I leaned against the window and squinted.

Could it really be?

I went for a walk to the gas station.

"Which number pump please?" said the attendant, not looking up from his newspaper.

"Actually I didn't come for gas," I said.

"Antifreeze? Lotto? Cigarettes? Vape? iPhone cable? Android? Taquito?"

"Are you from Sri Lanka?"

The man looked at me. He was wearing a tweed blazer over a white golf shirt with a Mobil crest sewn on the breast, and under that, a white turtleneck. He had a straggly mane of grey hair and a barbed grey beard. He looked like an old brown lion, living rough. He lifted a hinged section of the counter and came around to stand beside me. His lofty and disdainful and suspicious face turned sweet—the forehead un-creased, the crushed eyebrows became sunrises, the pursed lips busted into a toothy smile.

"Are you?"

"My parents immigrated from—"

"It is. It can't be, but it is! You are! You are! And you are here!" he said.

He made to leap toward me just as someone else came into the store.

"Hi there, Payatta, pump three and a pack of Marlboros please," said the customer.

The attendant clapped me on both shoulders, as much to make sure I was real as to let me know I shouldn't leave, and returned behind the counter.

"Now say, Payatta, is that fellow over there your—"

"No, no. No. He's just, he's an old friend, visiting us," said the attendant.

The customer, an old white man with a fat grey moustache, nodded at me on his way out. The Sri Lankan man came back from around the counter and again clapped me on the shoulders.

"Who are you then? What's your name?" he said.

"Prin," I said.

"No, what's your good name?"

"Umbiligoda."

"Umbiligoda … Umbiligoda … Kandyan?"

"I think so."

"Sha! That is an old Kandyan name, yes. My people are from down south. My name is Mandilu Joseph Gotoganawardene. My wife calls me Joseph. My friends call me Dilu."

"Didn't that man call you Payatta?"

"My customers. The Americans. They call me Payatta. As in, pay at a pump or pay inside store. Do you understand?"

"I think so."

"Just easier, no, for them and for us. But I *knew* you would understand!"

"I just saw the flag in the window and thought I'd say hello. I should get going."

"Why are you in Terre-Haute? When did you arrive? Just now? I saw nothing on the Facebook or WhatsApp to say a Sri Lankan was coming to town. I can introduce you to all the better Sri Lankans of Indiana. We can have a good chat over a nice chicken biriyani. My wife makes the absolute first-class A-level best. You must come home. You must come home! I can't close the shop now, but, but..."

"I really just wanted to say hello because I saw the flag, like I said—"

"Are you a new doctor at the hospital? What a great honour it would be to welcome you to our humble home."

"I'm not a doctor."

"Lawyer?"

"No."

"Engineer?"

"No."

"Then … Osteopath?"

"I'm a professor."

"A professor! Sha! Of what, biology or chemistry? PHYSICS?"

"English."

He nodded slowly.

I looked around. I was hungry—I'd thrown out that body-bag of chicken. I chose a big, dark plank from one of the beef-jerky displays.

"Please."

"I'm sorry, but I really do need to get going."

"Then take the jerky, please. A small thing between us."

"No, I'm happy to pay for it."

"And I am happy to present it to you on behalf of the Sri Lankan community of Terre-Haute. A bottle of muscle milk to wash it down? You're still a young man!"

"No thanks."

"May I inquire about your family status?"

"I have four daughters."

"You'll die surrounded by love! And your wife?"

"She's not here."

"Understood. Say nothing else. I have a daughter. Unmarried. Still young. Not old. Beautiful girl. Look!"

He showed me pictures of a glaring young brown woman on his phone. I nodded. He nodded. He smiled. I smiled. He nodded and began texting.

"They can be ready in twenty minutes. My wife is there, not to worry. I can't join, but still, even for a nice slice of butter cake? You know what I mean, no? Butter cake?"

"It can't be tonight. I start a new job tomorrow."

"Professor job? At the university?"

"Not exactly. It has to do with the basketball arenas down the road."

"My god."

12

THE NEWER ARENA had a canyon-like atrium that was cold and
dull. All was grey and empty. Cleaning machines droned here
and there. The arena's curved interior walls were covered with
a repeating set of blown-up placards—logos and crests and
coats of arms for Tracker Packaging, the City of Terre-Haute,
Vigo County, the State of Indiana, and the United States.

A security guard sitting beside an EKG backpack looked up
from his tablet. He checked my name and pointed to an escala-
tor. I was early, so I went to one of the deep, narrow concrete
corridors that led to the seats. Black netting had been stretched
over the higher banks of seats. The rows and sections closer to
the playing floor had been removed. The expanded space was
now a massive concrete slab with thick electrical cables coiled
and snaking around it, attached to nothing. Workers puttered
and stared at their phones.

I went back through the concrete corridor to the walkway
lining the bowl of the arena and passed empty steel-counter
concession stands before I found the meeting room. Its outside
wall was all glass. Inside was a conference table and blue
web-backed chairs on wheels. Video screens hung on opposite
walls. In one corner, two older men in khaki pants and satiny
golf shirts were shuffling along a side-table of coffee and Diet
Coke and pastries. At the head of the main table, a young woman

worked on her laptop, sipping a smoothie. A professorial-looking older man—wire glasses and corduroys and a spreading beard—sat next to a pile of books and loose papers and a fat leather dossier clapped full of more loose papers. Beside him was a bulbous coffee mug with a crest on it. He was staring at me as I entered, slowly nodding. Charlie's rare books guy.

My phone buzzed. It was Kyle, texting again—no, this time it was Hugh, reminding me of our call later that morning. *Then* Kyle texted again, to wish me good luck and also to remind me of our call later that morning (there was no call with Kyle later that morning). The young woman looked up from her laptop as I put my phone away.

"You must be Princely! Welcome! Now, do you prefer Professor?" she said.

"Prin is fine, thanks," I said.

"Prin, that's great! My name is Justine. Hello, hi. I'm the Project Lead. Welcome to Charlie's Angels! Sorry, that's the little nickname for this group."

"Thanks. I get it."

The professorial-looking older man snorted and sighed. He turned his mug so its crest faced me, and then turned it again so the crest faced him. Then he turned it back, and back again. This continued.

"Everyone, if we have our coffee and pastry and are ready to begin, I'd like to introduce Prin. And this is meant to be a transition meeting, between you and Professor. Correct?"

"That's my understanding," I said.

More snorts and sighs and mug-turning.

"Hi Prin," said one of the men in khakis.

"Prin," said the other.

"Okay then. I'm sure Prin will have a chance to catch up with Professor more directly, but why don't we give him a chance to learn a little more about the rest of us. Frank, Nick?"

"I'll go first. My name is Frank, and I'm head of procurement. I recently retired from Tracker, where I spent my whole career sourcing whatever was needed for machine retrofits and total changeovers and base materials for our products. I'm ready to go. Rides, games, concessions: whatever it is, wherever, I'll find it."

"But also, you'll work with our partners at Turnstyle Solutions, right Frank?"

"Yes, Justine. Someone just needs to tell me what we need."

"Any New Year's resolutions?" said Justine.

"I need to be better about doing my back exercises," said Frank.

He stood up and arched at the waist and pretended to paint the ceiling.

"Hi there, Prin. My name is Nick, and I'm in charge of the physical plant. I'd been at Tracker for thirty years when Mr. Tracker asked me to do this instead. Basically, my job is to ensure that the guts and bones of Heaven and Hell are working. And a little about myself, well, I think this is kind of funny. My New Year's resolution, as usual, is to eat less Doritos. But guess what I got for Christmas from the wife and kids? They went in on a trip to Cool Ranch, that new Doritos fantasy camp."

The men in khakis laughed.

I smiled and said: "I think that's what Dante would call contra—"

"CONTRAPASSO! Contrapasso. Contrapasso, Dante would call it contrapasso, a term only used once in the entirety of the *Commedia*, but which is its master-hermeneutic, as I'm sure our new colleague *must* know."

"Did you want to go next, Professor?" said Justine.

"No! What I want is release from this sudden contrapasso of my very own! Here I am, a rare books expert who curated the finest collection of privately held Dante materials west of

Boston, who personally recruited colleagues interested in ensuring the integrity of the publicly-engaged scholarship informing this ... theme park, and now I, now we, are meant to report to a ... scholar of marine life in modern *Canadian* literature? With a PhD from Marquette? Marquette! Where is the transparency in this decision-making? Where was the consultation? I never, ever thought I would envy the anonymous suicide of canto thirteen, but at least he could say, '*Io fei gibetto a me de le mie case.*' I'm sure you can look up the English translation ... in your Dover ... Longfellow ... paperback edition!"

He stood up, wiped some of the spittle from around his mouth, stared me down, smiled and nodded at Justine, and stomped out of the room.

"Prin, I am sorry. That is unacceptable behaviour. I will be escalating this," said Justine.

"This is just how professors can be sometimes," I said.

"He's the normal one. Wait until you meet the other two," said Frank.

"Which you'll be doing later this morning, Prin. I think this might be a good time for us to hear about you," said Justine.

"Sure. I'm from Toronto. My wife and I have four daughters and all of them are currently living in Milwaukee—"

"Big East refs are the worst."

"Easy Nick," said Frank.

"To be continued."

"Anyway, when I was lecturing about Dante around here last month, I had a chance to meet both of the Trackers, and in turn was offered this position."

Justine looked at me, waiting for more. They all were. But what? To let them know I was in on it? They weren't, were they?

"And so ... I'm here now and I'm happy to get to work. I'm sure I'll have more to say after I meet the other professors. The Dante professors."

"We looked forward to that, Prin. We've reached a bit of a standstill."

"Prin, listen. I mean, actually listen. What do you hear right now?" said Nick.

"Nothing."

"Exactly. This place needs to be a lot noisier, and pretty darned soon, if we're going to be open for Halloween," said Frank.

"And the issue is, Prin, the professors keep saying no to the options, and because they're the educational leads—"

"And you won't just let us ignore them—"

"It's my name, not yours, Frank, on the project compliance forms," said Justine.

"We're stuck. What we need is actionable Dante stuff. You know what I mean?" said Nick.

"The ground is frozen around Satan, at the end of *Inferno*. Could we put a skating rink in the arena?" I said.

"Exactly! I never thought I'd say this, but it's nice to have a Canadian on the team! We'll look at that right away. But that's not enough. We need more."

"Like what?" I said.

"You can tell Frank we need a tilt-a-whirl, we need those snakes from *Raiders of the Lost Ark*, we need the Mormon Tabernacle Choir, we need a two-headed dog—"

"Cerberus has three heads," said the Professor as he returned to the room. He drank the remainder of his coffee and then pocketed his mug in a stretched-out blazer pocket and gathered his books and papers. He put three pastries in a napkin and deposited them in another blazer pocket. He nodded and smiled at Justine as he left again, his head held high.

"Two-headed, three-headed, headless, it doesn't matter. We need to know, ASAP, what we need for the two arenas, and then Frank and his people will get the stuff for us—"

"And Nick and his people will make sure everything fits and works—"

"And I'll take care of organizing recruitment and hiring and making sure we're on budget, on time," said Justine.

"You three will do all of that, yourself?" I said.

They laughed and looked at each other, proud of themselves but too Midwestern to say so. They weren't in on it.

"Well, we have some help, of course."

"You mean the outside firm, but you three are in charge of the important stuff as far as Charlie's concerned," I said.

"That's right," said Justine.

"Charlie?" said Nick.

"Mr. Tracker," I said.

"At least he didn't say Hugh," said Frank.

"So, Prin, basically what we're saying is …"

"Follow that professor."

"Sounds good," I said.

"Does it really?"

They shook their heads.

The three professors were working out of the visiting team's locker room in the old arena. To get there, I took the path that parkgoers would eventually take, but in reverse. I left future Paradiso by walking down along the concourse that wrapped around the seats and playing floor. I went through a home-team tunnel to future Inferno. A wide tunnel connected the two arenas. I went into it.

Things became cold and dark.

I was walking underground now, between the two arenas. The moving sidewalks weren't working. Motion detectors turned on banks of purple and blue and yellow lights above me. Everything else was dark. An outer darkness.

I could see the bottle. It was beside the pack of extra shaving blades inside the shaving bag on the bathroom counter back at the apartment.

But not *pills*, for me.

Never *pills*.

Which is why I didn't take one before going to work that morning.

I only took them now and then, now and then. For when things came up or when I knew I was going to be in an airport. But the tunnel between the arenas wasn't supposed to look like the tunnel between terminals.

Or like outer space.

Had the pills made me an astronaut?

I didn't take them. Just now and then. Now and then. Right now, if only right now.

I breathed and breathed and opened my eyes—when had I closed them?

I turned and walked up the incline, back to the new arena, squeezing my hands into fists. Hating this. But hating *this* too.

That I hadn't brought a pill.

Also, that I wanted to.

Did I need to?

There were probably cameras down here. Who was watching? Would they send the footage to Hugh? How could I mind his father if I was losing my mind?

Okay Prin.

Okay, Prin.

Okay, Prin.

Don't leave, Dad. Where are you going now? When are you coming back?

I breathed and breathed and opened my eyes. Again, when had I closed them?

I said a prayer.

From somewhere, someone, inside the prayer:

Flush the pills.

Don't leave.

Can't you just flush the pills?

And not just because of who was waiting and watching. But God was waiting and watching, too. Weren't you? Aren't you? Aren't you always? What does *always* mean, between our minds and the mind of God? I could check Catholic internet.

Don't.

Don't leave.

I pressed and pressed and pressed all of it down and to the sides, black waves breaking into black nothing. This was all nothing—nothing!—except inside my head. Get outside of my head.

Don't leave.

I turned back from Paradiso and walked to the end of the tunnel and went into Inferno.

I found another guard. He gave me a paper towel. I wiped my face. He showed me the way to the visiting team's locker room.

I knocked. They didn't answer.

Should I call Hugh and ask him to fire the professors?

But then what, hire new Dante scholars willing to work on a theme park?

The old arena's main lobby was dark and steep and narrow. Greywhite columns framed entry gates to the seats, above which ran a frieze of Homeric young men, farming and playing basketball and reading the Bible.

I called Kyle.

"Done. A friend of a friend of mine can get you through any door in Terre-Haute. He's gunning for fire or police services or even correctional but needs to lose the weight, so these days he's gigging as an eviction-day mover. He can open that door loud or soft, and, for a little more, he'll deal with whatever or whoever is on the other side of that door, and he can do it clean or messy, and clean it up or leave it messy, whatever message you want to send the next tenants. It's up to you, the client," said Kyle.

"No, Kyle. I need you to bring baked brie, water crackers, and grapes to the old basketball arena beside the new one."

"Baked brie? I don't know about that."

"Ask your mom."

"Seriously?"

"Do you want me to see about a job for you or not?"

"Okay okay okay … MOM!"

Kyle arrived with the food, which included a pot of home-made pepper jelly, and after I failed to dismiss him we went back to the scarred locker-room door. I knocked again. I opened the food bag and put it down beside a splintered gap in the door-jamb. The door opened. I picked up the brie and entered and asked them to tell me about their research.

That night, after checking in with Hugh and Charlie, then Hugh again, I went to the apartment and flushed the pills. I called Molly to tell her. I called her ten times, in my head.

If I told her, she'd have questions. If I answered hers, would she answer mine?

Such as:

What's the Mormon understanding of friendship with married ex-girlfriends?

Better to stay cordial, as we had since Christmas, and fill the space between us with procedurals about the house renovation and homeschooling supplies and dance class pricing. The girls called to say good night and ask about my first day on the job and what the theme parks looked like so far. I told them the arenas were empty.

"Wait. Dad, your Dante park is inside a hockey arena?"

"Two arenas. And they're basketball arenas. This isn't Canada," I said.

"Wait. So what's going inside them?"

"That's what I'm here to help figure out. Maybe ask Mom if you can come see?"

"Really? You mean that, Dad? Guess what Dad just said! No! He means it!"

"When?"

"When!"

The heart-belling ring of their voices.

I meant it.

Not just so Molly would hear.

I did mean it.

"Soon, girls."

13

THE NEXT DAY, I asked Frank and Nick and Justine specifically where things were stuck with the professors.

"Start with the boat problem," said Frank.

"Charlie mentioned something about that," I said.

"Just pick one already!" said Nick.

The outside firm had recommended an all-ages boat attraction, and Frank had blown-up pictures from Disney World as examples—Pirates of the Caribbean, Jungle Cruise, and the "It's a small world" tour of the seven continents: all of them involved parkgoers climbing into a realistic ship for a ride, whether stationary and virtual, or fixed to an undertrack course. But apparently none were faithful enough to Dante and Virgil's boat ride over the River Styx with hell's fire-eyed boatman, Charon.

After arranging for them to move out of their shared locker room and into their own private offices in the old arena's luxury boxes, I brought the professors to the meeting room in the new arena, where Frank had set the pictures on easels.

Pastries were had, and then all morning they traded translations and debated whether Dante meant boat or ship, ship-ship or metaphorical ship, metaphorical ship or allegorical ship or anagogical ship. They didn't like any of the Disney options.

I called Kyle, whom I'd hired as my dogsbody ("Kyle Newton, Creatyve," read the business card).

"Which one do you think should be the boat ride in Inferno, Kyle? I need to let Frank and the others know our recommendation by lunch," I said.

"By lunch! Imagine what scholarship would look like if people made decisions by lunch," said another of the professors.

"I'm sorry, but this is part of my stated academic duty to the project. Right Kyle?" I said.

His eyebrows crushed in confusion. I kept nodding at him and soon he began nodding very very fast.

"Exactly! Stated academic duty! They're all old and boring!" he said.

Kyle was scrolling around on his phone.

"Wait. Look at this! What about a cigar boat, with flames painted along the side? That sounds like Dante, right?" he said.

I looked at the professors. They pulled their beards. I checked my watch. They bit their lips. I nodded and made for the door.

"Yes, we all have our stated academic duties to this project," said one of them.

"What about something like those duck-boats they have in Boston?" said the second.

"Painted dark and awful. Awful in the original sense, of course. With drivers dressed up as Charon. Proper ferries, with actual movement," said the third.

"Also, they are, if memory serves, repurposed amphibious military vehicles. I am sure that would appeal to the kind of people coming to this park," said the first.

"But you can't have a fleet of buses driving around inside the arenas," I said.

"Parking lot. Everybody hates the walk to the front gate, am I right?" said Kyle.

We all agreed.

Kyle beamed.

The rest of the week, we worked it out. From the parking lot, the duck-boats would take people into the old arena and deposit them at a bank of elevators, decorated as dark woods. People would go up to the top floor and begin making their way down along the concourse that encircled the playing floor, which had also been expanded, like in Paradiso, thanks to the removal of lower-section seating. When people reached the bottom, they'd go up and down inside a three-faced mechanical Satan eating famous betrayers, which was the outside firm's recommended main attraction. They'd also ride, play, and watch whatever else we put there. Arriving at the new arena, people would begin their journey in the company of a tour guide dressed as Beatrice; there could be gardens of white roses at the top ring of the new arena.

Frank and the others were happy they had something to work with at last.

"But what about the rest, Prin? What's the ride feature for the Satan? Keep it coming."

What was needed before the end of spring were all the things that went between the dark wood and the giant devil, in-between the garden and the roses. January and February, using the options list from the consultants, we worked ourselves into a pretty good rhythm. We came up with mud bogs, bumper cars, whirling teacups, a giant talking eagle, angels on wires, choirs, and ski lifts decorated with wings—demonic black wings and angelic white. They all liked the skating rink idea, too. Meanwhile, Frank and Nick and Justine figured out what could be sourced, built, and bought and went back and forth with Turnstyle Solutions and the work crews. Charlie came in every couple of weeks. He was happy that he finally needed to wear a hardhat and earplugs to walk the arena floors, which were becoming more and more noisy and crowded, Mexican music and Bon Jovi playing on portable speakers under the drilling and cutting and hammering and the flat, urgent beeps of lift trucks.

By early March, Terre-Haute had thawed into dull, ash-flecked brown. On the Saturdays I didn't go to Milwaukee, where, wedged between children on the couch, I'd nap to Netflix shows about sassy girls and their imbecile parents, I read Dante and studied theme-park attraction catalogues in Terre-Haute coffeeshops. On Sunday mornings, I would go either to a candle-guttered, widow-filled church downtown, or to a bright new suburban parish with comfortable seating that was always filled with families. Each a penance for the other.

Every other weeknight, I walked over to the gas station, bought something, and chatted with Payatta about how things in America "weren't like back home." After the third week of deflecting dinner invitations, I was returning empty, yellowy Tupperware containers to Payatta's wife. Charlie invited me over, once a week, for pizza and to watch a game. When I went, if I didn't leave by halftime, he'd start telling me Vietnam stories and asking me what I knew about Hugh's plans at the factory. We texted every few days. Hugh seemed to be in regular contact with Turnstyle Solutions, which confirmed the project was now progressing, on time and on budget. And Charlie was calling him less, which, as far as he was concerned, meant I was doing my job. I spoke to my parents at least once a week. After the first few times, I didn't tell them much about my life in Terre-Haute. They weren't interested. They only asked about Molly and the girls. They only wanted to know when I'd last seen them, and when I'd see them, next. Otherwise, I think they'd given up on humouring me. As if I hadn't been humouring them, for years.

As for Molly, we kept to a vague truce. I visited Milwaukee at least every third weekend, and also at Easter—a Good Friday of hot-cross buns and decade after decade of rosary with everyone else in gloomy and damp suburban woods; a Holy Saturday of egg-dyeing and then late hours in a cold, candle-lit church for the Vigil Mass, little ones sleeping under winter coats, then everyone awake and belled into bright glory; an Easter Sunday of ham and egg-hunting back in those same suburban woods, only now greener and warmer with ribboned children laughing in fresh light. We were, the two of us, alone very rarely. Whenever we were, the focus was on procedural matters. Wyatt didn't come up.

Many times, I could have talked about Dante and Beatrice, about devotion and falling away from devotion and being found and forgiven and brought along, brought home.

It sounded good, in my head.

I slept on the floor.

As for the children: at least they could explain my absence impressively. Their father was building a theme park! I promised they'd come see as soon as there was something good for them to see. I always came back from my Milwaukee visits with folders full of drawings.

The Monday after Easter, before I went to see the professors, I checked in with Justine and Frank and Nick. They all looked sour. When I came in, everyone stopped talking.

"What?" I said.

"Nothing to do you with you," said Frank.

"Or with us," said Justine.

"Oh come on Justine, you must have heard something when you did your updates with Call-Me-Hugh and Mr. Tracker," said Nick.

"I didn't," said Justine.

"What about when you're over at the finance office?" said Frank.

"Nope."

Nick turned to face me, instead, as if I'd asked a question.

"Prin, there have been rumours for years now that the company is up for sale, and we all know what Call-Me-Hugh thinks we should start packaging—"

"Don't even say it," said Frank.

"Let's move on," said Justine.

"Sure," said Frank.

"Well, maybe the point of this theme park is to make enough money to avoid that kind of scenario. Or maybe they've found investors for this, instead of that. I don't know," said Nick.

"Yeah. I don't know. What about you, Prin? What do you know? Huh? Don't you talk to both Trackers?" said Frank.

He got up from the table and did his back exercises.

"Pills," I said.

"What did you say?"

"Pills."

"What about pills?"

Frank had a hard, wild look in his eye.

"I was just wondering, if you have back pain, if there's a prescription."

Frank walked out of the room.

"Prin, I know you didn't mean to offend, but Frank's a little touchy about stuff like that, alright?" said Nick.

"I think we should focus on what we do know, thanks to the good work Prin's been doing with the professors, and staying on task, on time," said Justine.

Frank returned, his face red and wet from washing. There were soap flecks in his beard.

"Where are we with the teacup ride? Too bad we can't see a model in person, huh?"

"Right," said Nick.

No one spoke for a while.

"So, who's going to Tracker Derby next Saturday?" said Justine.

"That's still happening? I figured it would end when Mr. Tracker retired. But good. Sure. I'll go. I'll bring the grand-kids," said Frank.

"Tracker Derby?" I said.

"I've been going since I was a little girl. I love it! A few times a year, Mr. Tracker rents the town's roller-skating arena for his employees and their families. We didn't know if Hugh would continue the tradition, but he has, and in an exciting kind of way. I bet none of you know the big news about this year's version. It's going to be announced tomorrow," said Justine.

"Probably has something to do with Haute Wheels going out of business," said Nick.

"It's looked that way for years," said Frank.

"Kids don't even go to the mall anymore, never mind a roll-er-skating place. I bet Mr. Tracker kept Haute Wheels in busi-ness just by renting it out like he used to. What's Call-Me-Hugh doing instead?" said Nick.

"Hugh's hosting Tracker Derby next Saturday, right here, on the main floor of the new arena! This week he wants us to clear as much of the floor as possible, the cables and everything we can move," she said.

"That won't be hard. We're doing really well with Inferno in the old arena, but we need more actionable Dante for the new one, Prin."

"I know," I said.

"That's, that's actually a pretty good idea. Roller-skating, I mean. Is there anything like it in Dante?" said Nick.

"I'll ask the professors," I said.

"And everyone, just so you all know, apparently he's going

119

to make a big announcement there, too," said Justine.

"So you do know something!" said Frank.

"That's all I know. Alright? Drop it, Frank. Really. Or just ask him yourself."

No one spoke for a while, again.

"Are we invited?" I said.

"We all are, and also the members of our teams. I'm bringing my fiancé. You should definitely bring your family," said Justine.

"Yeah," said Frank.

14

THE GIRLS SAID YES!, and Molly said she'd drive halfway to Terre-Haute so I could take them from there.

"You might enjoy it too, Molly. You never know," I said.

"I could also use a bit of a break, Prin. It's just been me with them since March, more or less. It's been a lot," she said.

They were coming.

And she was driving them halfway.

So I skipped it.

That Saturday, I brought them to my apartment.

"Girls! This is where I live while I'm helping build the theme park!"

They started crying.

The single coffee mug beside the single bowl and plate; the age-ordered arrangement of their drawings on the fridge; the hoard of chips and candy I'd assembled for their visit; the tidy dustiness of the place—the Monday-night containers of salad and Wednesday-night souvlaki boxes piled neatly beside the drying, curry-stained Tupperware containers and stain-less-steel garbage can. I went into the bedroom to put away their bags and listened at the door.

"Stop crying!"

"You stop crying"

"I'm not crying!"

"Your mascara is running. Did Mom say you could wear mascara?"

"Maybe we should get him a dog."

"It's not mascara. Wait. Is it really running? I need a mirror."

"If we get him a dog, could we keep him in Milwaukee?"

"Who says it's going to be a boy dog?"

I looked out at the beige-and-taupe light of Terre-Haute in spring. My heart was flipping and banging around. I didn't record their talking, their tears, and send it to Molly. What kind of win would that be? And my children were here. With me. My heart felt steady and strong.

If only I could believe it. Believe it would last longer than a sigh.

Sursum corda.

I made a fast sign of the cross and returned to the living room.

"Girls, do you think the TV's too big?"

"Dad! That's impossible!"

"Can I turn it on?"

"No! I know how."

"Dad, if you had a puppy, would you name it Don T or Al Gary?"

"Shhhh, Pippa! And it's Dante Allegory."

"Alighieri, Maisie. Right Philomena?"

"Dad, can I get the Wi-Fi password?"

I took them to the gas station and introduced the girls to Payatta ("Please, call me Dilu-Siya"). He wanted his wife and daughter to come to meet them, or come over for dinner that night ("Chicken biryani and a nice love cake for dessert!"), but we were already late for the roller-skating party. Payatta sighed and bobbled as he took back the latest set of empty Tupperware containers and then insisted on free treats for everyone ("one per child please, from that shelf, no, not the King Size, but anything else, no, not the premium gum, well, okay, you have such nice plaits, and your mummy is not with us, what-to-do …").

"Is he related to our Siya?" said Maisie.

"Don't be racist!" said Chiara.

When we arrived at the arena, Tracker Derby was already going strong. Led Zeppelin and the low roar of rolling wheels, like a rock concert inside a waterfall. People were singing choruses and screaming warm words back and forth.

There was popcorn and candy floss, and the main part of the arena was half full of children and older people. Pulling on their roller skates, the girls pointed here and there, all over the building, debating where the angels and demons and rides should go. I saw Charlie standing at the rail of the luxury-box level. I waved, but he was looking at something else.

We began skating, and I saw what Charlie was looking at: Hugh, dousing his daughters in hand sanitizer. I also saw Frank, grinning and gliding around with two small children.

"Prin! These must be the girls! Hello ladies!" said Justine.

She was wearing black pants and a burgundy Harvard hoodie.

She bent in close, and over the rolling and the music, told the girls that her boring fiancé and boring dad wouldn't skate with her.

"Bye Dad!" said Philomena.

"Bye Dad!" said Chiara.

"Bye Dad!" said Maisie.

"Dad, wait for us here in Heaven. Don't go to Hell," said Pippa.

They were off, and I was hip-checked.

"Prin! Those were your daughters, right? I've heard so much about them," said Kyle.

"Really?"

"I love kids!"

"Really?"

"Is that them skating with ... with ... wait, who is that again?"

"Justine."

"Oh, really? Justine, from work? Oh right, right."

"Do you want me to introduce you?"

"No need! I can catch up with them. And this is kind of my chance."

"You know she's engaged, Kyle? And that her fiancé is actually here?"

Kyle rolled his eyes.

"He's not here, Prin. He's way over there, not skating. I overheard him explaining something something reconstructive knee surgery after the Harvard-Yale game, then, something something more reconstructive knee surgery after the Afghanistan thing ... loser!"

He shot off. I looked around. There were many little ones in the arena, all with older siblings or grandparents. Other than Hugh, I was the only parent here with his own children. The seating area was empty other than a few very old people and a severely disabled child in a wheelchair. Kyle was manoeuvring the child onto the rink, pointed at Justine.

Someone clapped my shoulder.

"Prin, are those your little girls over there? They're just beautiful," said Nick.

"Thanks, Nick. What about you? Anyone here?" I said.

"No, I'm solo this weekend. My wife's up in Champaign with my two daughters and their kids for the weekend."

"Is that where your daughters live?"

Nick cleared his voice and looked me straight in the eye.

"No. They're there for a tournament."

"Basketball?"

"My grandchildren are in competitive dance. All of my

grandchildren, Prin. That's right, even the boys do it. So did Walter Payton. Alright? Do we have a problem with that?"

"My daughters dance too."

Nick nodded, still looking me straight in the eye.

"I see Frank over there, I'm guessing ... with his grandchildren?" I said.

"That's right. They live with him and his wife."

"And his daughter?"

"Megan. Not a subject Frank likes to discuss, as you might have noticed the other day."

"When did she come up?"

"Pills."

"Oh."

"So did you see that Charlie, Mr. Tracker, is also here?"

"I thought I saw him up top. I wonder if he's here because of whatever Call-Me-Hugh is going to announce."

"Latest I heard is that he's going to pull the plug on the Dante project because he's sold the arenas to a South Korean video-game company that's going to hold tournaments in here and have the tie-in merch packaged at Tracker. Who would pay to watch a kid play Nintendo?"

"Do you really think that's going to happen?"

"No. People are just nervous over at the plant these days, Prin. Nobody likes Call-Me-Hugh or trusts him or understands the Dante park idea. They think it's some kind of diversion from what he's really trying to do. I mean, at least Mr. Tracker lived in town when he ran the company. You saw him at church, at games, down at the river for fireworks on the Fourth. We only see Hugh when it's something. And sure, this is nice, roller-skating in the arena, but I talk to people over at the plant. Something's going on. Slicker and slicker visitors, I hear. Not just product-rep slick, but Euro slick. Euro-lady-lawyer slick. You don't know anything, do you?"

"Pardon? I didn't hear you. The music."

"Sure. Keep your nose clean. By the way, Frank and I are really pleased with what you've been getting out of the professors. Grateful, actually. Things are finally moving."

"Good."

"There's always a 'but,' Prin. We're working at a much better pace with you here, BUT Frank and I are still worried those theme-park consultants are going to come in with all of their iPads and either Call-Me-Hugh or Mr. Tracker's going to call for a total changeover."

"Which is?"

"Replacing all your machinery, completely. As in, us. We can avoid it if we get moving and at least decide on the major rides for each park. Which is why Frank and I were talking, you know, about what we used to like in amusement parks when we were kids, and we thought, or, I guess it was Frank's idea, but I agreed, hey, why not fire things up by visiting one? Take it to the next level, like."

"Staff trip to Disney World?"

"Yeah right! Like the Chinese need more of my money! Growing up around here, Prin, people like us didn't go to Disney. Maybe a few saved up for a year, or someone got a Make-a-Wish trip, and probably Mr. Tracker took Call-Me-Hugh, but our dads worked on the line. We went to summer fairs and parks you could drive to and back in a day, before the next shift. There's at least one still going around here. It has kind of a funny name, and maybe not the best reputation anymore, but Frank and I thought we could drive out for a lookaround anyway. You could come along if you want."

"Okay."

Nick skated away to say hello to the girls, who were smiling and mugging with the boy in the wheelchair. Kyle stood beside Justine, his face contorted with cool and longing.

The deejay called everyone into a circle and held a limbo contest that Justine and Pippa won while holding hands after defeating two rail-thin accountants in the final. Afterwards, everyone did the hokey pokey. When the song finished, Hugh came into the middle on his rollerblades. The deejay handed him a microphone.

Wringing hands, biting nails, glaring eyes.

Pippa looked over at me, already bored. I looked at the others. They were pressing down on her shoulders, in case she broke for a victory lap.

Frank took his grandchildren and left through an emergency exit. The alarm went off and the door slammed. People jumped and held hands to their ears until the alarm and flashing lights stopped. You could hear Hugh breathing into the microphone.

"Hello everyone, it's me, Hugh. On behalf of my father and the entire Tracker Packaging family, I'm excited to welcome you here today, joined by my daughters Emma and Ava, who are also really happy to be visiting … I'm also really happy we were able to host the Derby here in this beautiful new facility that's going to be a great addition to Terre-Haute very soon, and that Tracker Packaging is proud to support, alongside some fantastic partners. We all know there's been some challenges in our town over the last little while. The good news is, well, I know I mentioned there was going to be an announcement, but we're not quite ready yet. I'll share the news over at the plant in a couple of weeks, with some special guests joining us. So for now, unless my dad wants to say anything … okay … I just want to say: enjoy the rest of the new Tracker Derby and … okay, thanks."

Hugh handed the microphone back to the deejay and said something and the music started but all you could hear were alarms and the emergency doors slamming again and again.

15

THAT SUNDAY AFTERNOON, Molly met me in the parking lot of a resto-gas station. I hugged them all and drove back to Terre-Haute, my soul brimful of soda water.

The next morning, Nick and Frank picked me up in front of my apartment for our visit to Dizzy's World, the only amusement park still open in the area. I brought along a multi-pack of Pringles left over from the girls' visit. It was my way of helping Nick stay off the Doritos. This got a good laugh, and I liked that these guys liked me, too. I didn't say much from the narrow bench backseat of Frank's burgundy crew cab F-150, which was space-shuttle clean and smelt like a lemon grove of baby wipes. With talk radio hollering—"Today, on the Perry Schlaffler Show: the brilliant host of *Breakfast at Tiffany Trump's*, the truth behind Jerusalem artichokes, and more of your calls about the Garyon Jackson case"—I listened to Nick and Frank trade stories about what they'd eaten, ridden, thrown up, and won on their many trips to Dizzy's World, back when they were young, and when they were dating their wives, and when their kids were young. Lots, in all cases, even if the rides and attractions had changed over the years. Neither of them had been to the park since the end of the American century.

Terre-Haute thinned out fast along Highway 42 after it stopped running beside the eastbound interstate. For forty minutes we rode through big, flat farmland, the ground in springtime looking like blanched brown rubble, no longer frozen but not yet furrowed. Industrial sprinklers lined the fields' far edges like giant steel crabs waiting for the go-ahead. Beside newer and older and busted up and fossilized barns were all kinds of cars and trucks, four-wheelers, dirt bikes, and at least one army jeep. Some were on blocks, others were tarped, all were American. The farmstead houses were generally older but dignified, or tiny and dollhouse-perfect, or tiny and maybe abandoned, with front curtains that looked like they'd been closed since the day the officer and chaplain knocked on the door with news from Normandy, Vietnam, Afghanistan. Beside the long, straight drives and bright, fat, hatchet mailboxes were shuttered vegetable stands, some with signs promising to *See you next summer*, others still offering fruit pies and silky corn *sweeter than sugar*. Closer to the road, there were cars for sale, and signs—homemade, professional, and professionally made to look homemade—asking you to choose adoption, love Jesus, support the troops, study Natural Law, support the police, bring back the gold standard, never forget 9/11, never forget 9/11 was an inside job, John 3:16, John 3:16, Make America Great Again, Make American Great Again, Again and Again and Again!, Comet is coming for our children, vote Yes or No to assorted Indiana Ballot Measures, sheriffs, judges, Just Say No to MAT Clinics, and also God bless America. Some of the farms had deer stands, and a few had billboards: half were advertisements to advertise *here*, and the rest were for bankruptcy-protection services, treatment clinics, churches, the nearest Cracker Barrel, and law firms specializing in workplace-accident settlements.

Just before farmland gave way to a sudden, sharp bolt of evergreen forest, a billboard. A circus showman with a spinning globe for a head promised fun for the whole family, just three miles and five minutes ahead. He pointed towards a park that looked like a walled medieval city. Surrounding the globe-headed showman was a constellation of starry-eyed, apple-cheeked children. The sign was faded and peeling, and the children's faces looked scabrous and anemic. Three more billboards counted down miles and minutes to the destination.

"Are you sure this place is open?" I said.

"There's cars in the parking lot," said Nick.

"There's people in the parking lot," said Frank.

"And what's the plan again?" I said.

"Yeah, Frank, this was your idea. Don't get me wrong, I like thinking about the old days and all, but what's the goal here?"

"We can't exactly drive to Disney World, and obviously we can't get tickets on short notice to that creationism park down in Kentucky."

"Do you mean Genesis Extreme, or BJ's Bible World?"

"Genesis Extreme. BJ's Bible World moved to Tennessee after they lost that court case. Whereas Dizzy's World is right here, near town. The plan is, we'll walk through and figure out if there's anything—ideas, or even models, at least for the main rides, like those spinning teacups for doomed lovers, right Prin?"

"Yes, Paolo and Francesca. Forever whirling around each other."

"See? So yeah, stuff we could use for the park. Then Prin brings it back to the professors and gets them on board and either we send it to the consultants or tender it ourselves. Okay?"

Nick and I nodded.

There were maybe a dozen vehicles in the gravel parking lot, rusted-out family vans and cars with garbage bags blocking the rear windows. At opposite ends were a BMW 323 and a Chrysler 500. Both were black, with tinted windows and fat mag-hearted wheels. Their engines were on, music was on, and their front windows went up and down for each rag-and-bone visitor. There were so many of them, it was hard to think that even in this little parking lot in a little town in Indiana, it had undone so many of them. Some were standing still, but most were slouching towards nothing in particular. They were just shuffling around the parking lot, back and forth, back and forth, between the black cars and their cars and a couple of picnic tables, back and forth between scores and getting enough money to get to score.

"Frank, are you sure this is a good idea?" said Nick.

"We're already here. And they're in the parking lot, not in the park."

"They're not really hiding what's going on," I said.

"We're not in Kansas anymore," said Nick.

"We're in Indiana," said Frank.

We parked away from the other cars and walked to the park entrance. The security guard was sleeping.

Three women approached us. The first had stringy hair. The second had almost no hair. The third had serpentine dreadlocks. All were pockmarked and scratching their chests. The first asked if we had any clean needles. The second asked if any of us was Arun, or when Arun was coming. The third asked for a ride to ... work? We kept walking. The women followed for a few steps, then turned back. Others came up and backed away, surprised we were real and here.

Dizzy's World was open. It seemed medieval-ish. The front of it was a palisade made of chopped-down telephone poles topped by vacant flagstaffs.

The ticket booths, single-person boxes painted long ago to look like ladies-in-waiting and men-at-arms, were shuttered and barred and padlocked and double-bolted. One had a message written in ballpoint pen on a piece of cardboard, directing visitors to the snack bar to buy tickets.

The counterman was big. He was big in the chest, arms, neck, and face. It was a cold spring day and he was wearing a clean, white T-shirt, as if to show off his muscles, but no: he was showing off his unmarked arms. We couldn't see his bottom half, and the top part of his bald head was cut off by the menu board, which was sponsored by Crystal Pepsi. In the back corner of the snack bar, a brown dog in a studded black collar worked over a big white bone.

"You law enforcement?" the counterman said.

"No," said Frank.

"NARCAN reps? You're supposed to call first."

"No. We'd like three tickets to the park," said Nick.

"Lawyers? Caseworkers? Church people?"

"No," said Frank.

"Family? Looking for somebody?"

No one answered. Nick was looking at Frank, who was texting.

"Got a picture? I don't know their names, but I'd probably know the face."

Frank was now staring at the counterman, chewing his lower lip, gripping his phone.

"Would you really know the face? Even from an old picture?" said Frank.

"Probably. I don't know. Maybe. Most of them come by for something every day or so."

"Are you saying that all of them are in the parking lot?" said Frank.

"No. That's not what I'm saying. I'm saying Park Security isn't what it used to be."

"Can we actually go into the park?" said Nick.

"You can. But if you want to ride anything or play a game, you need to come tell me. We're on reduced staff, and that's me."

"So then, three tickets," said Frank.

"Okay. None of my business what you do in there, but just so you know, law enforcement does come through, uniform *and* plainclothes."

"We're here for research," I said.

"And my dad read *Hustler* for the articles."

"We're working on the new Dante theme park in town. We're looking for some ideas that would make sense for the two arenas: Heaven and Hell," I said.

"You're in the right place. Fifty percent at least."

"I used to come here when I was a kid. Felt like heaven back then. I used to bring my kids," said Nick.

"Yeah, I know. Cash only," said the counterman.

Beyond the snack bar, the park was a broad spread of asphalt broken up by rusty kiddie rides, vacant concession stands, and empty game stalls.

"One summer, I won a Walkman for my daughter, right there. We went to Arby's to celebrate. Megan loved Arby's. Loves. We were right there," said Frank.

He pointed at a stall that had wire baskets full of baseballs. There were broken beer bottles all over the ground. Frank pretended to pitch a ball or two, then winced and pressed the small of his back. He pretended to paint the sky until the pinch went away.

"Does your daughter live in town?" I said.

"Let's keep walking," said Frank.

We passed Iron-On Maiden, a make-your-own-T-shirt kiosk, and a karaoke recording studio called Crewsade. Both were stripped bare. It felt like we were walking through the ghost of an amusement park. We came to the centre, a massive, plastic-and-metal elm tree attached to an industrial-sized winch. Above the tree's fudge-brown limbs and trunk, peeka-boo windows were cut into the metallic greenery. There was a small, arched door in the middle of the trunk. The door was closed.

"The twirling elf tree!" said Nick.

"Yeah," said Frank.

"I could spend all day in there, and it was perfect. I used to think that was what it was like, to be kind of like God—sitting still, above it all, in one of the windows, with everyone looking up trying to find you, knowing you're there, and smiling when they see you, and you smiling down at them and watching the whole world circling around you. Is there something like that, in Dante, Prin?" said Nick.

The door opened.

Head first, body part by body part, a young man crawled out, his chin dragging on the ground. Feet first, on her belly, a woman slid out after him. They were skinny enough to fit through the child-size entrance. They looked at us sleepily, then walked away slowly. After a time, two little boys also came out of the tree. They followed their parents, the bigger one holding onto the smaller one by his backpack.

"I really don't think this is the place for us," I said.

"Just keep walking. It's not the place for those kids either, but they're here. People's kids are here," said Frank.

We went past a boarded-up, burnt-out House of Horrors and a padlocked water ride, past little stages missing lights and wiring, and a puppet theatre with torn-off curtains. We came to the spinning teacup ride. Each cup had a toothy bar wench painted on it. Tea and Strumpets. There were people splayed out in a few of the teacups, false-dreaming. In one of them, there was movement. A man and a woman. Nick and I walked faster.

"Frank! We've seen it! Fine! Let's go! What the hell are you doing?" said Nick.

Frank kept looking.

"Let's get out of here," said Nick.

"I agree," I said.

Frank joined us.

"We're here for work. We came to get ideas for the park and we're being paid for this day and I intend to fulfil my responsibilities and my commitments."

"Easy, Frank. We all know why we're here. At least, I know why I'm here, and why Prin's here. What about you?"

"If you want to go back, fine. You can wait in the truck," said Frank.

He was already walking ahead, straight towards the park's main ride.

It was a small wooden rollercoaster. It was old, but didn't look broken down like everything else, maybe because it had always been wind-washed and a little rickety. A cut-out wooden knight held a sword sideways beside the entry gate, indicating how tall you had to be to ride the dragon. There wasn't much to it, as far as rollercoasters go. It had a short, flat run that led into a single, steep ascent, which turned into a gradual drop that crested as a long, easy curve that eventually returned you to the start. The ride wouldn't take more than a minute. The front car had a fierce dragon face, and the rest were patterned in electric-green scales. The middle cars had arching wingtips, the last one a barbed black tail.

"Actually, that's perfect," I said.

"For what?" said Nick.

"In the middle of *Inferno*, Dante and Virgil are stuck because they can't go any further on foot. They're surrounded by rivers of blood and deserts of fire. So they take a ride on this human-faced monster. I don't remember its name, but it's kind of like a giant scorpion or snake. So far, all the other professors have done to translate that part of the poem is paint the monster's body between two of the levels and have people walk down the ramp," I said.

"That's so boring! I mean, I don't understand ninety percent of what's going on in Dante, even after the PowerPoint version you had them put together for us, Prin, but even I can see something scary and fun—and also true to what happens in the story—in a rollercoaster that looks like a monster. I mean, this is what we really want for the park, right? We're not there yet, with the Satan ride, but people will come just for a good rollercoaster. Who wants to walk when you can roll? Right, Frank?" said Nick.

"Yeah, sure. That could work," said Frank.

He was texting and looking around, scanning, searching.

"Do you think we could replicate this to fit in an arena? Or source it somewhere else? Or even—not like it's getting any use here—if it can be reconditioned, maybe we could take it! Obviously we'd have to get engineering drawings, and then we'd have to safety it, and—actually, it might just be easier to go with a custom build based on this. What do you think, Frank? You're procurement," said Nick.

"Yeah," said Frank.

Nick wanted measurements. He counted the steps it took him to go around the ride, and then, groaning a little with the effort, he bent down and tried to figure out the power supply, the state of the track, the wooden frame.

I waited beside Frank until Nick came back.

"This thing would turn into kindling if we tried to move it, but Frank, with six months' lead time before we start test-ing everything in September, we could design-concept it now and have our main ride for Inferno, right here, ready for open-ing day. Right, Frank? And Terre-Haute people who come to the park are probably going to remember and kind of like that we're doing something inspired by Dizzy's World, right? Frank?"

"Yeah. Yeah, sounds good," said Frank.

He kept texting.

"Frank! You're worse than a middle-schooler with that phone," said Nick.

"Sorry. My wife keeps texting me."

"Prin, could you take a few shots for us? I just need to talk to Frank about something."

I took his phone and went around the rollercoaster, then along the platform, taking pictures. Every few, I looked back at Frank and Nick. Two sixty-year-old men in Dockers and hard-toed shoes, arguing. Nick hugged Frank, who didn't hug him back.

They agreed—Nick announced they agreed—there was nothing else to see in the park.

The passenger-side window of Frank's truck was shattered. The glovebox was open, and papers were strewn on the floor-mats. The highway transponder and garage-door opener were gone, as was the backrest on the driver's seat and the charger cable and dashboard mount for Frank's phone. The navigation screen was cracked and its metal lining scuffed and dented. Someone had tried to prise it out of the console with the bent, blackened spoon that was sitting on the driver's seat. The tins of Pringles were dumped out and thrown aside.

Pringles, all the way down.

We looked around. The same cars were there, and the same cragged, wandering people. A few were now watching us.

"Should I get the security guard? Should I at least wake him up?" I said.

"He wasn't sleeping. That's probably why he took this job. His paycheck's going right into his veins," said Frank.

"This was a mistake. Let's clean this up and get out of here," said Nick.

"Should we just sweep the glass out onto the pavement?" I said.

"We probably wouldn't be the first to do it. Hey, careful moving those papers around, Frank. They're covered in broken glass," said Nick.

"The Arby's coupons! The Arby's coupons!"

"What?"

"They're gone! Look down there. No, I'm serious. Come in here, and look down there. LOOK! My Burger King coupons are still there. My Jimmy Johns, my Potbellies, my Domino's. But the Arby's coupons are gone, Nick. Gone!"

Frank stepped back and away from the truck. His face was red and lit up and his eyes were big and glassy, like he was about to cry and just won the lottery and might stab someone. He kept opening and closing his hands, clutching air. He turned to look at the crowd in the parking lot and began running.

"Megan! Megan! Where's Megan! Which one of you knows where Megan is?! I'll give you money if you tell me where Megan is! Where's Megan! Megan! Who knows Megan?"

"Come on, Prin!"

Nick went.

I didn't.

Smashed glass.

Screaming, running men.

But they were in my head. And in front of me was a man running and screaming his daughter's name.

I caught up with Nick and we reached Frank, who was taking out his wallet.

Suddenly, everyone knew Megan.

Nick told them to get away and pressed down on Frank's hands to make him put his wallet back in his pocket. Most of the people wandered off, mouths agape. Two remained. Skinny and scraggly, windbreakers and dirty jeans, sunken-faced and sad-eyed. Fidgety and gumming their raw, red faces.

"Nick," I said.

"I know. Frank, we need to leave now," said Nick.

"She's here, Nick. It makes sense. The Arby's, the Walkman, it makes sense. When I used to drive Megan to the clinic for her methadone, we'd go to Arby's afterwards. That was the treat. And it was working! Damn it, it almost worked. She has to be here," said Frank.

One of the men fell into Frank, reaching for his wallet. Nick went to push him away as the other one started patting his own pockets. Looking for what? I saw a silver blade catch light.

"KNIFE!" I said.

"Where? Frank, watch out!" said Nick.

The BMW honked hard and long and everyone stopped and looked. The door opened and the music inside stopped and a very young man stepped out. He might have been sixteen. The Chrysler 500 drove up beside his car.

"End this shit! Right the fuck now!" he said.

The first one let go of Frank and the other put away a spoon and they ran off a few feet and stopped and turned back and did it again.

"This is a quiet and peaceful place for quiet and peaceful people. You all are fucking that up. You two motherfuckers standing over there: one more time, and you are banned from my parking lot, understood?" he said.

But they had already wandered away.

"As for you, Super Dads or whatever the fuck, you're going to get fucked up any second now by one of these people, and then the police will come and that's not happening in my

fucking parking lot. That is not happening. It is time to go. It
is time to go and you are never coming back here. It is time to
go and you better go or my boy in this car beside me is going to
make you go."

"Do you know Megan?"

16

WE DROVE TO Arby's. Nick and I stayed in the cold and messy truck.

"Any luck?" said Nick.

"No. I'll try this location again in a few days. Sorry guys. Anyway, I bought lunch."

The car smelled like steaming bodies.

"No need to apologize. I don't get it, but of course, I get it," said Nick.

"Thanks."

"Me too," I said.

Frank smiled at me and nodded, as if to a child.

He had no idea.

"So what now?" said Frank.

"You know I'll never turn down Arby's, but eating in here, with the broken glass and the Pringles and all?"

"Forget the sandwiches. What about Knight's? It's right beside the one-hour place where I get my windows fixed."

We dropped off the truck and then walked across a six-lane highway to a sports bar.

I took one side of a booth and Frank and Nick crammed into the other. We ordered a pitcher of beer and food from basketball-shaped menus.

"So," said Frank.

"So," said Nick.

"So," I said.

"So this is obviously on me. And I don't just mean lunch. I'll explain everything to Justine when we go back," said Frank.

"The teacup ride and the rollercoaster are good ideas," I said.

"Prin, my gosh, somebody pulled a knife, well, a spoon, on you today! I mean, you're an English professor from Toronto! This isn't what you signed up for coming down here."

"I've seen worse," I said.

Frank and Nick nodded slowly, both of them now smiling at me like I was a child describing my recent trip to Jupiter.

My arm hurt.

I was sipping my beer with flexed muscles. Could they tell?

"I can't really talk about it, but a couple of years ago I was involved in a terrorist attack."

"Are you serious?" said Nick.

I nodded.

They nodded.

The food arrived. Heads down, we said grace. Nick and I started eating. Frank's eyes were still closed. He opened them, blinked a few times, then smiled, waiting for me to say more.

"Sorry, but I signed a non-disclosure agreement, which means—"

"I know. Let me explain. We haven't seen her in a couple of years. No, no, don't worry, keep eating. And Nick already knows the story. That's why he's still eating. But Prin, I figure after what I just put you through I owe you more than just lunch. You have kids, right?"

"Four daughters. They were in Toronto when I went on that trip to—"

"That's beautiful. We had just the one. And you know, when things end up like this, you go all the way back. We've had custody of Megan's kids since they were little. So not only are you raising them, you're raising them and always thinking about what you might have done wrong with their mom when she was their age and trying not to repeat that. And you know, well you have kids, Prin, you know what they want to hear, right? Tell us stories about when mom was a kid, granddad! So you're always telling them about the time she saved the family dog. The damned pug always used to run around in front of the lawnmower, yapping away. Then one day I was in the corner of the yard where my wife had planted some kind of Chinese-lantern-looking fern, and I go under the branches with the mower, and the dog yelps and comes out with its paw half cut off. And it's little Megan to the rescue! She's the one who bandages it up, and it was a Sunday night and I know it's the family dog, but I'm not paying for any emergency vet here. No problem, says Megan. She's already figured out that Children's Tylenol will take care of the pain, and she grinds it up and mixes it into some Hamburger Helper. She does this for a whole week, and next thing you know the dog's yapping in the tall grass again. Stupid pug. And my grandkids love this story about their superhero mom who saves little dogs from the big bad lawnmower man, and I tell it to them every night and I am absolutely splitting inside, just cut in half, wanting them to have something good about their mom in their heads, and also wondering if that's when it started, grinding up Children's Tylenol because I wouldn't pay for a vet. And then the next night I tell the story, and the next night, and tonight, and tomorrow night, I'll do it again."

"Frank, we've talked about this, and you know, I know you know, you can't think that way. It's not right to put all that on yourself," said Nick.

"What should I do, read? My wife does that with all the latest mom-of-an-addict books. I get the reports. And she has all these people on Facebook she's friends with from all over the place, all going through the same thing. We can't talk to our neighbours about what's happened, but we can talk to people way up in Michigan and Maine. Did you notice, Prin, that Tracker Derby was all kids and grandparents? And none of us ask each other where *our* kids are. Still! Maybe because we all know. Anyway, my wife goes to Families Anonymous and stuff like that. I drive around. I help out at a few shelters in town, ask after her. Otherwise, I drive around. I know all the Arby's around here. I'd never checked Dizzy's World, but it showed up on one of my Facebook Dads groups, and when I knew we needed some ideas for the park, well, I'm sorry I pulled you two in like that. But that's what I do. I drive around, and I tell my granddaughters the same story—and, and, this splits me too: they never ask me for other stories, kind of like they know that's the story I can tell and that's the story they want to hear. The only story. Because I can tell other stories. The stories they don't want to hear. The stories other people don't want to hear—"

"Frank, do we really need to go there?"

"It's where I'm at, Nick, every day I go to work. Prin, do you have any loyalty to Hugh Tracker?"

I pointed to my mouth, which was full.

"Everybody likes Mr. Tracker. I think that's always been Hugh's problem," said Nick.

"Are you sitting beside me defending Hugh Tracker, Nick?"

"No, Frank. I was just saying. But go ahead, tell Prin."

"Do you want to hear it, Prin? Do you want to know what really happened to Megan?"

"Okay."

"You should know what kind of person we're dealing with these days, over at the plant. I guess we're all going to find out next week, when he gives his so-called big speech with his big news. Talk about fake news. I know you've heard some of the rumours," said Frank.

"Maybe not as many as you have," I said.

"Right. So, Prin, he's either selling the company, you know, or bringing in new business. And that's what he's supposed to be doing. But people are worried about what kind of new business he's going to bring in. Not just a new cosmetics-packaging contract or toy line, but—"

"Don't even say it, Nick," said Frank.

"A lot of people are going to get hurt, and good old Call-Me-Hugh's going to be just fine. Hugh's always just fine. He was a senior and captain of the cheerleading team and Megan was a freshman and made the squad. Back then, she was as good at gymnastics as Nick's girls. Right Nick? Anyway, he's Mr. Tracker's son, he's running the cheerleaders, and she's a cheerleader and her dad works for Mr. Tracker. Was one of his original employees, in fact. None of this is a big thing. It's normal. Been like that in towns like ours as long as there have been towns like ours. Every now and then, the forklift driver's kid marries the foreman's little girl. Not this time. Nothing was going on between them, so far as I know, but Hugh starts inviting Megan over for parties when Mr. Tracker's away on business, and God bless the late Mrs. Tracker, but she must have been either blind or deaf or hard-of-smelling. Megan starts in with the weed at those Hugh parties and comes home with the super-giggles. She was always a happy, happy kid, and she's over at the Tracker house, so why should we worry? That summer it's weed, it's still weed, just weed, and then some of her friends start doing stuff with their Ritalin, and next thing they're trading the Ritalin for other stuff, and next thing, my Oxycontin is missing from the medicine cabinet. I slipped a disc at work before I started working in procurement. I guess I got my office job because of that slipped disc, but anyway, my doctor wrote me a script for another bottle and it disappeared, too. Then I got a third and took out the pills and filled the bottle with Tic Tacs, and she didn't speak to me for a month. And I never took another script. I just do my exercises. But in the meantime school's still going okay for Megan and she's making her hours at Dollar General and how am I supposed to know the parking lot behind Dollar General might as well be real-life *Breaking Bad*? I hate that Bryan Cranston. Anyway, she doesn't look, well, she doesn't look like those people at Dizzy's World, and she'll still fall asleep beside me on the couch when I'm watching my games. Even when she's not speaking to me she'll come downstairs in her sweats and fall asleep, and I want to ask. I know I have to ask. But I don't."

"That makes sense," I said.

"Thanks, but you have younger kids. Anyway, I never asked her because I was worried she would run. So we never said anything. Even after I took the doors off the bathrooms and put them in the garage, nobody said anything around the dinner table. We'd have people over to the house, and they'd ask to use the bathroom and say nothing about the curtain we'd rigged up because you know, that would be impolite. But people knew. They had kids you couldn't pay to do laundry suddenly doing it all by themselves, and those green and orange stains kept showing up, and they weren't from gym class and soda pop, but all the parents did the same thing: they pretended. We pretended, and meanwhile, going to the doctor around here was like Halloween for people with bad backs, the way they were handing out prescriptions. We never talked about it with each other, but we all knew. But that's small towns, I guess. By the end of high school, well, she wasn't going to graduate, and she'd lost her job at Dollar General, and finally she came to us and didn't ask for money, she asked for help. Right away, we were ready with the treatment clinics and church-basement meetings, but those didn't work because the vultures, the dealers, they just park out front. And so we sent her to a residential facility in Montana, and she came back pregnant, and then again, a few years later, this time in North Dakota, she comes home pregnant, and with a boyfriend, and by that point we've burned through the home-equity line and taking extra credit cards and I'm working overtime at the plant to keep her in treatment and to take care of the kids and to pay for lawyers to deal with the ex-boyfriend, and it's not working. It is not working. We all know it and she leaves again: this time she's apparently found work in some shale town, and we go along with it, and also, she says she can't bring the girls with her and could we watch them just until she's settled, and we agree and we never see her again. That was two years ago.

"And so I drive around. When I'm not at the office, that's what I do. Even when I'm on the road, sourcing for Tracker, Dante, whatever, that's what I do. We get texts now and then, asking for money and pictures of the girls and stuff like that, and I like to believe she's home and just won't come by the house, because I can tell you she's not in Watford City, North Dakota. Anyway, I couldn't exactly retire last year like I wanted to, go out with Mr. Tracker just like I came in with him. I just couldn't, not with the debt I'm carrying, and Mr. Tracker must have known it and that's why he offered me this job with the theme park. And maybe Hugh didn't want me around, reminding him about Megan, if he even remembers Megan. I bet he doesn't. I don't know what's worse—if he does, or doesn't. Either way, I need the work, and Mr. Tracker knew that without my saying anything. I also knew there was no way in hell I was going to work for Hugh—who left his high-school parties for Baylor while my little girl's life went to hell and hell and hell and hell. And so I drive around."

"Can I interest anyone in dessert?" said the waitress.

"Just the bill," said Nick.

"Comes to me. Hey Prin, you must be wondering what kind of people you're working with," said Frank.

"Two years ago I went to the Middle East with my ex-girlfriend from grad school and one night something happened and even though it was just a few minutes on a rooftop—"

"That sentence finishes badly for you," said Nick.

"You didn't actually say that to her, to your wife, did you?" said Frank.

"I don't remember exactly what I said, but yes, I told my wife—"

"Big mistake," said Nick.

"You think so, do you? Why's that, Nick? Cheri from Dubuque?" said Frank.

"Don't you bring that up now, Frank."

"I told her, and the next day Wende was killed in a terrorist attack—"

"And you'd already told your wife."

"Yeah."

"See?"

"Cheri from Dubuque!"

"Anyway, I survived and came home and lost my job—"

"Prin, I'm so—"

"MY TURN! LET ME TALK!"

They snapped back in the booth.

Who had the knife now?

"I lost my job, more or less, and my wife and kids moved to Milwaukee in June, and my wife's ex-boyfriend from high school lives down the street."

"The bastard."

"What a son of a bitch."

"Thank you! Thank you. Yes. Thank you! Anyway, before coming here, my version of driving around was biking around,

Frank, and that wasn't doing any good, and I guess I didn't know what else to do because I wasn't going back to my therapist—"

"You had a therapist? Like a New Yorker?"

"I only went to a couple of sessions. Anyway, I also took pills for the anxiety attacks I would have in airports."

"That's fine, Prin. That makes sense. *That* makes sense."

"Thanks, Frank. I stopped taking them when I came here because I started to—"

"That's good, Prin. That also makes sense. You don't need to say anything else about it. So tell us about this ex-boyfriend. You want us to have a chat with him?" said Frank.

Nick nodded. My heart boomed.

I leaned across the table.

"He's Mormon."

"Maybe a little more?"

"He tells me he prayed me into Mormon Heaven," I said.

"What is that, like Mitt Romney's living room?" said Nick.

"So what's the plan? You have such beautiful little girls! It'd be a shame," said Frank.

"I've tried a few plans, so far. To be fair, she's tried, too. We keep missing."

"Keep trying," said Nick.

"It felt good, didn't it Prin?" said Frank.

"What?" I said.

"Raising your voice. Yelling in public. Being heard. Making people hear you."

"Jesus, Frank," said Nick.

"I brought mints!"

17

THE FRIDAY AFTER Dizzy's World, Hugh texted me on my way to pizza at Charlie's house.

"*Just agree. Say yes.*"

I replied with question marks and called but he didn't answer.

When I arrived, Hugh was sitting beside Charlie in the living room.

This was the first time I'd been in a room with both of them.

Son and father.

A grape and its raisin future.

"So, Prin. What do you think?" said Charlie.

"About? Is there a problem?" I said.

Did they know I'd gone to Dizzy's World?

"Prin, you know we have investors in the Dante parks," said Hugh.

"Yes."

"And for lots of reasons I don't need to get into right here and right now—"

"Go ahead, Hugh. Get into it," said Charlie.

He grinned like someone was pulling a coat hanger through his mouth.

"Dad, this isn't what I wanted to discuss with Prin, and I don't think he's interested, are you, Prin?"

"Agreed," I said.

Charlie's grin faded.

"Listen, Prin, there's a couple of things happening. You've probably heard that we have a big announcement happening at the plant next week."

"I got the email," I said.

"You did?" said Hugh.

He muttered something about listservs and began texting.

"While he's playing on his Game Boy, Prin, let me ask you the question Hugh keeps not asking," said Charlie.

Hugh put away his phone and looked at his father.

"Are you convinced?" said Charlie.

"Yes?" I said.

"No. You're not. What Dad means, Prin—"

"You're going to tell him what I mean?"

"Then do it yourself."

"Nah. Let's see what you think's on my mind. Then do I get to say what I think's on your mind?"

"What Dad means, Prin, is this: Are you convinced the parks are going to be authentic enough to convince people that, in coming to Dante's Indiana, they're getting some sense of what it was like to be in Dante's world? In Florence?"

"That was never part of the plan for the park, so far as I know," I said.

"But it should be, shouldn't it?" said Hugh.

"Agreed? Yes?" I said.

"Thank you. See, Dad? The thing is, Prin, our investors are European, and when they come next week, for our big announcement at the plant, they're going to ask how thing are going at the arenas. And, well, you know Europeans and how they can be. Right Dad?"

"Pizza's getting cold, isn't it Prin? And I doubt Jenny Craig here is joining us," said Charlie.

"It's called a paleo diet! But I do need to get going. Anyway, Prin, Dad and I have been talking, and we think it'd be a good idea to have a historical recreation of Dante's Florence featured in the arenas. That it'll be a value-add with our investors to help off-set the delays. Obviously I know we're not going to have it in place by the time they visit us, next week, but I'd like to tell them we're working on it, when they ask. And I'm pretty sure they will ask."

"Why's that, Hugh?"

"I just said why."

"But did you, really?"

"So. Prin. Can I tell them we're working on it?"

"Sure. I'll mention it to the professors and the rest of the team," I said.

"That's really great. Now, beyond assuring our investors, I think we need some more direct intel. And, well, I'd like to help out here myself. Maybe make amends for an earlier trip to Florence that didn't go so well, right Dad?"

Hugh grinned like someone was pulling the coat hanger through his mouth now.

"Pizza's basically frozen, Hughie. Get to it!" said Charlie.

"Prin, how would you like to join me and Dad on our big trip to Florence?"

"What?"

"Prin! Come on! Five days in Florence! All expenses paid! With the Tracker boys!"

"Not sure they have a Jenny Craig in Tuscany. Ask your phone, why don't you."

"What the hell, Dad? You want me to eat a slice of your stupid pizza?"

"Sure. There's enough. Or skip the pizza and tell me what's really going on here, Hugh. Suddenly you're coming over on a Friday night and worrying the investors aren't going to like what they see at the park and wanting us to rebuild Florence beside the gift shop? Why not let me meet with them when they're in town?"

"No. That's not the arrangement. I secured the funding. I hold the relationship."

"And I'm in charge of the park. What if I don't think we need a historical re-creation? What if I think a display from my collection would do the same thing? What if I don't want to go to Florence?"

"You don't know if you want to go with me? Then fine. I'm just trying to help here, Dad. I'm trying to keep a lot of people happy and on board these days, alright? Including you."

Hugh took a deep, halting breath. He got up and took two slices of pizza from the kitchen, folded them together, and ate them with squishy, snoffling crunches while looking into the backyard.

"Okay. Hughie. You got a lot going on these days, huh?"

He nodded.

"And historical re-creation or no re-creation, you really do want us to go to Florence together? Because it's the easiest thing to cancel."

"No. Let's go to Florence," he said. Still looking away.

"And what do you think, Prin? You want to come with us?" I didn't answer.

Charlie went to the kitchen to get his pizza.

Hugh took out his phone. I got a text.

"*I said, say yes.*"

"Yes," I said.

Hugh took two more slices of pizza and then walked out the door.

Charlie gave me my plate.

"Pretty convincing, wasn't he? Excited to go to Italy. With us, now. No offence."

"Maybe with the big announcement next week at the plant, and the investors coming to town, and wanting to do what's right for the park and also to keep that promise to you about Florence, he's trying his best."

"Yeah. Suddenly. Out of nowhere. That's what's got me worried."

"Welcome to Tracker Packaging!" said Kyle.

He met me at the main office, a building of brown-brown brick and aqua-tinted glass. He was wearing black running shoes, black jeans, and a black blazer over a black T-shirt that read STAND UP STRAIGHT WITH YOUR SHOULDERS BACK. Kyle introduced me as his client-colleague to staff who never looked up from their screens. Maybe they were busy, or used to Kyle, or just worried about Hugh's announcement.

"Let me walk you back to the main buildings through the staff way," said Kyle.

A forearm shot out and caught Kyle in the chest, pushing him back and to the side.

"This is a restricted area," said a bald man in a dark suit.

"My dad works here. Dan Newton? As in, Dan and Dale in the lunchroom? What are you, new?" he said.

The man said nothing.

"You know what? Let's go around," said Kyle.

"Is your dad actually here, Kyle?" I said.

"No he's not! Wait, is he? WHERE?"

We walked around to the back of the building. Kyle offered a running commentary on every childhood experience he'd had at the plant. We went along a road that ended at two large buildings. On the left was a storage warehouse. On the right was a manufacturing facility with a line of high windows along its upper storey. At ground level, big, burgundy, bat-like exhaust fans jutted out at intervals. Between the buildings was a dismal slope of old snow and broken pallets and rusty pallet-jacks, bordered by corroded drums and vats that young people in khakis and windbreakers were frantically painting red, white, and blue. Behind it all was a tailings pond, grey and flat and unshimmery.

People were shuffling around in front of open bay doors at the manufacturing facility. Beside me, Kyle began to jog in place.

"Do you need the bathroom?"

"Hi Justine!" he called over.

I looked for the Dante professors and for Nick and Frank. I didn't see Charlie anywhere, either. Instead, I saw lots of men in black suits. Also black cars, SUVs and sedans, and news vans emblazed with channel numbers and pictures of happy blonde women and laughing Hispanic men at anchor desks.

A school bus pulled up. A young man and woman wearing bright-orange hiking vests hopped out with iPads and leaned back into the bus, calling out instructions. They sounded excited and menacing. Very quickly, the bus emptied out a group of ragged-looking people in matching campaign T-shirts. They looked around, shielding their eyes against the overcast skies, staying by the bus in a loose group until the young man and woman began prodding them towards the open bay doors.

The plant itself was lit up by panels of fluorescent light that gave off a fluffy, throbbing whiteness. The floor was dominated by box-shaped metallic machines the size of chest freezers and minivans. Drills and rolling presses and hoses and cables ran to and from metal tracks and trays. Workers' benches were bolted to the machines near displays and keyboards and green and yellow levers and big stop-sign-shaped EMERGENCY buttons and red telephones. The workstations were all empty.

Above the floor, running along the perimeter of the building, was a walkway that backed onto offices and meeting rooms. People stood at the rails, watching. Massive blocks draped in American flags sat on a temporary stage bunting-skirted in American flags. A lectern was set up in front, displaying the Indiana State seal.

"I think this is more than just an announcement about Tracker Packaging," I said.

"#Flyswattercountry is trending on Indiana Twitter," said Kyle.

"Good to know."

"Really?"

One of the vested people from the bus was now standing on the stage, asking the very quiet crowd to calm down.

"LADIES AND GENTLEMEN. PLEASE JOIN ME IN WELCOMING THE NEXT PRESIDENT OF THE UNITED STATES!"

"Holy crap! Call-Me-Hugh's running for president! He's going to need a podcast, a digital … a digital youth … Fortnite, a digital youth Fortnite … AI … Twitch? Tik Tok? NFT?"

"Hugh's not running for president. I think the governor of Indiana might be," I said.

"Oh. Is that the other tall guy walking up to the stage?"

Hugh and the governor were joined on stage by a group of smaller, glowering white men dressed in tight patent-leather loafers and tight, shiny suits, and by women in blazers and skirts and bright, blown-out hair and pastel makeup.

Everyone sang the national anthem and then Hugh introduced his "great personal friend."

"Thank you, Hugh, and hello Terre-Haute! It's just so good to be back here with the real people of Indiana, instead of those Indianapolis elites. Last night, when my Bunny asked me where I was going today, I said Bunny, I am leaving Fantasy Island for the real world. Thank you, thank you. Now first off, let me address the rumours. I am not running for president … yet. Thank you, thank you. Listen, I am proud to serve this great state, especially when it lets me be part of exciting events like today's, here at Tracker Packaging, with my great friend Hugh and our guests. Look, today is not about me. It's about me lending my support to what's going on in places like Tracker Packaging, which is showing the world that, when it comes to fresh ideas, to renewing the American economy, to reminding folks about the superpowers of the American worker, this is the place to be. No one in this room is waiting for solutions from Washington and New York and Silicon Valley. Because the Midwest isn't the Middle Seat of America! This isn't flyover country. It's flyswatter country! Thank you, thank you. Now, let me leave you with a final thought before I turn things back to my great friend Hugh. Look, I'm sure I'm not the only one here who begins and ends his day by offering praise and thanksgiving to Our Lord and Saviour and then, if I remembered to empty the dishwasher, a peck on the cheek from the boss. I see some nodding out there. That's great. Thank you. It seems to me though, that for too long the people of Terre-Haute have felt like they're living the Book of Job. Why? Because people work hard, or they want to work hard, or they're ready to work hard, but something's been taken away from them: the chance to work, work hard, work with their friends and neighbours, or their family. We can blame Washington, we can blame Mexico, we can blame the Europes of the world, we can all blame the Chine-ocracy, thank you, that's what I call it in my new book, but is that what Job does? No. Is that what you do? No. Job endures, in his faith in God and in himself. You've endured, in your faith in God and in yourselves. And today, that faith is paying off. Today, we're saying goodbye Job, hello jobs. Listen, the details—FDA, API, V4, OEE—I'll leave to my great friend Hugh and our guests. For now, let me tell you the three little letters, no wait, six little letters, that matter to me and you more than any other: JOBs, and USA! Thank you, Terre-Haute, and God bless America!"

The workers applauded very politely. Campaign staff moved through the crowd, prodding the people from the bus to make more noise, make more noise, make more noise.

The crowd eventually went wild.

The governor dramatically sighed and nodded and mouthed apologies to Hugh and the others on stage and took a selfie with the applauding crowd. He returned to his seat and tapped on his phone as Hugh came to the podium. Everything, everyone, became as soundless as deep space. I saw Frank and Nick upstairs, on the second floor, listening. Nick was standing very close to Frank, who was gripping the railing.

"Thank you so much, Governor, for your inspiring words, and for your support, for all the different kinds of support you've given to get us here today at Tracker Packaging. I won't forget it, and when the time comes, I'm sure my fellow voters won't forget it either. Now, to turn to my remarks for today. Many of you in this room have known me my whole life. That's because, just like you, I grew up in Terre-Haute, I grew up right here, in these buildings. And over the years, and especially now that I've taken over from my father—and I'm not sure if he's with us today, but what about a round of applause for our founder, Charlie Tracker?"

Strong clapping.

"I hope he heard that. Anyway, I can tell you that I've really come to appreciate how unique we are, as a family-owned, mid-sized regional American converter company in a world, and an industry, increasingly dominated by corporate-owned, multinational packaging firms who make everything, and I mean everything, *everything*, in China. I meant, in the

Chine-ocracy! I like that, Governor. I'm going to use that now, after I finish your book, *Flyswatter Country*. It's really good, everybody. You should buy it. But anyway, you know, they say the only way to compete is to cut price or cut quality, but we've never gone in for the kind of down-gauging that gives you crinkly water bottles, and we never will. You also know how many times we've been approached to sell the company. We are not for sale. I'll say it again. We are not for sale.

"But, to compete, we need to make creative partnerships that leverage our strengths: those strengths are in this room, and in this town, and in this state, and in one other place, and that place is Poland. As I'm sure many of you know, Poland is the leading member of the V4, and with what's happening and not happening in the rest of Europe these days, I think we should really pay attention to Poland and the other countries of the V4, the Viségrad Group, because they are actually trying to improve things for ordinary people around the world, including right here in Terre-Haute. I met my great friend Karol here, back when we were doing our MBAs at IUB. Turns out we're both sons of great entrepreneurs. Anyway, we stayed in touch, and a couple of years ago he introduced me to his colleagues, who help him lead Jagiellon Capital, the investment group he took over from his father. They've been involved with the Dante theme park project in the old basketball arenas that, as you know, my dad's been working on since he retired. And I'd like to welcome, actually, those members of the Dante project who are with us today, and they're here because they are part of the larger Tracker family, just as our family is now part of the larger Jagiellon Capital family.

"What does that mean?, you may be wondering. I know you're probably worried because of the stories you've heard about American manufacturing these days. But we're telling a different story here. To explain it, I'd like Karol to come join me up here for a moment. Tracker Packaging, please welcome my great friend and fellow IUB MBA, Karol Młotek!"

One of the stocky men stood up. He came to the podium and nodded at Hugh to move.

"Thank you, Hugh, and Governor, for a chance to be part of this. I speak for all my colleagues from Jagiellon Capital in saying we see investing in Tracker Packaging as a great opportunity. We have a supplier in Poland that's looking for a packager who can bring their products to market with maximum efficiency and cost savings for everyone. That's Tracker Packaging, thanks to your FDA's new country-of-origin rules for end-product APIs, together with the V4's new most-favoured trading status with Indiana. Thank you for that, Governor. And we already knew about Terre-Haute because of the Dante park. We like this place. We like the Dante park. They're going to put fun back into the fear of God. Much better than atheist homosexual Euro-Disney. They say that when you plant a seed in foreign soil, it doesn't grow. But if you put a seed in its own soil, it will grow. That's what we'll have with this Made-in-the-USA product we're making together, here. You know, even when I tell them back in Poland what a good time I had at IUB, with Hugh and my other friends, the only thing they know about this part of America is from *Heaven's Gate*. So let's tell everybody a different story about what happens when Poles and Americans work together. Thank you."

He stepped away from the microphone, to little applause. The people on the stage gathered at the shrouded blocks behind the seats.

Kyle jabbed me.

"Search results: *Heaven's Gate* is a religious cult that committed group suicide in California in the nineties, or, hold on, he probably means this one: *Heaven's Gate:* a really, really long movie about Polish farmers who get killed when they come to

America. I could arrange a screening. I could even arrange a pre-screening for Justine, if she wants."

"Kyle, look up API."

"API? Seriously?"

"What is it?"

"Active Pharmaceutical Ingredient. Where are you from again?"

Hugh returned to the microphone.

"Okay, everyone, now it's time for the big reveal of the future of Tracker Packaging. Thanks to the partnerships Karol mentioned—with a raw-material supplier in Poland that Jagiellon Capital has identified, and also through the Indiana-specific trade agreements with Poland we were able to work out with support from the governor—Tracker Packaging is about to become the end-manufacturer of important and needed products made in America, by Americans, for Americans. Over the next few months, as we close out all of our current contracts, we'll have some re-training and crewing changeups. This summer, all machines currently on the floor will be swapped out for a state-of-the-art blister-feeding system with the best OEE rating in the industry. And in all of this, people, believe me: No layoffs, no phase-outs, no job cuts, no early retirements, nothing like that. In fact, when we reopen after Thanksgiving, I bet we'll need to hire more people. So please join me in—"

"PILLS! PILLS! YOU SON-OF-A-BITCH! YOU'RE TURNING US INTO A PILL MILL! YOU SON-OF-A-BITCH!"

18

"ARE YOU GOING to fire Frank? Does Hugh want you to fire Frank?" I said.

"Those are two very different questions," said Charlie.

"You know about his situation? With his daughter Megan?"

"I know there are lots of people in situations these days."

"But you knew this was the plan, Hugh's plan? You said so, when we were driving to the arenas that first day, back in January."

"What's that supposed to mean?"

"Pills. You said you knew that was what Hugh wanted to do. The company's going to package generic painkillers in the middle of a place that's been ruined by painkiller addiction. And people have to keep working because they're supporting families or paying off debts or paying for treatment. Frank can't be the only one."

"No."

"American contrapasso."

"I guess we all deserved that. Last I checked, though, Prin, you're not paid to sit in judgement of us, are you?"

Charlie stared at me and stirred his coffee. We were having breakfast at a Greek diner downtown. There were old people all around us, mostly men in hunting jackets with buzzcuts and canes. There were also older couples here and there, most eating breakfast with babies sleeping beside them in car seats.

This was a few days after the announcement at the plant. Nick had walked Frank out of the building before security reached him, and then Hugh and the governor and the Polish investors unveiled the row of new blister feed machines that would soon fill the factory. Not even the campaign ringers had clapped.

Work had resumed the next day at the arenas, outwardly at least. Nick stayed in his office, researching indoor rollercoasters; Justine focused on plans for a springtime hiring fair; the professors compiled lists of people and other things mentioned in the *Divine Comedy* that could be performer parts in the arenas; I researched Dante's Florence; Kyle watched *Heaven's Gate*. Frank stayed away. Eventually, Justine told us he was taking some time to decide whether he was going to stay on the project. We understood. We knew now where the money we were getting paid was coming from, or going, and none of us had quit.

No one had quit at Tracker Packaging, either.

Hugh sent upbeat emails with links to carefully edited local news coverage of the event. He texted me to ask how things were going with plans for the trip to Florence. Not knowing how to reply, I didn't. Hugh didn't seem to care.

Charlie leaned in.

"Question."

"Okay."

"Who are you really working for, Prin? Me? Or him?"

"I just want to keep working, Charlie. You know I need to."

"You and everybody else. Look, I get it. Given the plant's location, we, they, *they* can get pills to market faster than overseas generics and the various rules around country of origin versus country of manufacture for the active pharmaceutical ingredient are all working out to our benefit, their benefit, in terms of tax credits and per-unit pricing. I see the business case, sure."

"So you weren't surprised by the news."

"I thought Hugh had found Karol for Dante, but Karol and Hugh really found each other for this. They invested in Dante's Indiana to get me out of the way."

"You think so?"

"What Jagiellon Capital has put into Dante's Indiana is pennies compared to what they'll make with the generics eventually coming out of the plant."

"Why didn't you—"

"It's not my company anymore, Prin. It's Hugh's. It was his call. If it was me, I would probably have gone for another masstige line, or maybe tried to get state support for soybean packaging, or, who knows, maybe a new flow-pack line—Indiana corn on the cob, grown and packaged here—but Hugh's not me. Apparently he knew what he was doing all along. Karol knows what he's doing. I wonder if Karol's father knows what they're doing, or cares. Anyway, that's none of my business because it's not my business anymore. My boy surprised me. Hugh really knew what he was doing."

"People say he's making money off addiction."

"Would they rather he shuts down the company?"

"I don't know."

"Now what about Florence? I can't promise it'll be more fun than that little pizza party we had last week," said Charlie.

"Do you still want me to go?"

"We'll both probably behave a little better with you around, so ... no."

He smiled, defeated.

"I'm kidding, Prin. I see now that Hugh came up with this historical re-creation bull to give me something else to think about while he was getting ready for the investors. But actually, you know, it's not a bad idea. Might attract more high school classes to the parks. There's probably some extra State credits we can apply for, too. Whatever. So yes, you need to go to Florence and get some ideas," he said.

"It doesn't sound like you're too excited to be going," I said.

He looked around the diner.

"This is the first time in memory, Prin, that I have eaten in this establishment and not a single person has said hello."

"I doubt people are blaming you," I said.

"It is what it is. Maybe I deserve it. I don't. But. Maybe I do."

"Do you think, if the park works out, Hugh will change his mind about the plant?"

"No. Too late for that. But maybe others will. See you at the airport."

Just after I checked in for the flight, Hugh texted me. Something had come up. He wouldn't be able to join us in Florence. He thanked me for taking Charlie to Italy and asked me to call when we got back.

The plan, all along.

I looked around the departure lounge but couldn't see Charlie.

Boarding would begin soon.

He called me.

"Did you hear from Hugh?" he said.

"Just now," I said.

"No surprise there, huh?"

"Where are you, Charlie?"

"I'm in the airport."

I could hear boarding instructions in the receiver. I looked around.

"Are you sure you're at the right gate?"

"I am."

"I can't see you."

"That's because I'm going to Kentucky, Prin."

"What?"

"I've set up some meetings with some people down there. Potential new investors. I'm going to check out Genesis Extreme. I'm not going to let Dante's Indiana be a front for what Hugh and his Polish buddies and that damned governor are doing to my company and my town!"

"Does Hugh know you're doing this?"

"He will when you tell him. Are you going to tell him?"

I had to tell him, didn't I?

"Prin? Still there? I asked if you're going to tell him. Or are you going to enjoy a nice trip to Florence? Hotel's already paid for. And then I'll tell Hugh, myself, when I get back. Give me your word you'll let me tell him."

"He's going to check in with us, thinking we're both over there."

Charlie laughed.

"No he's not! Not anymore! Not now that's he's got everything in place. Give me your word you won't tell him," he said.

"I'm not sure I can do that, Charlie. I just want to keep working."

If I told Hugh, Charlie would fire me.

If I didn't tell Hugh, Hugh would fire me.

"For who?"

"For whoever lets me bring them home. Remember?"

"I do. And I still respect that. So keep working. Go get some ideas for a historical re-creation. And just so you know there's no hard feelings between us, why not take somebody with you? No need to go alone."

Five days in Florence, with Kyle?

"I don't think any of the team could come on this short notice."

"I meant your wife, Prin. Ticket's on me."

Invite Molly?

What would she say?

Would it matter what she said?

"Look, it's none of my business, but sometimes you need to make the call and take the chance and do something bold. That's my advice. See you back in town. Don't call Hugh. Call your wife."

I called.

"Dad. I'm taking Molly to Italy!"

"Really? She said she'd come with you?"

"I haven't called her yet."

"You call me, first?"

"I wanted, well, yes, I did. I wanted to let you know I don't actually like this," I said.

"Good son."

"Thanks, Dad."

"But shitty husband, Prin. Call Molly."

"I know my wife's name, Dad."

I grinned and braced for the yelling.

"Just call her, Prin."

He hung up.

I called Molly.

"Do you want to come to Florence?"

"What?"

I explained a version of the situation.

"Prin, I can't just go to Italy tomorrow."

"Why not? Your mom can watch the kids, and it'd only be for a few days. When was the last time it was just the two of us, anywhere except your sister's sewing room?"

She laughed a little.

Actually laughed. Then sighed again.

But now I really did want her to come.

"And I checked: the hotel has heated floors, so no problem for me," I said.

She laughed a little more. Sighed a little less.

"Prin. Prin, you know that's not how I want things to be."

"Me either. So come with me."

"Okay."

"Really? Okay? Molly, that's—"

"Prin. I don't think we're going to solve everything by spending a few days in Florence."

"Maybe not. But I'm glad you're coming, anyway."

"Really?"

"Really."

Really.

19

I SPENT MY first two hours in Italy in a lost luggage lineup.
Through thick, lipstick-smudged plexiglass I learned that my
suitcase would arrive the following day and be sent directly to
the hotel. In the meantime, the airline gave me a care package:
a translucent toothbrush; a tiny, beautiful tube of toothpaste,
its firm, silver-and-tricolour-striped paste resembling a ruddy
minnow; unisex deodorant; a packet of chocolate biscuits; and a
white undershirt big enough to hoist as a sail.

My hotel room wasn't ready, and my phone's travel plan
wouldn't be activated for another three hours, so I left my book
bag behind the front desk, checked a map, grabbed handfuls of
biscotti from a bell jar, and walked to Dante's house in cold,
bright morning light.

It was down a cobblestone side street lined with shops and
scooters and scruffy brown men standing around selling leather
goods at "best price, best price, best price." As soon as one of
them caught my eye he'd shoot to life and ask, "What country?
What country for best price, boss? Let me guess country for
best price, brother! Boss! Brother!"

I agreed to UK, Spain, Portugal, and Goa, and declined
each and all the best prices. In the in-flight magazine, I'd read
about a prestigious and little-known leather-making school

beside one of the city's Dante churches. I'd take Molly there when she arrived, the next day.

Ahead of me was a narrow, dark house in a dim corner of an alley. Inside, it smelled damp and was all dark wood and heavy stone hallways and steep, narrow steps, which led from floor to floor, exhibit to exhibit. What Dante and his family ate and wore, who they warred with and were healed by. I took notes and pictures. But why would we give park space over to this when we could just move a couple of Charlie's display cases into the lobbies and cordon them off? I went through the museum and reached the gift shop, where a young man in a burgundy NYU sweatshirt was begging the clerks to let him use the bathroom.

I picked out a guidebook to Dante's Florence and a couple of accordion-style picture-books about the house itself, a packet of illuminated-manuscript postcards and boxes of Divine chocolates for Charlie and the others. These were small, sweet saints and sea-salt sinners made by a centuries-old chocolatier from Ravenna, where Dante wrote the *Divine Comedy* in his exile. The little pieces were modelled on figures and symbols from the poem—there was a line of white-chocolate roses and, as the box's centerpiece, a white-chocolate man gnawing a dark-chocolate man's nougat head. The plastic coverings weren't properly sealed and the chocolates were covered in a grey film. Nevertheless, Charlie would get a kick out of them. Maybe he'd even see a new business opportunity here, too. I flipped through a children's edition of *Inferno*. I returned it to the shelf. It was meant for children given wine with their lunch.

Back on the street, I saw an alley church made of rough brown brick. I stepped inside. In front of the altar, a guide stood lecturing a sheaf of tow-headed teenagers. I genuflected and sat at the back of the church on a pew the colour of dark syrup. I checked my watch. There was still an hour before my phone plan started, two hours more before our room would be ready, twenty-two hours before my luggage arrived, and twenty hours before Molly landed.

The church had wispy, rich-red paintings of the young poet adoring and pining for his beloved. To my left was a simple side-altar framed by flat, fluted columns, underneath which was a grey slab covered in folded notes and dried roses. I went over to read the austere stone plaque pressed into the wall above the slab. The name of the buried person was—was it?—her name was Beatrice Portinari. Was this really *Beatrice* Beatrice?

I checked the guidebook. This had indeed been Dante's family church, the place where he'd married Gemma Donati. It was also the Portinari family church: from the thirteenth century onward, many of them were buried here, including Beatrice and her devoted maid.

It *was* her!

I knelt before her grave, empty-handed.

But I didn't need dead flowers and letters.

I could leave something living and real instead.

I began to pray.

I prayed for help, for her help, for Molly, for me, for us.

But Beatrice wasn't a formally recognized saint.

But certainly she'd died and gone to heaven. She must have. How could she inspire what she inspired and not have gone to heaven? Maybe you'd get a reason or two if you asked Dante's wife … Just in case, *just in case,* I also prayed for the holy soul of Beatrice Portinari, should she still be in Purgatory, to be granted admission to Paradise.

I waited.

Someone came into the church through a side door. I looked over.

Did the sunlight suddenly seem just a little brighter?

Was another soul seeing God face to face and refracting that glory down upon us?

Maybe?

Either way, once more I prayed for Beatrice, and for her intercession, for Molly, for us, for both of us, for us, that on this trip we might turn back to each other, return to our life together and to both know and want and, yes, love, that this was what we were doing, together. Not *sursum corda* but *sursum cordibus*.

That our lifted hearts might be one.

I got up from my knees and backed away from the altar and tomb. Two college girls wearing backpacks and clear braces, their hair in ponytails, took my place. They were clutching their phones to roses bought from the brown men at the church door.

I was hungry. I went in search of a Florentine speciality Molly wouldn't want: Lampredotto, a sandwich of hard bread and soft intestines smothered in green sauce. On a side street, in the long, cold shadow of the Basilica of Santa Croce, I found a trolley car tricked out as a sandwich shop calling itself *Aviditas Vitae: Lust for Life*. Waiting in line, I remembered the snack bar in Dizzy's World: the Crystal Pepsi sign and the bone-crunching dog in the corner and the human anvil with his clean arms and white T-shirt and cash only. The whole operation, the whole place, the people, the time: everything had felt out of joint with itself, busted, broken, stuck. But it was still going, like a smashed-open clockworks, still ticking.

Something else was going on here. Inside the sandwich trolley was an older man in Phil Donahue glasses. He wore a short-sleeved V-neck sweater and gold chains around his neck, like a tangle of angel hair. He stood in front of posters of Padre Pio, Iggy Pop, and the Pope, working the till and handing out paper napkins and bottles of beer with milk-coloured cups popped on top. Beside him were two young men in matching grey-wool driving caps chopping up intestines and scooping and dipping and pressing together orders for those in the lineup, all of them men, whether in suits or garage coveralls or school blazers or walking shoes. I leaned forward.

How did you order?

How did you join this flow of food and money and talking? The old man and his sons never let up in their back and forth of yelled and sung words, their rising and falling rhythms oblivious to the saucy, synth-beat Italian pop blaring in the background.

I leaned back. Father and sons, in rough and real harmony, a rough and real harmony unbroken by whatever breakages there must have been between them. I couldn't imagine anything like this between Charlie and Hugh.

Between Kingsley and me.

Me and Kingsley.

When Dante meets Cacciaguida in Paradise, he listens to his forefather and he talks to him. The distance between them, poet-pilgrim and crusader knight—centuries and planes of existence apart—might as well have been the space between the counter and the cash inside the sandwich trolley.

When my travel plan started, I'd call him. And not just tell him I'd called Molly like he said. But listen, and talk.

"Lampredotto," I said.

"Sauce?" said one of the brothers.

"Yes."

"Soft?"

"Sauce?"

"Yes, yes, sauce. I know. But soft? Also, soft?"

The counterman turned to his brother, his face full of despairing confusion. The brother came over, his Mezza Luna knife dripping goop, and pantomimed dipping a bread roll into a plastic jug of steaming gravy. The old man called out, annoyed. The brothers called back, shoving their palms at me as if they were lifting a heavy table. A new conversation started.

"Sorry, sir, you know this is not halal. It's okay?"

"Catholic," I said.

"Hey! Cattolico! Hey!" said the first, then the second, then the third. And with that, they returned to their wheeling.

I paid for the Lampredotto and was given a bottle of Peroni the size of a bowling pin. I didn't want a beer any more than I wanted to tell the old man I didn't want a free beer. The American college kid in the NYU sweatshirt came around the corner, stepping lightly in Vans wrapped in images of Our Lady of Guadalupe. I passed on the bottle, we fist-bumped, and I took my lunch to the church square.

The rest of me felt tired and creased and stale from travel, but my stomach was now warm and very pleased with the hot, savoury sandwich. Chewing and squinting through the sunlight that arced in from the riverside, I studied the great, imperious statue of Dante—it was made of a cold-looking, harsh-white stone that hadn't faded and softened and been ruined by the romantic grime of centuries, like the other old stones and statues in Florence.

Could we put up a replica in front of both arenas?

I took out my phone, but before I could take a picture it began buzzing. The travel plan had started. Messages and notifications pulsed and pulsed. My mother had called and texted me fifty times already, demanding I call IMMEDIATELY – EMERGENCY – URGENT – LIFE AND DEATH.

I smiled. I stretched. Who was cordial now? I basked in the sunlight of the church square. I bought an orange and found a free bench, where I sat and peeled it and savoured each slice, really chewing up the pulp and pith. My phone kept buzzing.

Finally, I called her.

She was sobbing and speaking. I couldn't understand a word. I didn't need to.

"Mom, I'm fine. I'm fine. I'm in Florence. The only issue is that my luggage is delayed, but other than that, I'm fine. I'm fine, okay? And Molly's coming, Mom. Please, stop! Really, things are okay! I'm okay! Molly's coming!"

But she kept going on about the terrorists, the terrorists, my father and the terrorists. So Kingsley was worried, too. He'd even talked to *her* about it. My parents, long divorced, at last together about something, back together, about me.

"Mum, listen to me. Trust me. And tell Dad, too. I'm in Florence, not the Middle East. There are no terrorists here. Don't worry. I'll call him myself."

"You can't! Prin! Prin, listen to me. I am not saying terrorist. Can you hear me? I am not saying terrorist."

"Mom, yes, I am listening to you. And I hear you. You are not saying terrorist. So what *are* you saying?"

"I am saying TERRACES, Prin. Terraces. They took him to the Terraces. Your father's been taken to the Terraces."

"Dad?"

"Yes. They found him in his room. On the floor beside his bed."

20

MY FATHER DIED while I was peeling an orange. He had a heart attack and was pronounced dead in the condominium's intensive-care unit, the Terraces, before the ambulance arrived.

I spent the rest of my day on the phone, and when I wasn't on the phone, or standing and staring at nothing, time filling and sucking around me, I went into churches full of art students and tour groups and got down on my knees and prayed for my father, for his soul, for its swift and kind admission to heaven, to the face and mind of God. Then I looked up and around to see if there was any difference in the light, even the smallest increase in brightness, whether candle or late slanting sun. But there wasn't, not yet, for Kingsley.

I prayed more.

I called Molly. My mother had already called her. She was repacking for Toronto instead of Florence.

Each of the girls took the phone from Molly.

"Sorry Dad."

"Sorry Dad."

"Sorry about your dad, Dad."

"He always gave us the candy in the end."

They didn't say much else. On speakerphone, we prayed together for him. There was depth in their voices, a depth of feeling, of knowing something distant and unreal as something suddenly here, present, real. It was more the case now than it had been two years earlier, when I'd tried to explain to them what it meant that I was sick. They were very young, and it had been prostate cancer, early detection. This wasn't *cancer* cancer. Likewise, I wasn't sure if they really understood what had happened to me when I nearly died in Dragomans. There'd been a kind of family NDA around that. It was made of very delicate glass and was set on a pyramid of playing cards. No one even breathed in its direction. The fear of total collapse.

Whereas Kingsley's death was clear and undeniable. They would have to buy black dresses and tights. Someone they knew, and loved, had died, was gone from them. Gone from everything. Gone. It had finally happened, and it would happen again and again. And some day, they wouldn't be talking to me, but about me. About Molly. Another day still, they wouldn't be, either. They'd be elsewhere. Where? We knew where; we believed. But still. I prayed more, and not just for Kingsley.

After speaking with Molly and the girls, I called my sisters, who'd been living in Australia in the years since they met their husbands while backpacking with phones and flowers through Europe. They had already heard from Lizzie. The earliest they could get to Toronto was Friday morning. We'd have the funeral the next day. I called Molly again, and she'd already made plans to arrive in Toronto on Wednesday night. Meanwhile, I was stuck in Florence.

Gone from me, too, he was.

Lifted up, we were.

Both of us. *Both* of us? All three?

The next morning, I loitered in the hotel lobby on a gilded bench beneath a vaulted ceiling frescoed in fruits. On the bench to my left, two German tourists were barricaded behind metallic-blue suitcases. On my other side, an Italian man in torn jeans and expensive-looking sneakers was thumb-wrestling himself. His T-shirt read *Ricorda Montaperti*.

Because of some EU declaration I had signed, it was impossible to arrange for my luggage to be kept at the airport so I could pick it up before boarding the same return flight to Chicago. I would have to accept the luggage at the hotel, so I booked a one-way afternoon flight to Toronto for the next day, Wednesday. If everything worked out—traffic, the border, air traffic, customs—Molly and the girls might even be able to pick me up from the airport on their drive back to Toronto. I'd written to Hugh and Charlie and to Justine, letting them know I'd be cutting my time in Florence short and wouldn't be returning to Terre-Haute for at least another week. Hugh called me but I didn't answer and he didn't leave a message. My inbox filled with messages from people in Toronto, Milwaukee, Indiana, Sri Lanka, and from all the suburban-white-people places that Kingsley's batch-mates and cricket chums had migrated to.

I had twenty-four hours on my own in Florence.

No one expected anything of me until I returned to Toronto.

Not even that I answer all the emails. All sympathetic and understanding.

What would my father have wanted me to do with such time?

Did it still matter? To both of us?

I got up from the gilded bench and stepped over the thumb-wrestling Italian and told the four or five people working behind the hotel's tiny front desk to send my luggage up to my room when it arrived. I left my phone with them—everyone back home was sleeping, and I was sick of tapping out gratitude—and asked them to deliver it upstairs, too. I accepted a vial of mouthwash and stepped out into the city.

I went past church after church, gallery after gallery, school group after tour group. I crossed the river on the Sri Lankanish Ponte Vecchio—crowded, old, crumbly, damp market stalls full of gold and smelling of fish—and had a beer and a hot, crusty sandwich in a shoebox bar. A woman let her dog pee on the antique barrel beside the bar's entrance just as the owner was stepping outside to smoke. I stepped around their cursing and walked and walked around on the far side of the Arno until I reached a big, green park that ran up and behind a grand and massive museum made of toast-coloured brick, the Pitti Palace.

I found an entry-point along the curving wall of the Boboli Gardens and walked until I found myself standing in a brace of tall trees shot through with cold noon light. I stopped. I was breathing hard. I didn't realize how fast I'd been walking.

I prayed *Sursum corda*.

Lord, lift up my heart.

Nothing.

Lord, let me find my way. Let me find my way back to the life I had once had, with you, the life of finding and being found, of being found ready and found worthy, of being who and what had been granted me.

Nothing again.

Was I asking for the wrong thing?

To go the wrong way?

Not back.

I felt a palm pressing against my chest: not lifting up my heart like I'd been asking, but cleaving it, opening, deepening, warming it. Maybe this wasn't about returning.

Who knew, then, that Thanksgiving would be the day my father would make his most radical act of love? He said he'd give me gas money to go see Molly and the girls. Who had taken me in the car, the big blue Caprice, when I was a small boy, to pick up my mother from work, and held me on his lap and pointed out all the birds and cars of the world. Who had arrived before my mother finished her shift again and again and let me drive, sitting on his lap, while he smoked cigarettes. I had steered and Kingsley had revved the engine and we'd laughed as we veered around the mental-hospital parking lot waiting for my mother to finish work. What a lavish waste of gas money that had been!

Forty years later, my father would have given me even more lavish gas money, to go to my family.

But I had liked the idea of it more, the spurning of it, the idea of being spurned even for thinking about trying.

I looked around the park. Students were sketching minor ruins, couples were picnicking and little ones gambolling. On one side a path sloped down past a square neoclassical building. It was made of the same soiled white stone I had seen elsewhere in Florence, only this place didn't feel neglected so much as indifferent to the scrubby surroundings. The building was topped by a black cross on a broad, steepled canopy made of wire-mesh. It looked deserted. But it was full of a strange life. The canopy was full of birds beating to break free.

On the other side was an uphill path that led to a clearing with tall, soft-looking grass. In the middle was a large, white oblong stone. A memorial? A tribute? Art? Whatever it was, it had no life to it at all.

Canopy and stone, each seemed entirely itself and yet more than just itself. *Sursum corda, corda mortem.* I wanted to walk to both, but I sensed I couldn't, or shouldn't. I didn't move out of the stripe-lit wood.

Make of either what you want, Prin.

You can, and you will.

But do more than your usual head- and heart-work.

Decide.

Go.

What would Kingsley do? Yell until everyone returned to him, and no one ever did.

What would Charlie do? Keep trying.

What would Dante do? Wake up far from home and write his way to heaven, even if he had to go to hell, go through hell, first: and he did it, and he was not alone. He did it and he was not alone because someone wanted to see him on the other side.

Molly: did she want to see me on the other side of whatever was between us? Yes. Yes she did. But for Kingsley, she would be flying to Florence right now. And how I wanted to see her! I had thought so and said so and worried so, and a day before I had prayed so at Beatrice's tomb. But now, more than all of that oxygenating of myself and the Holy Spirit, I really wanted it. Her. Our life. The life ahead of us.

Decide.

Go.

I went.

I went uphill, fast and easy, straight at the white oblong monument. I slapped my palm on it. I looked around. No one noticed. I slapped it again. How cold it was! As if all the sunlight in Florence were here, in this, absorbed and defeated. Unlike Dante's statue in the church square, which, I imagined, would feel cool in all seasons, all times. Was the oblong statue more like the body, laid out in a funeral home, waiting to be outfitted as he'd requested?

Inferno was hot and then freezing cold, according to Dante.

Heaven was, well, what? Beyond weather? Beyond fun? I hoped not, for the sake of my father. Terre-Haute, too.

I looked away from the statue, over at the birds beating vainly in their steepled cage. Kingsley, in the oldest chambers of my heart.

Purgatory was temperate, a place to stroll in a cricket sweater.

21

TEN DAYS AFTER the funeral, I returned to Terre-Haute. Early springtime in Indiana: the dismal remains of snowbanks. What had emerged was not yet green. I drove to the arenas on a thick-feeling Monday morning along roads lined with unburst trees, under clouds that looked like blotted tissues. The air itself like a glass of inky water.

But there was no augury here.

I could have stayed heavy with the life of this past little while—Pippa swinging her legs in the funeral home and catching me watching her and missing my smile because she gulped and then sat up, straight and solemn, glassy-eyed and trembling in the overstuffed chair; the life-insurance company notepad I found in Kingsley's kitchen, with its numbered list of things he was going to do the morning he died, which included (#3) Email them the forecast for Florence. *Them.* But there was more ahead than behind, than before. Work on the house in Toronto was progressing well. And Molly said she would bring the girls herself to visit in a few weeks. Not meet me halfway at a resto-gas station with big-rig parking and free showers, but come with them and stay for a visit.

There was more life ahead than behind, than before.

"Bitter-pill-to-swallow" stories filled the Terre-Haute news. In between commercials for pillows designed for the working man's lower back, talk-radio hosts pointed out that money behind the Dante parks and the packaging plant was coming from the same bank account ... dark money, euros, roubles, renminbi ... in the end, isn't it always shekels?

One of the evening-commute jockeys held a naming contest for the pills that would soon be manufactured down the road from Dante's Indiana. But the winning entries—Paradiso and Elysian—were already FDA-approved sleep aids. Half the town seemed convinced that renewal was only possible if Hugh's plan worked and the plant started packaging pills. The other half was convinced that exactly this would be Terre-Haute's total and final ruin.

Hugh hadn't contacted me since I returned, and I didn't try too hard to check in with him, either. Charlie sent me a message, saying he'd see me at work on Monday.

When I arrived, with chocolates and picture books from Florence, the conference room in Paradiso was dark. There was a sign taped to the door. Our Monday morning meeting had been moved to the staff lot behind the arena.

Charlie, Justine, Frank—Frank hadn't quit—Nick, and the Dante professors were standing beside a tractor-trailer. It was painted in lush greens, as a garden of hairy, smiling men and women in loincloths and animal-skin dresses. They were surrounded by deer, rabbits, raptors. Above them, the sky was filled with ivory doves and pterodactyls.

"Prin, it's good to see you and to have you back with us. I am sorry for the loss of your father," said Charlie.

Everyone offered condolences for Kingsley.

"Thank you, everybody. So, why are we meeting here, beside this truck?" I said.

Justine smiled tightly and with quick hand motions deferred to Charlie. He banged on the truck's back doors, which opened into a dark space that glowed red around the edges. A deeper red throbbed from inside. A man in a cowboy hat stepped out and smiled. He was very, very thin for an American white man in his fifties. Flappy-skinned, as if his insides had been cooked in a sous-vide bag. The man pressed a button. A hydraulic lift covered in straps and buckles and braces lowered to the ground. He took off his hat and held it to his heart.

"Good morning! I said, good morning! That's better! Now friends, on this absolutely beautiful day of His creation, who's ready to take the first step on the road to glory?"

The lift went up at a steady groan. We stepped off, into the front part of the trailer, which was painted black.

"Welcome to the beginning of the rest of your lives!" said the man.

He went over to a small podium. Behind him, an arch-shaped door was cut into the black wall. Something red was behind that door, throbbing. The man smiled. He looked at Charlie. He kept looking at Charlie.

"You can go ahead, Pete."

"Thank you, Mr. Tracker. So, as I was saying earlier, friends, good morning! I said, good morning! That's better! Now, friends, on this absolutely beautiful day of His creation, I appear before you by the grace of God and on behalf of American Weedin' Eden Ministries. Can I get an AWEM? I said, can I get an AWEM? I said—"

"Pete, can we get to the presentation?" said Charlie.

"Mr. Tracker, you are a man of God and a businessman, and I appreciate that sometimes the last needs to be first. Let me get right to it. My friends, while Weedin' Eden has dozens of projects and products that bring people closer to Our Lord, you've probably heard of two more than any of the others. Am I right?"

"Genesis Extreme," said Frank.

"And also? Also?" he said.

"America's Got ..."

It was one of the Dante professors.

"Come on, my friend, you can say it. I know you can. We're all here, waiting on that last word. Can you say it? Can we say it, together? Can we all say it? Just like the lucky one of those two criminals crucified on either side of Him, *America's Got ..."*

"... jesus ..."

"JESUS!" said the man.

"Jesus H. Christ!" said another of the Dante professors.

"That is indeed His full name and rank, correct. And He's the inspiration for the talented folks that perform on inland America's highest-rated television show, which broadcasts live from our very popular Biblical attractions park, which Mr. Tracker recently visited. Of course, these days, with gas prices and electric cars and the godless people locking down freedom and paving the interstate over and over again right at our exit, not everyone can make it to our location in beautiful down-home Kentucky. That's why our Gospel-true geniuses designed this fully accessible mobile ministry unit. But before I tell you more about what this is, I'd like to take the opportunity to tell you more about what this is, right here. I'm pointing at where they stapled my stomach, just in case you can't tell. You might say I'm the prodigal son, or more like the prodigious son, as you'll hear in a moment. And so, friends, this is my personal testimony and witness. It begins on a rock, outside a truck stop in Tennessee. The Bible says—"

"I'm sure it does," said Justine.

Charlie gave the flappy man at the podium a hard nod.

He smiled at Charlie and smiled at Justine, seething. Then he closed his eyes and prayed, looked up, and pressed Play.

The trailer shook with big drums and driving, heavy strings and whooshing, whirling winds. The podium mechanically jutted to the side, and the arch-shaped door opened onto the throbbing red darkness.

"SHALOM," said a deep, deep, deep voice.

We walked into the next room of the trailer and sat down on stone benches. Actually, they were made of wood, but spackled in stone paint. I began worrying a chipped edge. The door closed behind us. There was no sound except the hiss of the air conditioning.

"IN THE BEGINNING, GOD CREATED THE HEAVEN AND THE EARTH. AND THE EARTH WAS WITHOUT FORM, AND VOID; AND DARKNESS WAS UPON THE FACE OF THE DEEP. AND THE SPIRIT OF GOD MOVED UPON THE FACE OF THE WATERS. AND GOD SAID, LET THERE BE LIGHT ..."

There came a great buzzing sound, holy legions of honeybees.

"AND THERE WAS LIGHT."

The room went electric white. Lightbulbs all over the ceiling and across all four walls. Bars of light were inlaid in the floor. It smelled like burning. Someone fell off a bench.

The lights dimmed. Nick climbed back onto the bench. Screens lowered, and the voice of the Bible told of God's wondrous creations as hairy and scaly CGI versions multiplied. Mists sprayed, a young brontosaurus family went gambolling across the Edenic green, and the floor quaked. Two people ate an apple—the sound was sucking, draining, bone-crunching, like a man gnawing on another man's head—and then a flaming sword descended.

After the show, we were given DVDs and laminated defenses of Biblical truth, as well as brochures advertising "MCU @ GEx," the full version of what we'd experienced in the tractor-trailer.

The man drove off and Charlie took us to lunch in town. He'd made a reservation in the private dining room of a dry-goods factory that was now a museum of a dry-goods factory.

"This is a firing lunch," said Nick.

"Why do you think so?" I said.

"Off-site, and after what we just saw?" said Nick.

"And look at those sandwiches. They've been under cling wrap since Jar Jar Binks was in short pants," said Frank.

I looked at the side table pressed against the pitted brick wall. The white-bread sandwiches were triangular, each with single piece of meat and cheese. A few had thin green lines of leafy courtesy. The sandwiches were all frowning at the corners from the tight cling. I added the box of greying Dante chocolates I'd brought from Florence.

"Everyone, please, help yourselves to some lunch. Or maybe we should sit down and talk, first," said Charlie.

Everyone sat down.

"So, what'd you think of the presentation?" said Charlie.

The Dante professors raised and lowered their hands but said nothing. Frank and Nick made like infants who'd just discovered their thumbs.

"Do you want me to start?" said Charlie.

"That might be helpful. It'd be good to understand your thinking here," said Justine.

"Well, I have some news," he said.

We were being fired and replaced.

"As you know, the Dante parks have been supported, so far, by some investors from Europe. But I think we all know now, after the big to-do at the plant a while back there, that they're focused on something else. Something very different. And while I am not going to pass judgment on my son's decision—"

"Others have," said Frank.

"I know, Frank. I know. But he's still my son, alright? And we're committed to our children, no matter what, aren't we?"

Frank nodded and looked away.

"Look, folks, I have let Hugh know that I'm not interested in continuing the Dante parks with funding from his Polish friends because of their plans at the plant. But I am interested in continuing on with Dante's Indiana. We need new backers. While Prin was in Florence, I went to Kentucky and visited Genesis Extreme and met with their leadership, the AWEM people. And they're interested in backing us. And it turns out they already work with Turnstyle Solutions as their design and supply group, which is very helpful. I asked them to send Pete and his rig to us, so you could see the kind of work they do. You're all invited down to Kentucky, too, by the way, to see their big park which, I have to say, is impressive. Anyway, they like our Dante idea and respect it, and will keep sending the major work to Turnstyle Solutions, but, well, they do want a little more control over what's happening inside the parks, which is understandable."

"Is it?" said Justine.

"And the other good news is that they have a lot of back-up rides and extra tech like what we just saw, all ready to be finished off here."

"But what do they know about Dante?" I said.

"They probably think Geryon's a dinosaur," said one of the professors.

"And he's not! There are no dinosaurs in Dante!" said another professor.

"Wait. Wait! Stop talking. What is Geryon, in Dante?" said Justine.

"A monster with an innocent face. The embodiment of deceit," said Charlie.

"Also, it's the name of our main ride in Inferno," I said.

"The fabricator just sent me some mock-ups. It's looking pretty cool," said Nick.

"Hang on. Haven't any of you been following the news about the latest police shooting in Chicago?" said Justine.

We shook our heads.

"So you're going for the total changeover, Mr. Tracker?" said Nick.

"No. Or not necessarily. Well, it's like this—"

"Hang on. I'm sorry, everyone. None of you know what I'm talking about? Garyon Jackson? None of you see the problem here? None of you even want to know what the problem is?" said Justine.

"The problem that I see right now, Justine, is that this is a firing lunch, and some of us are not exactly getting a lot of new job offers these days," said Nick.

"So let's get to it then. Yes, people, this is a firing lunch. But it could also be a hiring lunch."

"Meaning what?" said Frank.

"Meaning, with two weeks' notice, you're no longer working for the entity that hired you to be my personal project team for Dante's Indiana. But I'm also saying I have convinced the AWEM people to let you to continue on, you know, as Charlie's Angels," he said.

He smiled.

"Does it mean we have to say things about Jesus?" said one of the Dante professors.

"Well, they probably have some covenant documents you'd be expected to sign, but we can deal with that later."

"And you think Dante's Indiana is going to save Terre-Haute from Hugh?" said Nick.

"Not from Hugh. I don't like it put that way. He's still my son. But an American small town whose main business is packaging painkillers for local distribution—"

"Beating that, that's your plan?" said Frank.

"We have to give it a try. And sure, I can work directly with Pete and others like him, but you all know I'd rather have my own people involved," said Charlie.

"I'm in," said Frank.

"Same," said Nick.

"Me too," I said.

The Dante professors nodded.

Justine took a breath, held it, blew out short and hot, and slammed the cover on her iPad.

"I can't believe none of you know who Garyon Jackson is!"

"I may have heard the name in the news," said Charlie.

"And?"

"None of my business," he said.

"Right. Because this is your business. But not mine. Next week, I'm supposed to spend three days in a skeevy old basketball arena interviewing people who want to work minimum-wage jobs in Hell. Protesters are gathering in Chicago right now. Recruiters message me all the time. Sorry, Nick, but that's me. And my fiancé's in Charlotte and I could have gone there, too. I can go anywhere. I can be helping change things, anywhere. But I chose to come home, and work with all of you; work for you, Charlie Tracker, because I grew up listening to my Daddy say how much you believe in this place and in the people who work for you and the people who live around here. And this is what I get, for believing in Charlie Tracker and believing in what you're trying to do here? You say Garyon Jackson's murder is none of your business and you want me to work at Jurassic Jesus Park?"

"I understand, Justine. You're a heck of a project manager with a great future ahead of you, and we'll miss you, but I understand. You don't want that kind of thing on your resumé, right? Won't look good on Wall Street and LinkedIn and those kind of places, right? Take all the time you need to pack up and all, and you'll be paid to the end of the month, and finally, well, thank you," said Charlie.

Justine looked stunned.

"As for the rest of you. I really don't want a total change-over. I want us to keep our hands on the controls as much as we can. That means at least showing them we're capable of it. So, can you do that in the next little while? Can some of you go down to Kentucky and meet them?"

"I'll go," said Frank.

"I'll go with you," said Nick.

"I'll drive, this time," said Nick.

"I'll go too," I said.

"After the job fair, please. I need you all there," said Justine.

"Thank you, Justine," said Charlie.

She shrugged, staring at the trapped sandwiches.

22

"HI! WELCOME! HI there! Hi! Sorry, can you hear me? Are you here to audition for a performer role, or are you interested in joining the guest services team?"

"Dental? Is there dental?"

"Area three," I said.

"Sir, you can go over to area three? Sir? Hi there! Hi, sorry, can you hear me?"

"Dental? Is there dental?"

Pressing her lanyards against her chest, the HR temp Charlie had hired for the job fair leaned forward and pointed. The man in front of us didn't move. The line grew behind him.

"I'll take him," I said.

I went around the table and motioned for the man to follow. We walked across the playing floor. He had a sharp smell. Cheese rind, scalp. He was wearing a winter coat over jeans and a tank top that showed fuzzy white hair on a birdcage chest. His unlaced construction boots looked like gutted woodland creatures. His mouth like a clear-cut forest.

"That coffee?" he said.

"Yes, and there's sandwiches, too. Help yourself."

We had created area three in the old arena to receive "general" job applicants to Dante's Indiana. Most were weather-cheeked and rheumy-eyed; many had limps; others, blued gums and green tattoos.

Among them, this latest man asking about dental made his way to the coffee table. Head down and shuffling, he joined a longer line.

"You in charge around here?" said another man.

"I'm part of the group that organized the job fair," I said.

"Okay. Can I get the paperwork from you?"

"You'll be given papers if you apply for something specific, in area one or two," I said. "I think we'll be considering applications from this area later."

"No. I'm talking about my paperwork. Mine. Can I get that from you?"

He limped forward, pulling out a messy sheaf of papers from his shredded silver ski jacket. I turned to go back to the main intake desk.

"Come on, I'm not asking for money, man! I don't even want a job here. I just need someone to sign my papers saying that I applied for a job this week. Can you just sign saying that I was here, please?"

"Same! Terms of my peace bond," said another, now approaching.

"I need mine for my alimony waiver," said a man in a three-piece suit, also following me.

"If I don't have any priors, just domestics, do I still need to tick the box?" said one of the many men who looked like a homeless department-store Santa.

"Loose square? Who's got a loose square for me?" said an old man in a Bulls cap.

"Stop begging this poor man for what you all need! Listen, honey, I'll do anything you—you!—need! Just let me show you. I work hard. Just ask," said a righteous-faced older woman with tremolo eyebrows. She wore a pink blazer over a tight black skirt. There were bruises on her bare legs.

Someone near her made an awful comment and people snickered and laughed. She turned around, slipped her heels into her purse, and began swinging it at them.

A guard came over.

"Okay, sir. Thanks. I think it's best if you just escort people to the area and then ask one of us to take over. You can go back to your desk now. We've got this under control."

He was big and bald and had thick, clean arms. The other guards were also big and bald. They all wore tight yellow SECURITY T-shirts and were now strutting through the milling, riled-up crowd that had gathered around the old woman, who was still swinging her bag at laughing men, but growing tired. The rest went back to sipping coffee and thumbing cracked screens.

"We've met before," I said.

"You law enforcement?" the security guard said.

"No."

"NARCAN rep? Lawyer? Caseworker? Church people?"

"No."

"Family? Looking for somebody?"

"We've had this conversation before. Don't you remember?"

"Man, do you know how many times I've had this conversation?"

"We met at Dizzy's World, last month. I was there with two other men. You were at the snack-bar. We were looking, well, for ideas for this place, and also, my friend was looking for his daughter."

"Yeah, I know. Yeah. Cash only."

Walking through the parking lot, the morning of the second day, I saw an older woman in a business suit being harassed by a fat man in a red hat. Was she a new HR temp? Had the young woman from day one had enough? She was being patient with the fat man, but then he took one of her hands and was pulling her away.

"Hey! Stop that! Security!"

They both looked at me. The man let go of the woman and she pecked him on the cheek. He walked towards an old pick-up truck that was pulling a camper.

"That's just my husband. He wanted me to help him with something on the computer but there's already a lineup to put in your application, isn't there? Can you tell security to leave him alone? We won't park overnight."

I saw her again later that morning, when I took my shift at the area two intake, beside Nick and Frank. She was applying for a position in the gift shop. She used to be the store manager of a Sears outside Cincinnati.

Unlike the crowd moving around and around in area three, the people in area two waited in neat lines for their chance to approach the hiring desk, their faces expectant, pallid, humble.

"Prin, we got this under control. We don't need you here," said Nick.

"Why don't you go over to area one and see how the auditions are going?" said Frank.

"I'll go in a minute. But first, what do you think? Are we getting good applications?"

"Yeah, not bad. Seen worse. Seen better. Kind of what we expected, right Frank?"

"Back in the day, the line-up for these kinds of jobs would have been all teenagers from the high school and a few second-chancers, guys back from the service, parolees, gambling problems. Feels like the numbers are way reversed now, but yeah, fine. We'll staff-up behind the scenes. I'm with Nick, Prin. I'm wondering how we're doing with the performer options over in area one. Could you bring us some Danish when you come back?"

I left area two and walked across the arena floor. Other than barking dogs, the sound was a steady murmur. The light coming down from the wide overhead lamps was dull and vague, as much grey as yellow. I looked around. People from all three areas lined the walls of the arena at repeating intervals. They were charging their phones. A few were also charging ankle monitors. One of them kept calling out. He wanted to do his interview from there, attached to the wall. If he crossed the arena floor he'd be violating parole.

Area one was cordoned off by burgundy ropes that Kyle had salvaged from a shuttered hotel. There were lots of locals trying out for Dante characters: ex-gymnasts and exotic dancers, some very young, and others not at all; middle-aged mom- and dad-looking people in old Halloween costumes—sexy angels and fat devils. One woman was wearing a deer costume.

People in dress khakis and newer sweatshirts were there to audition their dogs as assorted beasts of Hell. One couple and their German Shepherd were down all on all fours, trying out as three-headed Cerberus. Other dogs were barking and pulling and snapping in the line-up. The woman in the deer costume was torn at the flanks.

Kyle saw me and waved and asked the couple standing beside him to hold on a moment before they entered the audition room. They were wearing a tuxedo and bridal gown, backwards, which made it look like their heads had been twisted around.

"There's an issue with the latest audition. Can you go in? Also, any dog treats? Please?"

Stepping behind the curtain, I saw Justine's face before I saw the other faces, the faces she was staring at. She looked terrified. The Dante professors sitting on either side of her looked stricken. They were all staring at the man standing on the audition stage in front of their table.

He was young, and thin, and bald, and barefoot, and wearing a rough woollen cloak. His face was painted blood red. In his mouth were the naked legs of a very small man. A dull metal band ran around his forehead, on which were mounted two other faces, one painted shock-white, and the other black as night. These hung down on either side of his own face. In each of the side-mouth faces was the upper half of a very small man.

He was chewing the bodies, working them like he was trying to split skin from shell, shell from seed. The whole time he stood before us silent, and sobbing.

Justine looked at me.

I looked at him.

He looked past me.

I went to him and offered my hand, as if to a child coming off a high step. He took it, still chewing, still crying, and I led him out of the arena through a back door that opened onto a loading dock where workers were eating lunch. They got up and moved away, filming us. I guided the young man up a delivery ramp and out into the grey-white light of the parking lot behind Inferno. He let go of my hand, which was now warm and wet.

He smiled and, from his cloak, took out a round black bag with brass clips, the kind you'd use for carrying a bowling ball or stethoscope. With his free hand he lifted the metal band off his forehead, and with it the side-faces and their chewed bodies. He placed it all in the bag and then pulled the very small man's legs out of his mouth and put them in the bag and shut it. The clips snapped in a final bite.

"Can I call someone for you?" I said.

He wiped his mouth.

He wiped his eyes.

Walking backwards, saying many things I could not hear, he left.

23

BY THE FAIR's third day, we had enough applications for service positions but not enough for performers. The line for auditions was down to an older black woman in light-blue jeans and a green sweatshirt. She came in and saw Justine and snorted. The front of the woman's sweatshirt had a silk-screen image of a young man's face. Under a black leather baseball cap and above a neck covered in gold chains and tattoos, his face was sweet and innocent. Beneath, it read JUSTICE FOR GARYON.

"This line's shorter, so I came here to apply for night cleaner. I can't work days until my grandbaby's old enough for kindergarten."

"Your sweatshirt. It suggests some familiarity with the *Divine Comedy*, yes?" said one of the Dante professors.

"Excuse me?" she said.

"Well, there's a typo," said one of the other professors.

"I said EXCUSE ME?"

Justine stood up at her desk. She glared at the professors and walked the older woman to the side. Justine began to say something but the woman stepped back, wound up her whole body, swayed once, twice, and then told Justine she didn't know and never would know and something about a credit card. The woman took off her sweatshirt and shoved it at Justine. She flattened a yellow T-shirt over her stomach and walked out, screaming someone's name. A little girl in cornrows came out of nowhere and ran after her, holding a beeping, hot-pink tablet.

Justine folded the sweatshirt neatly and held it against her chest and wiped her eyes and turned to face us.

Kyle stepped in to ask if we were ready for the next audition. He saw Justine's face and stopped moving.

"All you see is a spelling mistake on a sweatshirt. *They* can't spell names from Dante, but let's give them a job anyway. The lady who just walked out of here could have been Garyon Jackson's mom. She knows a lot of women who could have been his mom. Everyone she knows could have been his mom."

Justine began digging her fists into the sweatshirt. She started shaking it. She stopped. Now she was shaking.

"And do you know what she just told me? That I could never, ever be his mom. And she said congratulations for that. And she's right. She is right. I will never be late picking up my son from an intersection near the airport where he's selling boxes of chocolate out of his gym bag to pay for football equipment and then gets shot by an off-duty cop who thinks he's reaching for a gun. You know why? Because no son of mine will ever be selling chocolates at an intersection near the airport. He'll be at lacrosse practice and I'll be waiting for him in the parking lot, on a conference call. Congratulations, Justine! You fucking did it! My parents, my teachers, my coaches, pastors, professors, Mr. Tracker, my fiancé's parents, all of you. Four hundred years, 1619 until right here and now, all blended up in my morning smoothie. 'Look at Justine, what a credit to her race! What a credit to all of us!' That woman who just walked out of here, you want to know what she said? She said, 'Congratulations, girl, you a credit card to our race.' A credit card. Do any of you even know what I'm talking about? I don't know if it's worse that you were pretending you didn't know anything about Garyon Jackson when we had that lunch with Charlie, or if you really don't know the murdered child I'm talking about. Not someone from your stupid fucking poem. Not the disgusting name of your rollercoaster. I'm talking about a real person. A real person who's dead. That's it, people. I quit."

"Well, she only promised she'd stick around that long anyway, right?" said Charlie.

We were having breakfast, a few days after the job fair.

"Charlie, if you'd heard what she said and what this woman said to her—"

"I know. Justine called me. We talked. I heard her out and said no and wished her well."

"You said no to what?"

"Listen, Prin. I've known Justine her whole life. I told you, at the start, just how special she was, didn't I? That's why I brought her into this. I did. Let's not forget that. But I said no, and I wished her well. So long as she doesn't give up everything she's got going for her for a pair of marching boots. Talk about a mess of pottage. You do everything possible so they can be successful, and something about them always just gets in the way."

"They? *They?*" I said.

"Kids. Justine. Hugh. Even Frank's girl, in a way. Maybe if we could ask your dad about you. Maybe, in a few years, if I ask you about your girls. I hope not, but always seems to be that way. I mean, think about Dale's boy. That dope-on-a-rope who works for you. Kale."

"Kyle."

"Yeah. That's what I meant by 'They.' Understood?"

"Okay."

"So that's that about Justine. Now. About Kentucky: you're leaving later today, right?"

"That's right."

"Who else is going?"

"Kyle, Nick, and Frank. And my wife and kids are going to meet us there."

"That's really good, Prin. I'm glad that plan worked out. A little good news."

"Thanks. Here's a little more. Nick checked with the fabricator and there's still time to change the design. We're thinking of making it just a generic winged devil. They're flying around everywhere in *Inferno*, so it's still in keeping with Dante. And the professors are fine with it, too."

"What are you talking about?"

"The rollercoaster. We're going to change the name," I said.

"I already told Justine the answer's no."

"She asked you to change the name? I guess she didn't know we were already going to."

"She came to see me. We spoke. It didn't take long, and it didn't go that well. But I respect her father. He's a good man, and maybe he'll talk some sense into his daughter."

"You mean, you'd be willing to hire her back?"

"That's not happening, Prin."

"Why not?"

"Well, for starters, the rollercoaster's our main attraction, and its name is Geryon. It's the right name. And it was your idea in the first place, wasn't it? You brought this to the rest of us after you made that trip to Dizzy's World! Prin, this is your idea. Own it."

"Fine then. It's now my idea to change the name, Charlie. I know the spelling is different from the name of that poor kid who was shot, but I'm not sure people will appreciate the difference. What about something like Hellrider, or Hellraiser? This isn't just about Justine. It's about making sure people don't protest and boycott the park. You know, that could happen."

Charlie stirred his coffee and began flicking and snapping a packet of sugar substitute.

"'That poor, innocent kid who was shot,' huh? You really think he just had boxes of chocolate in that bag? I guess we watch the news on different channels."

He sat forward.

"We are not renaming the rollercoaster. And if crazy people yell about it, that'll just make regular people want to come here more. Dante sent friends to hell and enemies to heaven. He split Muhammad in half and shoved lots of your popes into damnation, one on top of the other. And he did it because that's what it took to tell the story. Having a rollercoaster named for a treacherous monster with a sweet black baby-face is the right call."

"Who said his face was black?"

"Excuse me?"

He seemed to grow by a half, across the diner booth.

"Listen, Prin. I'm no Supreme Court nominee. And I'm not going to tell you about all the men I served with in Vietnam and would have died for in a heartbeat, in a heartbeat, or about how many men and women—and their daughters, until they quit—have had good, good jobs under my watch. A lot better than their other options, I'll tell you. This park has to be true to Dante if it's going to work. And I guarantee our friends in Kentucky are going to agree with me."

"I still don't understand why we can't just change the name of the rollercoaster and stay true to Dante."

"Because being true to Dante means making some tough calls about people, and they're tough calls because they can be true. They are true! Am I wrong?"

"You're right about Dante."

"That's good enough for me. What about you?"

I gave him my answer and left.

24

I DROVE TO a church and joined a confirmation class confession line. When it was my turn, I confessed that I'd just lied to my boss. Maybe.

"Maybe?" said the priest.

"I'm not sure yet, Father."

"So what's the sin here?" said the priest.

"I told my boss I would do as he asked, about a work situation, but I'm not sure I'm going to," I said.

"And why not?"

"I don't think he understands the situation properly."

"So pride."

"Pardon?"

"You're here to confess the sin of pride. Correct?"

"Okay."

I left the confessional booth and knelt in the first bench before the altar to do my penance.

I left the church and went to Payatta's, to drop off Tupperware. As usual, he invited me to a proper dinner again, and, as usual, I declined. I had a real excuse this time. I would be in Kentucky for work for a few days.

He didn't just bobble his head and wince and sing "What Prin!" and send me on my way. Instead, he said, very calmly, that there would be no more take-away suppers until I came home for a proper dinner. I didn't want to go. It felt like a betrayal of my own parents, to have dinner with a Sri Lankan couple in Terre-Haute.

No it didn't.

I just didn't want to spend a night looking at family photo albums of dead people and Ceylon gardens while agreeing to fifth and sixth plates of food.

No. He deserved more than that.

I told him I would come for dinner, definitely, when I returned from Kentucky. The following Sunday night.

"You're not playing the fool?"

"No. I promise I'll come."

"I can tell my wife and daughter?"

"Yes."

"Because if they air the saris and polish the oil lamps and take the bus to Indianapolis for dry fish—"

"There's no need, Payatta, for them to do all of that."

"Right. We'll just eat a bag of Burger King on the bathroom floor like Americans."

"Okay. I understand."

"You do? You understand what it means, your coming home to have dinner with me and my wife and the daughter?"

"My parents are Sri Lankan, Payatta. I understand having a guest for dinner."

"No. This is more than just having a guest for dinner. You understand what this means, for me, for wife, for daughter?"

"I do."

His eyes became glassy and he cleared his throat and bobbled his head once, firmly.

"We have been waiting a long time for this occasion to take place, son."

"Sounds good. See you soon."

He smiled and started texting.

* * *

I drove four hours from Terre-Haute to Kentucky along a broken-shouldered highway, Kyle sitting beside me in silence. I made jokes about Teslas and Sloppy Janes, in vain. The most I could get out of him was that he was "working through some thinking through" about "where things are at, and not just with me and Justine, but with people, with America."

Ongoing highway construction near the park, even on a Saturday, meant we had to detour onto serpentine local roads. We crawled and curved around mountains dotted with fading red and green Monopoly-like houses and drove past live-in scrapyards and shady cemeteries and red and white churches. We were slowed down by a big rig hauling frozen peas that had a sign on one back door saying, "If you don't like my driving, talk to my boss!" while the other back door had a picture of the boss, bearded and doe-eyed, waiting for you to call him by his name.

"Jesus, seriously?" said Kyle.

His first words in hours.

"You mean about the guy's driving?" I said.

"Just being stuck here, like this, all this time, and if it weren't for the racist, murdering police state of Illinois, Justine would have been here, the whole time. I could have had hours and hours with her, Prin. Also, yeah, I mean, that young man would still be alive."

"Kyle, I appreciate you had a lot of feelings for Justine—"

"Had?"

"Have a lot of feelings for Justine, and that she has definitely acknowledged your presence, but you were never dating."

"Not yet."

"Also, she's engaged."

"For now."

"Probably until they get married."

"But who knows? I mean, if you think about what happens to young black men in America these days—"

"Jesus, Kyle, seriously?"

"No. I'm just saying, but no. Sorry. I need to do a little more working through my thinking through."

Eventually we began to see Moses, many Moseses: big fibre-glass cut-outs, beards blowing in the wind. They were set up at half-mile intervals along the road, pointing straight ahead to the park. Beneath the final Moses, a man in a lawn chair was reading a scientific journal beside a homemade display of maps and charts showing the ascents of man and beast. Beside him was a cardboard cut-out of a bearded Victorian and holding a sign.

Honk if you're evolved!

We drove between the soaring legs of a giant angel holding an electrified sword and found a spot in the overnight parking lot, which was filled with camper trucks. To get to the main gates, we took a bus wrapped in the parted Red Sea, alongside other parkgoers and their luggage and strollers and wheelchairs and wheelchair-strollers and coolers and oxygen tanks and travelling dialysis kits with ROLL TIDE bumper stickers. Kyle sighed and put away his phone.

"There's just no filter to make this look good."

We showed our passes at the main gates and were taken by golf cart to a smaller bus, this one wrapped in bullrushes and driven by a Gulf War I vet who loaded our bags with his good hand and hummed hymns on the way to the park hotel, Rahab's Hideaway.

We could have walked from the main gates in less time but what did I care? I jumped out of the mini-bus to find Molly and the girls.

"Hi Prin! Girls, look! It's your dad! It's Prin! Hi Prin!"

Wyatt. Waving and laughing.

Kyle elbowed me.

"Who the fuck is that? He looks like the guy who was sleeping with the babysitter the whole time."

"Mom didn't invite him, Dad," said Philomena.

"Dad, he totally invited himself. Dad, he didn't even bring his kids. He said he had to 'research' it first to make sure it was appropriate. He said Mormon views on evolution were 'evolving.' Dad, he's trying to make puns with us now," said Chiara.

"What a cheugy," said Philomena.

"He's going to be busy for a while," I said.

God bless Kyle.

He was in the front entrance of the lobby, asking Wyatt about the accuracy of *The Book of Mormon*, which he'd confused with *Angels in America*. Wyatt was nodding and laughing and shaking his head. His hands were opening and closing into fists.

He'd invited himself. Not been invited.

Why didn't she tell me he was coming?

Because it didn't matter?

Because it did?

But then there she was in the lobby, in a long blue dress, and my heart fired with an ancient flame. Not ancient.

We hugged, hard. We kept hugging.

It didn't matter.

Sursum cordibus!

The girls didn't make gross-out noises or shoulder their way between us to break it up. Instead, they closed around us in the lobby.

We checked into our room. The girls divided the bath products, which had been made in Michigan by Iraqi Christians. We met Wyatt and Kyle back in the lobby and took golf carts into the park. Kyle kept it up with Wyatt. I told him there was no need. He said it was good training.

He challenged Wyatt to a Bible trivia contest inside an escape room modelled on the mighty faith of Daniel. Just the two of them.

Molly waved goodbye.

Wyatt froze.

He glitched back to life and laughed and nodded and went into the lion's den with Kyle.

And now it was just us. The children asked if we could use the motorized scooters. We decided to walk. The mid-May Kentucky weather was invisible and perfect: balmy and dry, the sun filtered by cottony clouds and high, bushy trees. Ahead of us was a massive lineup, more than an hour long, for the most popular ride at Genesis Extreme—David's Sling, which put people in cars shaped like smooth stones that went flying above the park's main causeway and into the smoking, smashed-in forehead of a snarling, brass-helmeted Goliath.

No one wanted to wait for the ride or to sit through any of the park's hourly talks, concerts, or testifying sessions. The girls were excited to attend the live studio taping of the latest episode of *America's Got Jesus*, but that was the following afternoon, and thanks to my VISavedP pass, we didn't need to camp out the night before.

We also had spots already reserved at the park's newest attraction, a virtual-reality experience called the Marvellous Christian Universe. We'd see both of these on Sunday after going to a Spanish-language Mass in an office portable beside the cooking-oil barrels.

"So what should we do now?" I said.

Beaming, the children pulled out their girl-edition park maps and began arguing for other options: we could ride rafts down the Ultra Euphrates; we could visit Studio Exodus and paint lintels and doorposts with the blood of the lambs that parkgoers with boy-edition maps were invited to slaughter next door at the Passover Test Kitchen; we could join "Project take back the Rainbow" by helping stitch together the largest technicolor dreamcoat in the world; we could fill bags of rice for people starving in the Sudan and write letters of encouragement to the prime minister of Israel; we could meet Jim Caviezel; we could visit Patmos Labs, where we could 3D-print pieces of the ten plagues of Moses, either to take home or to throw at Pharaoh during one of the thrice-daily re-enactments.

It was all too far away by foot, and by now the scooters were all checked out. Anyway, we were enjoying just walking together—we hadn't done something like this since our trip to the zoo on New Year's Day, two years earlier. The girls kept turning around to see Molly and I both smiling "for-true-life," as Pippa liked to say. We bought treats at Ole Honey's Milk and Honey Café and went to the only attraction that had no lineup.

The Jesse Tree Maze was laid out as a series of roots and branches off a cross-like trunk, which you could only get through by walking and also knowing Jesus' genealogy. The children darted and veered around corners from begat to begat and we trailed behind, Molly beside me.

Both of us smiling for true life.

25

"SO MOLLY, WHAT do you think?"

"About?"

"This place. Do you think the people who made this can help us finish Dante's Indiana?"

"I'm not sure. I don't really know what's happening there these days, Prin. But do you really think your boss ..."

"Charlie ..."

"...wants Dante's Indiana to look like this?"

"No, not like this, but he thinks working with these people is the only way we're going to have the park ready and good enough."

"Good enough for what?"

"Hopefully, to prevent the other big project in town—the changeover at the plant, to package pills—becoming the main attraction."

"That would be terrible."

"I know. As would some other things going on right now."

"Like what?"

"Just a situation with one of the rides and someone who recently quit. I'll tell you later."

"Okay. Do you really think Charlie wants giant angels standing in front of the arenas? The girls looked up when we drove under."

"He wants a giant Dante. Legs together."

I smiled. She smiled. We were both quiet.

"Prin, you can't help yourself! You need to know what's changed, right? It's not enough for you that something has, is it! Because something has changed. I feel it. Don't you? Maybe we both sensed it in Toronto but …"

"My dad's funeral."

"Exactly. Anyway, this isn't exactly where I thought it would happen—"

"But you always thought it would happen?"

"Yes. And I felt it right when I saw you, when we hugged. Didn't you? I was thinking about it in the car. Maybe my mother's praying a new novena. Maybe both of our mothers are. I don't know, only that I wasn't expecting that it like this, but, yes Prin, it's happened."

"I was actually thinking that it would be in Toronto, when we moved home. After the renovation was finished. In the backyard."

"That's a such Prin thing to say. So specific to you, and unknown to me. But never mind. Never mind."

"Molly, I agree, it doesn't matter where, or when. It has happened. That's what matters. Thank God."

"And what do you think has happened?"

But there was no challenge in her voice. There was, instead, a real searching.

"Molly, I don't want to talk and talk and talk about what's changed or what's happened and then suddenly nothing's changed, nothing's happened, again."

"Me either. So let's not talk and talk and talk, but maybe talk a little. The kids are having fun ahead of us and now's as good a time as any. I don't just want to hug and hold hands and get on with things. I think we've done that before. I don't think we should, again. Do you?"

Again, no tiredness, no give-up. Not short and cool either. Her voice was clear and warm.

"Okay. So then?"

"I was riding the bike the other day, in my sister's basement, and suddenly I just felt it."

"Forgiveness?"

"No."

"Oh."

"Stupidity."

"Molly, I know. In going to Dragomans and doing what I did, taking a risk like I did, I was so stupid—"

"Prin, you don't know! Yes, fine, you've been stupid. Yes. But so have I."

"No, Molly, it's me."

She stopped walking.

"Maybe this time I'm the one who's figured something out about myself? About us? Maybe even about you? Can you let that happen?"

Chiara and Maisie motioned for us to go to the right side of a bend in the next branch.

"Yes."

"Really, can you?"

"Okay."

"Okay. This is what made me feel stupid. I thought: 'What I am doing, riding an exercise bike in Milwaukee every day while the kids learn about Herodotus at my sister's kitchen table and my ex-boyfriend from high school is dating me in his head?'"

"Are you serious? I knew it! Even Kyle, after just seeing him—"

"Prin, this isn't about Wyatt, either. But I know that's not easy to hear, so let me say, again, it's in his head. Most of the time, I don't even think he knows it's in there. Or maybe he does. His wife is kind of a ghost. When she's not working, she's on the bike or at church."

"Mormon church."

"I think he's incredibly lonely. Anyway, it's not in mine."

"Not in yours."

"And never has been."

"But was it, ever? Molly, was it?"

"This morning, I was packing the car for the trip—"

There came a dull and constant beeping. Just ahead of us, a couple in motorized scooters were reversing out. We had to wait.

I didn't pray that my heart be lifted up. It wasn't under the bridge with the trolls. It was here. I prayed that it stayed right here. Beside hers. Wherever it was and was going.

"I was talking to myself with the trunk open, trying to remember if I'd dumped out the hot water and added coffee to the thermos and then there's Wyatt, standing beside me, and he says, 'You always forget to do that!' and he's smiling and at first I thought he was remembering an old joke between us, from when we dated in high school and once mixed up our thermoses and he was worried he was going to Mormon Hell—"

"I love you, Molly. But it's just hell."

"I love you, Prin. Worried he was going to ... hell for drinking coffee, but he wasn't remembering. He was actually talking about the present day, about us, meaning me and him. He was talking like he knew something about me, about us, something—"

"From inside?"

"Yes. From inside, and the only person in there is you, Prin. When Wyatt said what he said, it felt fake and crummy. And I didn't just feel stupid. I felt fake and crummy, and I thought, how did I get here? Did I mean to? Did you mean to, Prin? Did you want to? Dragomans? Wende? Staring at Wyatt with the trunk open, I knew my answer, and I knew that it was your answer, too."

"My answer is no."

"Yes."

"Yes?"

"Yes. Mine too."

When it was time to go to my meeting with Nick and Frank and our hosts, Kyle said he'd join Molly and the girls for dinner at The Psalm.

"I'm the fifth wheel around here, not Utah jazz-hands."

But Wyatt said he was really tired from all the Bible trivia with Kyle, and that, anyway, he should probably check in with his wife and boys.

"Sounds like a good idea," I said.

"Thanks! So, hey, still enjoying heaven?" Wyatt said.

"Mormon Heaven."

"Yeah. It will be," he said.

I kissed Molly and left them at the hotel restaurant.

AWEM's corporate offices were located on the top floors of a building built into the backside of Goliath's head. Frank and Nick were waiting for me outside one of the boardrooms. Frank was doing his back exercises and Nick was looking between the doors to figure out what in there was smelling like a lot of warm beef.

"So what do you think?" I said.

"You first," said Nick.

"Do you want me just to say it?" said Frank.

"I'm not sure what you're going to say, Frank," I said.

"That this place is scary the way going to watch soccer in Brazil would be scary. Right?"

"I'm not with you yet," said Nick.

"Soccer in Brazil. Soccer in Brazil! Imagine if we were

starting a new pro team in Terre-Haute and we recruited a bunch of guys from Rio to join our team."

"And you see how good they are at it," said Nick.

"Exactly!"

"But now imagine the Brazilians understand that it's our team, that they're the hired guns, and they want to help us win. That wouldn't be bad, would it?" I said.

The elevator dinged.

"We'll see," said Frank.

The doors opened. Men of all ages emerged wearing short-sleeved dress-shirts and corduroy pants that were either flaming orange or livid green, as well as corporate nametags and big golden crosses and buttons that said, "Ask me about my pants, *please!*"

"Gentlemen! Welcome! I'm Adam, the founder and CEO of American Weedin' Eden Ministries. So. Dante! I'd rather Magic Narnia Kingdom if we're going with literary inspiration for a theme park, but maybe we'll do that ourselves somewhere else. I'm just glad to be working with Charlie. I'd also like it if his company was packaging up our DVDs instead of the godless Chinese, but we're signed up with them for another five years, and anyway, I understand his son's doing something else with it now. Charlie mentioned the new plan. Let me say, I think it's terrible. Sinful, even."

"Amen to that," said Frank.

"Amen indeed, my friend! Especially when I have super-smart brethren in Brazil doing some stuff with pharmaceuticals, but a God-friendly line. Chastity pills, for virtuous young Christian gentlemen. Some kind of vascular inhibitor, blood pumper, or maybe anti-blood pump, whatever. Young men take it and don't get too excited around the girls, or even at the idea of girls. The clinical trials are going well. Thinking of calling it V3—for Virginity, Virtue, Victory. They'll be looking for a North American packager and distributor pretty soon. But the timing's off. It's too late for Tracker Packaging. And now here's another way to work with Charlie. In other words, what the Inferno, let's do it!"

The others chuckled.

"Pills? From Brazil?" said Frank.

"Too late for Tracker Packaging. He just said so. Leave it," said Nick.

"Now, gentlemen, I know he sent you down here so we could get into the nuts and bolts of it. We'll do that over some warm beef in a bit. But first, hey, say, who wants to skip the lineup and ride the Good News? Get a sense of what we can do for you up in Terre-Haute? I said who?"

We were taken by golf cart to David's Sling. After putting on an oversized MIND THE GATH T-shirt, I rode in the first of the five smooth-stone cars, alongside Adam. After the safety bar came down across our legs, we lurched forward and waited for the others to get into their cars.

"So! Before we fell Goliath, tell me, what's your story in His story?" he said.

"I'm working for Charlie Tracker, who, as you obviously know, is the person behind the Dante theme park that we're building in Terre-Haute. And we're here, as you also obviously know, to talk about working with you and your colleagues."

We began to move.

"It's actually a two-way interview, friend. You can ask me anything you want. But I still want an answer to my question. What's your story in His story?" he said.

We began accelerating.

"You're asking me a more personal question, about my own faith commitments. Alright. I'm Catholic—"

"WAY WRONG! Try again. I'll say it as many times as I need to. What's your story in His story? Try again!"

Now we were moving really fast, straight at Goliath, and Adam was yelling in the wind.

"TRY AGAIN!"

" ... Jesus? ..."

"AMEN! Now say it like you RCs believe you eat it! Hang on, here we go, straight into the big dumb Gath's head."

We smashed through and dropped at a steep pace into a rumbling dark cavern and then shot out onto a lower loop. We came to a stop at a sign that read "Whose son *art* thou, *thou* young man?" and returned to the golf carts.

Adam patted the seat beside him. I walked past and sat in the second cart with Nick and Frank, who were also wearing new T-shirts.

"Did you ask your guy about his pants?" said Nick.

"No," I said.

"Did you, Frank?"

"I did. Did you, Nick?"

"I did."

"And?"

"Don't ask them about their pants."

"Okay. But what did you think of the ride?"

They both nodded.

"I think we know what to do with Satan now. A ride inside the bodies of the bad guys."

In unison they moved their arms up and down, eating imaginary Judases.

We left David's Sling and went through the rest of the park, past all the attractions, which were turned off and shuttered for the night. We came to a broad path that led to a windowless rectangular building overlooking the highway. It was surrounded by floodlights that illuminated its façade, which was painted to look like burgundy leather with a thick golden cross at its centre.

"Is that a giant Bible?" said Frank.

"Look! The front cover is opening!" said Nick.

We parked off to the side and walked into the Marvellous Christian Universe.

It was dark and empty.

We were given white headsets with black screens that covered the upper half of our faces.

"Before we start, I just want to say welcome to our main attraction and yes, our main attraction is the Bible. Everything we need is inside," said Adam.

His colleagues nodded and said Amen.

"Now, you definitely would have seen this building from the highway, if the highway were open, but as you know, by some strange coincidence, right after we built this facility, construction started right at our exit. Months later, no progress, just lots of progressives. Ha! But don't worry, we're going to deal with them in the courts. We've had to do it before—in case our guests don't know, the Kentucky Supreme Court has ruled that only a true-born woman, soup-to-nuts, can audition for Salome on a television program with closely-held religious beliefs."

His people nodded.

"Amen."

"Awem."

"And I know, Dante folks, that you experienced our road-show of righteousness when Pete brought the tractor-trailer to visit you in Terre-Haute. We usually send it to children's hospitals and mobile-home communities and correction facilities and detention buildings, and I was glad we could make that little stop, just to give you a taste of what we've created here. Now you'll get the full experience. And after that, like I said, we'll break bread over some warm beef. It's then that I'll say a little more about where all of this came from, other than the Bible. It'll also be a chance to talk about what you've been seeing and liking around here and what we've already worked up for your Dante park and what we're hopefully going to do together. I'll just say this for now. On our latest call, Charlie let me know you're having some talent issues, recruitment-wise, for Heaven. Correct?"

We nodded.

"So I'm thinking this: Next month, when I figure we'll be bringing our planning team in anyway, why not use one of your arenas to do a special edition of *America's Got Jesus*? You can recruit for Heaven directly from our show. How's that sound? Good? Good!"

Just then, Hugh texted me. "WTF? JUSTINE?!"

"Okay! Gentlemen, gear up and take a knee," said Adam.

His colleagues nodded and donned their headsets and knelt. They prayed. They got up. We remained standing, Frank doing back exercises and tipping a bit with his headset on. An intercom voice told us to move apart from each other, far enough that, if needed, we could die for our friends without bumping into the sinners dying on either side of us. We stretched out our hands, moved around until we stopped touching the fingertips of other men. And then we entered the Marvellous Christian Universe.

Driving orchestral music started, it was like the Super Bowl and presidential debates and Bible movies all in one, only louder and darker, more victorious. Then total silence, without form, a void, black. We were taken from this sucking shapelessness into a fresh new world of blues and greens and dappled things. We went for a soaring ride across an Eden in full flower, first on the fluffy wings of a pterodactyl, and then on the scaly back of a brontosaurus that smelled like straw and cow manure. From there we were dumped into a searing, dusty exile on the far side of a flaming sword. Generations of people lived and died. Cities rose and fell. We entered the ark and rode floodwaters in search of a dove bearing an olive branch. Eventually, a baby boy cried out in a manger that also smelled like straw and cow manure, and then we stood on another searing, skull-covered plain, beside a beloved young man and a weeping mother as the son cried to his father for abandoning him on the cross. We entered another shapeless void, dead quiet until voices began screaming, cursing, muttering, sighing, and laughing with fishbone tongues and rusted throats. Then shrieking. Then silence, again. Three days later, we were blinded by the light of resurrection, and in the blinding brightness we heard new voices, small and scared. Burning tongues of fire warmed our heads. Later, we sat in a cave with a man once young and beloved, now old and visionary. This John told us of many other things, of all the lambs and dragons and gates and rivers and cities ahead of us before there came new beginnings and final endings. It ended with him opening a copy of the Bible towards us, asking what our story was going to be, in His story.

Charlie called me after we drove away from the giant Bible. Hugh had already texted again, twice, the same message.

"Hi Charlie. We're just on our way to dinner. Can I call you afterwards?"

"Forget dinner. Find a TV and turn to the news."

"Why?"

"That poor, innocent kid. Justine. She got a new job."

26

"DADDY! WE'RE WATCHING TV! Mommy said! Look! She's so pretty! Justine! And I skated with her first, when we went roller skating with her!" said Pippa.

"Dad! So pretty. So, so pretty. And now Justine's famous! I skated with her the longest," said Maisie.

"His name's Garyon. Not Gary. His name's also Geryon, with an 'e,' or something like that, according to Dante? Dad, what's happening? Is what Justine's saying true?" said Philomena.

She was sitting apart from everyone else and biting her nails, her feet curled up.

"Kyle told us Justine was on the news. Was this the complicated situation you were going to tell me about?" said Molly.

"Dad? Dad, is what she's saying, true? Is it?"

"I skated with her as long as you did!"

"No you didn't! You got tired. Dad, is Justine just on this channel? Isn't she on other channels? Should we check if she's on any Netflix shows? Can we watch Netflix now?"

"Girls! Just, everyone, can you give me a few minutes to watch and see what she's actually saying?"

I sat down on the edge of one of the two beds. The children jockeyed and climbed around me, hot little wars breaking out over who would sit where and who would hold the remote.

"Dad, do you want me to hold your phone for you?" said Maisie.

Said with an air of such careful, such graceful indifference, I nearly gave it to her.

Instead, with my free hand I kept checking it. My phone was pulsing with messages and missed calls, from Charlie and Hugh, Nick and Frank. Kyle.

Justine was being interviewed by a news anchor with a pained face. She was identified as a "community activist" and "whistleblower." She was wearing the sweatshirt the older woman had shoved at her the day she quit Dante's Indiana.

"Before my experiences with this company at a senior management lunch, and then at a job fair I was directing, I didn't believe what has happened was possible. I believed him," said Justine.

"Who? Just so viewers are clear," said the anchor.

"Mr. Tracker. Charlie Tracker, who hired me."

"And what did you believe about him? And what's changed?"

"He's been very good to me and my family, and to our town. He's done a lot. But then some things came to light."

"You're a woman," said the anchor.

"Yes."

"A woman of colour."

"Yes."

"A young woman of colour."

"Yes."

"Working in a majority older-white-male workplace and industry. Justine, is there something else you want to tell us about what's been going on for you?"

Justine paused.

My phone stopped buzzing.

"No. Nothing like that. Not to say others haven't, but that

hasn't been the situation for me. That's not reason I'm here today. The reason I'm here is that I had no other choice."

"What do you mean?"

"With witnesses present at the lunch I mentioned, I tried to inform Mr. Tracker about my concerns, and was told I could quit if I didn't like his plans. I decided to keep trying to advocate for positive change from the inside and then was publicly confronted by a fellow member of the Black community about the situation. I was humiliated and offered no support from either company leadership or HR. At that point, I chose to leave my position. But I had one more conversation with Mr. Tracker, and that was when I asked him directly to change the name of the rollercoaster—"

"Which, for viewers just joining us for this exclusive interview, is the main feature of the theme park set to open in a few months in Terre-Haute, Indiana. Now this rollercoaster is, I understand, designed to look like a monster and, despite your repeated requests, this ride will be named after a black male character from Dante's *Divine Comedy* who is eternally burning in hell. Is that all correct?"

"That's my understanding, yes."

"And as of now—and I want to say again that no one associated with the theme park has responded to repeated interview requests—you are alleging that the people behind the park plan to name the rollercoaster Geryon, correct?"

"That's right."

The anchor looked directly at the camera.

"And as viewers know, this is also the name of the Chicago teenager, Garyon Jackson, whose recent shooting by an off-duty policeman near O'Hare Airport has ignited protests in Illinois and elsewhere. Correct?"

"Correct."

My phone began buzzing again.

"Dad! Is it true? Is this really happening? Are you really doing that?" said Philomena.

"Dad would never do that! Right Dad? You would never let us give you ideas for something like that, right Dad?" said Chiara.

"Why don't you go down to the lobby and call Charlie? Girls, let's see what else is on."

"NETFLIX!"

"Dad, what about the headline?" said Philomena.

"It's not true."

"See? I told you," said Chiara.

"Promise?" said Philomena.

"What's that supposed to mean?"

"Prin, go make your call. I'll talk to Philomena," said Molly.

I looked at the television. Justine was gone. An expert on the whitewashing of the Middle Ages was being interviewed. The screen was now showing a portrait of Dante, the plan of the poem laid out behind him, a rollercoaster crashing through it, and the headline.

BREAKING: RACIST THEME PARK SET TO OPEN IN INDIANA ...

I drove back to Terre-Haute the next day. Frank and Nick decided that staying on task was the best way to help, so they remained in Kentucky and went through the rest of the park on Sunday with their hosts. Molly and the girls stayed too, to try David's Sling and go to the MCU and attend a taping of *America's Got Jesus*. The girls called to tell me they liked the ride more than the Virtual Reality, and "Jazz Hands for Jesus" more than "Abs-Salom, Abs-Salom" at the talent show. The rundown was really just an excuse to tell me Wyatt had rented a car and gone back to Milwaukee on his own. Meanwhile, Kyle had disappeared. He texted his mother and me together, promising he was safe and would be home soon, and we'd understand, then.

The Sunday before Memorial Day weekend was beautiful in Terre-Haute. Driving into the city, my windows were open and the air smelled good and clean. The sky, filled with wispy clouds, was the softest blue. What for months had been taupe and brown had suddenly burst out green, everywhere. For once, the city didn't feel out of season.

When I turned onto the main road that took you from downtown Terre-Haute to the arenas, I saw sharp, black shapes hanging in the sky. Helicopters. I slowed down but kept driving until I saw barricades ahead. Police were standing around them, their cars parked in chevron formation, doors open and lights flashing mutely. Then, like burning leaves, I heard the voices.

I stopped the car.

I texted Molly to keep the children away from the television. It was too late. She said the girls were worried about the situation in Terre-Haute, worried for Justine because of the angry crowds. They wanted to do something.

I suggested they make cards.

My phone rang.

"Prin, where are you?"

"Charlie, I'm driving to the arenas, but—"

"Get out of there! The police have cordoned off the main roads because of the protesters. They're marching on the park. We're meeting at the house, instead," he said.

I made a U-turn and drove away from the whomp and whir.

Charlie and Hugh were in the living room, as were others. Hugh was sitting on a bar stool brought in from the kitchen island. He was bright red, his eyes bulging, his lips swallowed into his face. He looked like he was boiling from the inside. From his reading chair Charlie was watching Hugh, too. He looked worried about him, or about whatever Hugh was looking at on his phone. Probably both. Across from us, a man and a woman were sitting on the couch in almost identical business clothes. Beside them, slouched down, was another man, with dreadlocks that looked like they were made of honey and bits of toast.

"Prin, thanks for cutting short your time in Kentucky and coming in on a Sunday. We can talk about Genesis Extreme another time. Say, how's the family?"

"Of course. And thanks, they're fine."

"Hugh, do you want to start things off? Hugh?" said Charlie.

"No."

"Well, can you at least tell us what's so interesting on your phone? We should probably keep each other informed about things, with everything going on. Don't you think so, son?"

"Do *you* think so, Dad? *Now* you think so?"

He went back to his phone.

"Can you at least introduce your friends to Prin? You brought these people here. I certainly didn't."

"Thanks, Charlie—"

"I'm Mr. Tracker," said Charlie.

"Right! Mr. Tracker, we can do that! We can introduce ourselves. Hi, I'm Heather," said the woman on the couch.

The man beside her shifted to face me. In unison they smiled and pulled out business cards and placed them on the far side of the coffee table. The other man on the couch, heavy-lidded and dred-haired, nodded in my direction.

"Prin, we're with Zephyr, a crisis communications group based in Indianapolis. Hugh has retained us to work with you and the rest of the team for the next little while," she said.

"I've run a company for decades and never had to work with PR types—"

"Crisis communications, Mr. Tracker."

"You want crisis communications? Vietnam, the summer of sixty—"

"You're a veteran?"

"I am."

"Thank you for your service to our country, sir."

"Why you sarcastic son-of-a—"

"No, I mean it! My dad, too. Desert Storm."

"And your father lets you keep your hair like that?"

He shrugged.

"Could I ask Kevin beside me here to start us off?" said Heather.

No one said anything. Kevin opened his laptop.

"Okay, so, thanks, Heather. So, right now, #Dantesowhite and #TerreHate and #racistrollercoaster and #JusticeforGaryon are all trending on Twitter. Also, #Justine2024. Geolocating multi-platform social-media activity and word-clustering a data set out of that and then cross-referencing that data with meeting announcements and calls-to-action on social suggests high hundreds, not including media, are making their way to your site."

"So everyone who hates us, thanks to Justine, is coming for us now?" said Charlie.

"Not exactly," said Kevin.

"You're disputing that Justine is responsible for this mess?" said Charlie.

"Whoever named the rollercoaster is responsible for this mess," said Hugh.

"So now you're blaming Dante?"

"No. I'm not blaming Dante for naming the rollercoaster," said Hugh, staring at me.

The woman beside Kevin pulled his laptop towards her.

"What Kevin means, Mr. Tracker, is that it's not just critics and opponents who are gathering at the site."

"Who else?" said Hugh.

"These groups have pretty obscure names and they change a lot, but, well, some of the organizations that have called for action in Terre-Haute, to support the theme park, include the Dark Knights of Columbus, the NSA, even something called ... I'm actually not comfortable saying this entity's name," she said.

"Did you just say the NSA is coming? As in the National Security Agency?" I said.

"As in, Not Sorry, America," said Charlie.

Everyone looked at Charlie, who looked right back.

"Does this make things better or worse?" said Hugh.

"Each side, and lots of groups and organizations on each side, will have their own storylines. Old media is going to amplify everything. It's going to be lot of noise. A lot of noise. What you want to be is the signal in the noise," said Heather.

"Because if you're not, then it's Justine," said dreadlocks.

"I could call the governor," said Hugh.

"Like he's going to do something that doesn't help him in the primaries. Or who knows? Maybe he'll call in the National Guard," said Charlie.

"He just might. Which is fine by me, Dad. Because this is about more than your stupid Dante hobby now. And the governor knows it. If our Tracker Packaging investors think this place is a mess, Indiana is going to lose a major new investment opportunity and all those jobs ..."

"Anyone else see the governor of Ohio is already trolling our governor about this? He's tweeting about the international investment opportunities in his calm and quiet state."

"Everyone's running for president these days. Hugh, do you really think your investors are going to walk away because of some college kids and hobo librarians yelling into their phones? My investors aren't going to do that," said Charlie.

"Dad, Karol told me they've decided to put an immediate hold on funding *my* project until this situation is resolved. Even if they're not part of it anymore, the park and the plant look connected to people. And we've already ordered the new machines! We're on the hook for that if they walk, and it'll take months to find a new investor. The plant would shut down, Dad."

Charlie was studying him. Nearly grinning.

"Not we, Hughie. You're in charge over there. Remember?"

"Which is why we need to fucking resolve this now! And why you're going to work with these people to do that."

Charlie nodded, more to himself, and his mouth did a funny thing. He nodded again.

"Anyway, like Hugh says, we need to deal with this now and be done with it as soon as possible. You're the paid professionals. How'd you just put it? What's the signal in the noise?" he said.

"Not what. It's who," said dreadlocks.

"It's what?" said Charlie.

"Who. Right now, the signal in the noise is Justine. No matter what's going on with all of those other groups and what they're saying on all the platforms, she's the face of this. In a couple of days, she'll be on CNN and they'll be talking about a run for Congress," he said.

"#Justine2024," said Heather.

"Right?" said dreadlocks.

"So what do we do? Release a statement?" said Hugh.

"Saying what?" said Charlie.

"Affirming your commitment to Equity and Diversity and Inclusivity. Both of you."

"Problem," said Charlie.

"Are you not committed?" said Heather.

"Of course we are! I personally recruited Prin to work here. And he, he's, he is …"

"Sri Lanka! Ha! Look who's committed now, Hughie!" said Charlie.

"I don't think that'll be enough, sorry. And just releasing a statement is cold and corporate. You need to make the statement yourselves," said Heather.

"I don't think so," said Charlie.

"Why not, Dad?"

"That kind of thing, coming from me, about Dante's Indiana? It'll spook *my* investors."

Charlie and Hugh stared at each other.

"If you can't agree on releasing a joint statement, there's also the nuclear option," said dreadlocks.

"What's your name?" said Charlie.

"Zephyr. This is my company," he said.

"Alright. Go on." said Charlie.

"It's actually pretty simple. We take a deep look at her life," he said.

"Whose life?"

"Justine's! I know publicly this is all about Garyon versus Geryon, but really it's about Justine. People can't get enough of her. So …"

"We dig," said Heather.

"And dig and dig," said Kevin.

"And dig until we come up with something," said Zephyr.

"You won't. That's not Justine. I've known her since she was a little girl. You'd have better luck selling hunting rifles at a petting zoo."

"Not a problem. We can be creative."

"You can be creative, with the story of her life?"

"She's destroying the company you built, Dad!"

"I'm as mad at her for this Judas stuff as you are, Hughie, but do we really want to ruin the girl's life?"

"It doesn't have to go that far. We can work up a menu of options for you. Whatever we go with, we can dig *that* up and do a little pink slime work until it becomes red meat. And I don't mean just CNN. I mean CBS, NBC, ABC—the channels people who go to theme parks and work at packaging plants still watch."

"Fox?"

"Pink slime work?"

"Exactly."

"What is? What's pink slime?" I said.

"The solution! We've done this for other clients, usually political campaigns rather than business plays, but for sure, we can do it for you. With a VPN and an international wire transfer, next thing you know the *Terre-Haute People's Post* is up and reporting that certain things have come to light about Justine. Just say go, Hugh," said Zephyr.

"Go," said Hugh.

"No," said Charlie.

"These are my hires, Dad. Do it."

"Okay. You win, Hughie. Joint statement."

His mouth was still doing a funny thing.

Zephyr's firm arranged for Hugh and Charlie to release a video describing their personal and company commitments to Equity and Diversity and Inclusivity and doing better. By design, the video began trending locally and then regionally on Twitter. Critics retweeted more than supporters. CNN interviewed Justine. Other networks followed. The protests grew.

Sirens, horns, chanting, vuvuzelas.

Locals stood on their front stoops and yards, guarding their property and selling parking spots to out-of-towners.

Perry Schlaffler announced on his radio show that he was coming to town and invited his listeners to join him in a celebration of Great Americans and Great Books.

Terre-Haute was now being attacked and defended for hosting a company and a theme park dedicated to celebrating dead white males *and* dead black males.

Hugh flew to Poland to reassure his investors. Charlie went down to Kentucky. He told me that if things worked out like he was hoping, he wouldn't be coming back by himself.

And Kyle kept texting me "Closer, closer."

Molly wanted me to come to Milwaukee; Philomena and Chiara were fixated on the situation in Terre-Haute.

A weekend of talking to my older children about race and justice while filling water bottles. Driving many children to many things. Not much time with Molly, just Molly. And she'd probably be tired, anyway. Or the bed would be full of children and water bottles.

Sirens, horns, chanting, vuvuzelas.

Marchers in Terre-Haute.

The loud, hard world.

I was needed.

Again.

The crunch of goldfish crackers under my boots.

Wasn't I needed?

Wouldn't I always be?

The right thing was to ask Molly.

But then an automated dinner party reminder came through. The lion from the flag of Sri Lanka, sipping champagne. How could I go to Milwaukee this weekend?

27

COOKING OIL, CUMIN, rosewater, mothballs, burning flowers: I could smell Sri Lanka from the double driveway. Payatta opened the front door. He was wearing a dark suit. His wife was beside him in a green sari, their daughter beside her in a crimson-and-gold sari, legs wrapped tightly. A showroom for dead mermaids.

"Ayubowan! Gracious welcome, esteemed professor, to our home. I present my wife."

She smiled, clasped her hands in a prayer-like greeting, and half-nodded, half-bowed.

"I present my daughter."

She smiled and did the same as her mother.

I stopped beside the garden hose and did the same.

Still smiling and clasping, Payatta's daughter whispered something to her mother, who whispered something to Payatta, who scowled at them and smiled at me.

"Please, esteemed professor, enter."

I entered a very fragrant house full of leatherish furniture and oversized portraits of stern old brown people and graduation portraits of Payatta's daughter. There was a mirror-backed entertainment cabinet, lit up by pot lights, full of satiny, coconutty, elephantine Sri Lankan knickknackyness. A rooster-topped oil lamp, as tall as Payatta, stood beside the stairs, each of its four bowled levels filled with water and flowers and floating candles shaped like coconut flowers. The dining-room table was laden with enough food to feed a wedding reception.

"Payatta, my goodness, this is too much. Had I known you and your family were planning such a feast, I would have brought my family with me."

"You have such beautiful daughters! They will get nice and fat, living with us!"

"My wife who would love to be here for this meal. She loves Sri Lankan food."

"Loves? Not loved?" said Payatta.

"What do you mean?" I said.

"SEE! I told you, Daddy!"

Dinner was quiet. My phone kept buzzing in my pocket— "Closer! Closer!" messages from Kyle.

Why did Payatta think I could marry his daughter? Had I really never mentioned Molly in all of our gas-station chats? Did he think I was a wedding-ring-wearing widower with children who were taken care of, magically, by someone else, somewhere else? I guess that wouldn't be so strange in Sri Lanka. But I felt bad for him and his wife. I felt terrible for his daughter. She was in her late thirties and wearing a sari meant for her younger self.

"So, do you work in the area?" I said.

"She's like you! Almost a doctor!" said Payatta.

"I work at a pharmacy."

"She graduated third in her class!" said Payatta's wife.

He had yet to tell me either of their names. Perhaps there was no point, if I wasn't marrying into the family?

"She graduated third because there were two Korean boys in the class. Not fair, no?"

"Daddy! Enough!"

"No point, no?" said his wife.

"I'm sorry, what are your names?" I said.

The doorbell rang.

"Who could that be?" said Payatta.

"Dad, you didn't! Remember what happened last time you invited two of them?"

Didn't what? Two what?

Payatta went to the door.

"CALL THE POLICE!"

I went to the door. Kyle was standing there, with several black people.

"May I present, please, my client, colleague, ally, and friend, Professor Prin!" he said.

Unimpressed eyebrows.

"Hello. Would you excuse us for a moment?"

"What do you expect us to do? Stand here on the front stoop? You're not even going to invite us inside your house?" said a woman in her fifties.

She was wearing a "Justice for Garyon" T-shirt over a hoodie.

"Kyle, what's going on? Who are these people? And how did you know I was here?"

"I follow Payatta on Twitter."

I had no words.

"Excuse me, please, everyone, come inside," said Payatta's wife.

Now Payatta had no words.

"Something smells good!" said one of the men as they walked into the front hall and took off their shoes and made for the dining room.

"Kyle. Kyle! Wait. Who are these people? What is going on?"

But Kyle had no words, either. He was looking at Payatta's daughter. He followed her. One of the strangers stayed back in the hall. She was about my age, maybe. Her face was lined and careworn, her eyes bloodshot and glassy.

"My name is Rachel."

"Hello. I'm Prin."

"Rachel Jackson. My son is Garyon."

Kyle had spent the past two weeks searching Chicagoland for Garyon Jackson's family. He found them, and convinced them to come to Terre-Haute to meet Justine.

"Then what?" I said.

"Pardon?"

We were in Payatta's onion-filled kitchen while the others enjoyed the Sri Lankan matchmaking feast in the dining room.

"I said, then what, Kyle? What do you think will happen after the family meets Justine?"

"Ayomi looks like she has an old soul," he said.

"What? Is that Payatta's daughter's name? Kyle!" I said.

But he was already gone.

In the morning, I went back to Charlie's and told him about Garyon's family. Charlie asked me to find out where they were staying so he could send food.

"Do you want to meet with them?" I said.

"Not sure that'll do much good, Prin. Friendly fire maybe."

"Should you ask Zephyr?"

"Send the sandwiches. Some flowers, too. Also, before you fire Kyle—and you will fire Kyle for this stunt—get him to ask about their favourite TV shows."

I left Charlie's house and texted Kyle, who told me Justine was ignoring his messages and the family was getting upset.

I called Justine, who didn't answer. I called many times and eventually she texted me back, asking what I wanted. I told her I wanted to talk about a situation with Garyon's family. She said I'd have to come see her in person.

I drove to the arenas, pulling onto a side street before the police barricades. I paid to park on a front lawn and tried to follow Justine's directions on foot. I became lost, almost immediately, in the crowds, hundreds of people cut through here and there with grotesque Uncle Sams on stilts—vamping, vampirish, piratical, undead. But no trolls. No need for. Thank God. Lines of smoke disappeared into the spring-blue sky above wilting flags and thrusting banners. Behind it all, as if fixed in place, hovered the helicopters, more of them than the first time I noticed their presence in town. There were now both the bug-like news-copters and larger black-green military machines. The governor had vowed to keep the peace and keep Indiana open for business.

Black preachers were delivering sermons. Their listeners were holding hands and swaying, chanting, singing. Academic-looking young people, white and slight, were giving lectures to each other about how to be anti-racist, about the whitewashing of the Middle Ages, about the misogynistic, Islamophobic, homophobic, transphobic, speciesist, and fat-shaming affects and effects of the *Divine Comedy*. Climate activists shouted over cancellers of capitalism (multinational, suburban, finance, surveillance, extractive, carceral, corporate, crony, Christian, Zionist, Goop, pharmaceutical, theme-park), while representatives of radical caucuses and grassroots presidential campaigns and healthcare and immigration-rights groups collected signatures. An Octavia E. Butler reading marathon had been going for twenty-three hours. Beto O'Rourke was standing on a table, pleading. People were drumming. The air smelt of roasting coffee and chickpeas. Anyone with a free hand was filming. I called up to an undead Uncle Sam for directions. He smiled and did his best, but had to keep moving or he'd fall down.

Closer to the main drive leading up to the park, where Justine asked to meet, booted men dressed in black were standing in a semi-circle, saying nothing. They stared across a line of policemen pacing between them and another group. In between the two groups was an empty monument base, where the Dante statue would eventually go. The base had been spray-painted and egged. The other group were counter-protestors: jeering, bearded men of many ages in hunting vests and concert T-shirts, some slinging rifles and crossbows. One man wore Viking horns. Another, bagpipes. There were also many women, of uncertain ages, red-faced from screaming and bony and straggle-haired. All were white and weather-cheeked.

How many had applied for jobs at Dante's Indiana?

How many were going to lose their jobs at Tracker Packaging?

Burly cameramen in shapeless jeans and white sneakers panned back and forth.

Behind the counter-protesters and nearer to the park's main entrance, sitting in the cabin of his snowplough, Perry Schlaffler was addressing a crowd carrying flags and crosses and cardboard snowflakes. Steve Bannon was sitting beside him in black jeans and a Hawaiian shirt, smiling and waving around a red light saber. A banner stretched across the plough itself.

EVERY MONTH IS DANTE MONTH!

My phone rang.

"Justine?"

"Hi Prin. I see you. I'm over here."

"Where?"

I looked around.

She tapped my shoulder.

"So?"

"It's about Kyle. He's been trying to reach you," I said.

She shook her head.

"Of all the ways a guy has tried to get with me—"

"No. He really did find the family."

"Wait a minute. He actually found Garyon's family and brought them here? To meet me? Why?"

"I think it's part of a larger plan," I said.

"Was this Hugh's idea? Or Charlie's?"

"No. It has nothing to do with them. But yes, Kyle has his own larger plan. More of a personal plan, I guess."

She shook her head.

"Another white guy offering to help me, strings attached. And he's using the family for this? And now I'm supposed to be part of that?"

"I don't think Kyle means any harm."

"They never do, Prin. That's the problem," she said.

"The family really does want to meet you," I said.

"I don't want it to happen here, in the middle of this. They don't deserve that," she said.

"Do you want me to figure something out?"

"No. I'll deal with it myself."

"Can I ask for just one favour, then?"

"So brown guys are just as bad as white guys?"

"Okay. Don't worry about it."

"Fine. What is it?"

"Can you ask the family the name of their favourite TV show?"

"That'd be weird. Why?"

"Charlie wants to know. I think he's trying to make amends."

"With them? Or with me?"

"With them."

"So he's still not changing the name of the rollercoaster."

240

"No."

"So he's not making amends. With me or with them. And you're still working for him?"

"Yes."

"Why? Because you're just happy to be recognized for your contributions? I'm tired of that. I'm done. Why aren't you done? Aren't you tired of being the model minority, Prin?"

"Who do you think's the new model, Justine?"

"Go to hell."

28

"LIVE FROM THE banks of the Wabash River in beautiful
Terre-Haute Indiana, welcome to Heaven-in-the-making! It's
America's Got Jesus: DANTE EDITION!"

The host was a hip-rocking little blond man in an elec-
tric-blue suit, peppy, with an elvish grin and a sharp, short hair
frosted white at the tips and eyes so blue they looked rinsed
in washer fluid. He brought the cheering crowd to a crescendo
and then made a sweeping, cutting motion as he dance-jogged
across the stage and pirouetted at the end. Everyone went silent
just as he stuck the landing and shot his arms out, palms wide.
A screen lowered behind him. He stood at attention.

A young woman and a very old man appeared on the stage.
Both were in motorized wheelchairs. The young woman was
wearing a long, brown skirt and beige blouse; the old man
was wearing faded-grey dress pants, a dark-navy blazer over
a white shirt and red tie, and a big, blue baseball cap with the
word VETERAN embroidered in gold across the front. On the
screen behind them, the Stars and Stripes writhed regally. A
military tattoo played.

The young woman and old man smiled and nodded, encour-
aging each other. They closed their eyes, took deep breaths,
reached for each other's hand, and then began to stand up,
their legs shaking. The host's face bloomed into concern, then

horror, at what might go wrong. He readied to spring into action and held himself there, coiled. They continued to rise. The crowd was so silent you could hear the crickets making their leg music. We were watching from Adam's mobile luxury box, a converted freight container. My ears strained to hear the chants of approaching protestors, but there were none. After arriving in Terre-Haute and visiting the arenas to plan for the show, Adam had asked why we wanted to put a sheepfold between a goat farm and a wolf pack. He said they wouldn't perform the show at the arenas, so Charlie arranged access to a public bandshell by the river. All approaching roads were controlled by ID-checking police, and the parking lots patrolled by the national guard and licensed safety officers from Genesis Extreme.

Finally, the old man and the young woman stood, squeezing each other's hands and holding them up, just a little, in triumph. With his free hand, the old man took off his cap and nodded at the young woman. She smiled and wiped a tear from her face. She wiped a tear from his face. Then she sang "God Bless the USA."

The singer and the veteran teetered back into their wheel-chairs to a standing ovation. They motored away.

The host introduced the judges—a perky high-school drama teacher and conversion-therapy coach; a lion-haired Latina gospel singer; and a very old and severe Englishman who murmured to himself and held a paisley handkerchief to his mouth. The host's name was Jace ("as in, the two best syllables in all of creation!"). He reminded the crowd that everyone appearing in this special episode wouldn't just be sharing their talents with Our Lord and all of us, they'd also have the opportunity to audition for a role in the heavenly section of America's most exciting new theme park. He added that audience members and viewers at home would receive a fifty-percent discount on admission for their first visit to the park when it opened in the fall.

And so it began.

Joey and the Technicolor Dreamcoats were a band of Filipino-American first cousins outfitted in tight, bright suits. They performed a high-energy Broadway-style number about mercy and forgiveness.

Suga Cain and Abel, a hip-hop duo from a Philadelphia street ministry, rapped about brotherly love and keeping.

Ten sisters from an Iowa soybean-farming family swayed in white, cottony gowns, holding electric torches and singing a Jesus-hacked version of "Wishin and Hopin."

The Rapture Captors, a bungee-jumping squad from an Ohio Bible college, swung down from a beam and saved the elect.

Noah's Barks were a family of Alabama dog stylists. To stormy orchestral music and oohs and aahs from the crowd, the groomers used clippers and hair dye and stick-on eyeballs to transform six standard poodles into six pairs of Biblical animals, and then, to wild applause and flashing phones, the dogs walked two-by-two into a kennel tricked out as a little ark.

To awws from the crowd, the dog-groomers' children swept away poodle fur while the next act, a young woman, set up her prop.

Jace introduced her as a freestyle Bible reenactor and stood to the side while the very, very narrow door was wheeled out in front of her, ajar. Snarling, she dislocated her shoulders. Gasps. A few people cheered. Her arms now dangling, she used her chin to motion Jace towards her. He rushed over, concerned. The crowd was silent. She asked him to hold the microphone to her sweating, grimacing face.

"Luke … Luke … Luke 13. Our Lord told us that, in order to be saved, we have to make every effort to enter through the narrow door."

She motioned for Jace to step back. Then she stepped forward, passed through the narrow door, cracked her shoulders back into place, and lifted her arms in victory. The crowd stood up, cheering and applauding.

"Couldn't she have just gone through the door sideways?" said Zephyr.

Two people weren't standing: Justine and Garyon's mother. Jace noticed and went over.

"This wasn't part of the plan, was it?" said Zephyr.

"What plan? I just thought it'd be nice to give them free tickets," said Charlie.

"People, you need to trust in God and in our man Jace. I do. He's just great with the African-American ladies. They like how little and pretty he is. Like a Jesus-loving Ken doll," said Adam.

Jace was crouched at the edge of the stage, looking concerned. The crowd were back in their seats and the young woman, whose arms appeared to have locked in victory formation, was being helped off-stage, her narrow door wheeled behind her. Jace beckoned Justine and Garyon's mother to join him. They refused.

Then he looked up and made a face—he had a bright idea! Jace shrugged, smiled, and jumped down to them. He bent down on one knee beside the older woman.

"How are you tonight, ma'am? You didn't seem too impressed with Debbie Narrow Door's performance."

"I was just wondering about that line she said. You know, from Luke? About doing everything we can, to get to Jesus?"

"Is there someone in your life that you're worried about right now?"

Garyon's mother looked down and shook her head, and Justine leaned over, blocking Jace. Then she looked up, squeezed Justine's hand, and looked back at Jace.

"Are you okay?" he said.

"Doing alright, all things considered," she said.

"And is this your daughter beside you? Hello. Shalom, welcome."

"No. This is just a very good friend in a time of great trial. I don't have any daughters. I only have a son," she said.

"And where's that lucky young man right now?" said Jace.

She put her head down again, and Justine held her around the shoulders, glaring at Jace.

"Ma'am, are you alright? Is your son the one we should pray for, all of us right here, right now, to get through the narrow door to Jesus?"

She shook her head.

Justine leaned in, her face furious, but then Garyon's mother held up a hand and whispered something to her and nodded at Jace.

"Whether you are at home or with us here in Terre-Haute, my fellow *America's Got Jesus* Americans, take a knee," he said.

"WE'LL TAKE TWO!"

Everyone in the audience stood up and turned around. They removed the cushions from their seats and put them on the ground and knelt. The people in the wheelchair and motor-ized-scooter sections stretched out their hands. Performers and poodles emerged from the wings and gathered in the middle of the stage, as did the old veteran and the young woman who sang at the opening of the show. We knelt in Adam's box. Most of us.

"Okay ma'am. We're ready. Can I ask your name, and the name of the person you'd like us to pray for?"

"I'm Rachel. His name is Garyon. Garyon Jackson. He's my son," she said.

"And where is he, right now?"

"I pray to Jesus he is in heaven, in through that narrow door," she said.

"He passed?" said Jace.

"He was killed. Murdered, by the police. By the racist white police," said Justine.

Murmurs and hissing noises. A few boos, and shushes, too.

"Everyone, quiet down. This is America. Free speech. Everyone is entitled," said Jace.

"Boo all you want. They killed my son, and I want justice. Lots of people do. Folks have been around this town for a while now, and I thank them. I do. Lots of people need lots more justice these days. I will lend my name, and his name, and our story. And I hope we can get some. We're going to keep on trying. But nothing changes that my boy is dead. So right now, this mother just wants to know that he's safe and sound with Our Lord."

"Everyone, let's pray to Jesus Our Lord and Saviour that the young man, the son of a good woman, that Garyon Jackson, has gone home through the narrow door."

There came a greater murmuring, a warm hum like the engine room of some great ship, its pistons and gears made of human voices, human hearts. After a while the murmuring subsided. Jace looked up and around. Moving the microphone away from his mouth, he leaned over and said something to Garyon's mother, who shook her head and said nothing.

29

AFTER THE SHOW, Charlie and Adam met Garyon's family and offered them lifetime passes. Garyon's mother said he did love rollercoasters, but that she was tired and just wanted to go home before the next rallies, which would take place in the state capital. Her relatives accepted the park passes, and they left. Justine left, too. A few days later, her father told Charlie that she was moving to Charlotte, where her fiancé worked, and that she'd become Assistant Vice-President for Inclusive Ventures at a healthcare conglomerate. Charlie told us there were no hard feelings and that he'd take care of the honeymoon if the newly-weds wanted to visit Italy.

Adam went back to Kentucky, but not before he gave each of us his personal business card, which was the Bible. Zephyr took one, too.

Thanks to *America's Got Jesus*, we recruited at least two dozen performers for Paradiso. The Noah's Bark people insisted on a licensing agreement for co-branded merchandise, premium location and performance times, and an option to sell puppies from their breeding program on the arena floor. The Dante professors returned to their work with Charlie's personal library, and Kyle spent most of his time in chat rooms, practicing conversational Sinhalese, as I was informed by the HR temp who gave me his termination papers.

"Kyle, this isn't an easy conversation, and I'm glad things

seem to have worked out, overall, with Garyon Jackson's family, and I'm also personally grateful that you introduced me to all of this, but, I'm sorry, we're letting you go," I said.

"I was planning to quit anyway."

"You're quitting?"

"Prin, I need to get on with life."

"You're that serious with Payatta's daughter? What about Justine?"

"What about Justine? She's engaged, you know."

"Right."

"Anyway, about getting serious, with Ayomi, yes. The thing is, I'm not going to go any further until I can show up at the house with a plan to provide."

"So shouldn't you keep working?"

"You mean, start working? Do you really think what I've been doing with you and Dante's Indiana is work?"

"What are you going to do instead?"

"I've signed up for a State retraining program. They don't know it'll just be *training* for me. Anyway, who knows what's going to happen at Tracker Packaging, but maybe I can get a job there sometime. My dad keeps saying he's going to retire. Probably lots of them will in the next couple of years, if the plant doesn't shut down first."

"Kyle, this all sounds, well, don't take it the wrong way, very mature."

"With Ayomi, I have a new life ahead of me. Now I'm a man with responsibilities, and I'm in a situation where I need to earn some money."

"Kyle, are you doing that on purpose?"

"What, am I quoting Dante? Is that from Dante? Does he say it somewhere?"

"No. That's what I said to you about my own situation, in New York, when we first met."

Kyle grinned.

"You knew that," I said.

"Yep. You didn't think I was listening!"

"No. I guess there's always been more going on with you than I gave you credit for."

"Well, I'm thirty-eight, so—"

"You're thirty-eight?"

But then I saw it, the crow's feet around his eyes, which for once weren't beading or bugging out but looked soft and tired. And he was losing his hair. Ayomi must have made him stop gelling up the front.

"Not too old to hug it out one more time, bro."

He smiled, shrugged, and we shook hands. He walked out of his office empty-handed —he'd never brought anything to work except earbuds and energy drinks.

Hugh returned from Poland and quit Tracker Packaging, which had lost its investors. He became Jagiellon Capital's new American prospect consultant. During the Garyon protests, the governors of Ohio, West Virginia, Maryland, and Maine, all of whom were also considering presidential runs, had each extended tax-break packages to companies from Viségrad Group countries willing to invest in one of their many calm and quiet factory towns, which were full of Americans willing to work and to buy American. Charlie came out of retirement. The company had enough contracts to carry on through the summer, but nothing beyond that, just new equipment designed to make millions of blister packs for pills.

And so for the first time since Charlie Tracker had come home from Vietnam and started his business, the Tracker name was dirt in Terre-Haute. On Reddit and Facebook, father and son were both urged to go to hell, as in *hell* hell: first the Trackers had embarrassed the town and created all kinds of chaos and invited all sorts of crazies with their racist theme park, and now they were putting a lot of people out of work. People began posting pictures of the toxic-waste drums that had been piling up for years beside the main building and suggesting someone should call the State about the fire hazard the Trackers had created.

No one was surprised by Hugh's skipping out. Everyone was surprised at the news Charlie was leaving town, too.

"Are you working on something? Do you have a plan?" I asked, the last time we spoke.

"Not yet. But I'm not coming back until I do. And I'm coming back. Remember asking me when you could start? Why you wanted to come here in the first place?"

"I do."

"There's no Ravenna in America for either of us, Prin."

"So what now?" said Molly.

"We keep working on the park and waiting for Charlie to return."

"With the Kentucky people?"

"Yes. Apparently, because they've been using the same consultant, they already have a lot of prefabricated material and tech, back-ups from Genesis Extreme, which just need to be modified and reloaded for Dante's Indiana. That's what they'll be doing over the summer. They almost don't need us around at this point."

"Then what are you doing there these days, Prin?"

"I'm, well, Charlie asked me to make sure his staff still feels part of this."

"And do they?"

"I think that's where I can be an example for the others."

"Which means what?"

"Making sure our views are heard when it comes to things like finalizing details about the rides and the performers. I guess I'm still a go-between passing on suggestions and proposing changes from one side to the next, using the kind of language each group needs. Like I've been doing all along. But Molly, what are you really asking me?"

"Why you don't come home? Do you really think they couldn't do this without you?"

"I think there'd be a lot more disagreements and arguments."

"And then the park wouldn't open?"

"It would still open."

"And would you still be paid?"

"My contract goes to December 31."

"Come home, Prin. We miss you. I miss you."

"I miss you too! But the house isn't ready yet, Molly. Two months more."

"Then stay here in Milwaukee with us, until then."

"But I promised Charlie."

"Ask him if you can go back and forth to Terre-Haute when you need to."

"He's hard to reach these days."

"Prin."

"What? Things are good now, aren't they Molly? Between us?"

"Yes. But is that enough for you?"

No.

"No. Not anymore. Not now."

30

I MOVED TO Milwaukee for the rest of the summer. It was good. It was better. The bed was better. I took calls with the professors and Nick and Frank and the Kentucky people while driving children to quarry pools and matinees and soccer practices. The calls became less frequent as the summer passed.

The plant shut down at the end of August, and, a week later, trial-runs started at the park. The Kentucky people hired former employees from Tracker Packaging to go through Inferno and Paradiso. Nick and Frank took a road-trip to New Mexico to attend Cool Ranch, the Doritos fan-experience centre. Only the Dante professors held on—they were fighting with the Genesis Extreme academics over how much Dante and how much Bible would be preloaded in the digital display screens and exhibits being installed in the arenas.

Nothing from Charlie.

Not even his location.

I moved back to Toronto. We all moved back, together.

No more Ravenna.

That September, I began offering a Dante seminar at The New U. There was the matter of the NDA that formally precluded me from teaching, but when I agreed to give up researching, they modified the clause. The university's lawyer enrolled in the class ("this is the original lawyer's joke book!"), as did Connie, who had lost her husband, Enrico, a few months earlier. She brought focaccia to class and read aloud from the original Italian so beautifully. Sister Contra Melanchthon signed up and shredded me with shortbread-nibbling questions about mediaeval theology. She sat between Connie and the condominium's newest resident, Marcus, who'd retired from his security-desk job. He looked away every time Sister Contra asked him to stop leaning and just switch seats with her.

Greeting everyone in the hallway and checking for food in my teeth, that my zipper was zipped, *etc.*, Lizzie explained that, with her son and his family back in town, she didn't need to take the class. She was already in heaven. Standing beside her, Kareem reminded each of my students as they made their way to class that Islam was a uniter, not a divider. Did he know that Dante had placed the Prophet Muhammad with other sowers of division in deep hell, where he was split from top to bottom? Was that really why they weren't taking the class? Only once did my mother catch my eye and wink: were we both thinking about Kingsley? He would have taken my class just to find out what Muhammad looked like in the *Divine Comedy* so he could get Kareem the perfect costume for the condo Halloween party.

As for the seminar itself, we talked mostly about Dante, about whether he was a good Catholic or a bad Catholic because of what he wrote about others, and also about how being one kind of Catholic usually led to being the other kind, and back again, always back again, as much in Dante as in life. With the old nun nodding, I suggested you were probably neither a good Catholic nor a bad Catholic if this never happened for you. Like the people in hell's lobby, Marcus added. We also talked about how the crisis Dante experienced at the beginning of the poem, and at midlife, in the middle of the journey of his life, was the crisis we all have, and not just in the middle of life.

They also had questions, every class, about where I had been and what I had seen and done while working on the theme park; about whether the condo could organize a bus trip to Indiana when it opened; and also about living in America, about living with Americans, about whether the people, the arguments, the portions, the handicapped parking, everything, were really as big and scary as they looked on television.

I could only say so much; I'd only gone so far into American things, this past year, and now there was no need, no reason, no way, to go any further. It became easier, every day, to skim Zephyr's daily social media report, and ignore the Urgent!!! emails from the Dante professors about whatever was going on with the Kentucky people in the tunnel between the arenas. I only looked for a message from Charlie. And still, nothing.

Our new house was much more than we had expected. We'd gone from a century-old shabby shoebox to a glass-and-steel land yacht. Only in retrospect did Molly and I realize how many design decisions we'd just passed on with all of those bank transfers: the house felt like a testing facility for off-white paint. It wasn't fully finished, either. Pot lights were missing in most rooms, Molly's exercise bike only fit in a Wi-Fi dead zone, the air conditioning made one of the bathrooms vibrate, and our feet were perpetually covered in white dust. But we had more than one bathroom, we had air conditioning that didn't drip through the ceilings, and we had a laundry room that didn't smell like dead bacon rat.

We kept marvelling at all the extra space. We kept sleeping in the master bedroom, all of us.

There were new kinds of shadows on the bedroom walls; racoons had shrieking, thumping disputes at 2 am over our garbage cans, and the girls had forgotten how bright and loud a city neighborhood was at night compared to a Milwaukee suburb that backed onto storage warehouses. Eventually, the girls began sleeping through the night in their own rooms. Eventually, the random morning checks stopped, too.

There was never a pillow and blanket on the floor beside our bed.

They'd known so much, all along.

The contractors hadn't been able to get the pool installed in time, only dug out. Flaming-orange construction fencing ringed the giant hole in the backyard.

Molly didn't want the pool. She'd never wanted it, in fact. It had been her older sister, after Molly told her about seeing one at a friend's house when they were little. At her sister's command, Molly had drawn pictures over and over again. It had been a kind of torture. Torture, not longing, had been what I'd heard in her voice, the one time she'd told me about the pool, years before.

We agreed the backyard should be filled in so the children would have a place to play, or so the children and a new dog would have a place to play. That was the new nightly dispute at the dinner table. When I asked if I could be the one to name the puppy, it was all over.

I began calling and emailing to see how much of the pool deposit we could get back, to put into savings, and also land-scaping and a Weimaraner.

But if we didn't need money for a pool: what had I done, spending nearly a year away from my family in Terre-Haute, Indiana? Had it all been done in vain, and wrongly?

One night in late September, after the children had gone to bed, I asked Molly.

She answered, "Prin, was my going to Milwaukee something done in vain, and wrongly? Or is that what made it possible for us to come home, together? *Here* and *now*, do we still need to be asking these questions? Do you want to? I don't. I don't want to be stupid, anymore. Do you?"

"Well ..."

She took my hand. She held my eye. I blinked and pulled her close. We kissed, kissed again, and got on with things.

I needed and was needed, wanted and was wanted, and wanted to be. Here. Here I was: here we were. Will and desire, fire and sun, all revolving as Love's all and one, clement and quiet, in the east end.

31

"PRIN, WHEN ARE you coming back?"

"Just before Halloween, Nick, with the family, to go through the parks when they open."

"Can you come earlier? Can you come by yourself?"

"Why? Is something wrong with the park?"

"No."

"Did Charlie come up with a plan?"

"No. I haven't heard anything. Have you?"

"No. What is it?"

"It's Frank."

"What's wrong?"

"He found Megan."

"Oh. Oh no. Is she …?"

"No, not that. She's come home."

"That's good, isn't it?"

"That depends."

"On what?"

"On what home's like."

"Isn't Frank happy?"

"He's terrified."

"Of Megan?"

"No. Of course not."

"Then what's the problem?"

"Terre-Haute. It's not the best place right now for someone with her, you know, issues."

"Nick, I can't do anything about Terre-Haute."

"Neither can Frank. I'm worried he might try."

"What's that mean?"

"I don't know. And I don't want to find out. That's where I could use some help. And most of the other guys around Frank these days aren't helping."

That night, I told Molly about Nick's call. We talked about it, we talked about how to talk to the kids about it, we made more jokes about stupidity and plans for them to come to town for the park opening a few weeks later, and then she said job or no job, I was being asked to help, *actually* help. She sent me to him.

We found Frank in his garage.

He was staring at a bathroom door that was leaning against a stack of winter tires. He had a phone and a power drill in his hands. There were bags of hinges and boxes of screws at his feet.

"Hi Frank."

"Hi Nick. Oh, and Prin's here too. Hi Prin. When did you get back?"

"Just the other day."

"Why? Something wrong at the park?"

Nick nodded at me.

"I just had to check on some things," I said.

"Right. Okay. Well, good seeing you. Listen, I put a Netflix on for the girls because I've got some stuff to do here, so, if there's nothing else, I should probably get back to this."

"Put the bathroom door back, Frank. She'll know you trust her."

"Will she? Do I? I don't even know when she's coming to the house, Nick. *If* she's coming to the house. I've taken the door off and put it back on so many times since we found her that I've pulled the hinges out. And the frame's so chewed up from other times, I don't know if I could mount it again, even if I wanted to."

"The day you can't rehang a bathroom door is the end of days for America, Frank," said Nick.

Frank smiled. But he was sad, and very tired. The skin around his eyes looked like it was filling up with shoe polish. He put down the power drill and arched his back and winced as he pretended to paint the garage ceiling.

Nick had told me Megan texted Frank while they were in New Mexico at the Doritos fantasy park.

Dad, can I come home?

He'd driven straight to a women's shelter outside Las Vegas. She was in no condition to see her children, to be seen by her children. Frank and his wife wanted to keep her away from town too, from old friends. And so now one of them was with her at all times in a motel room outside Terre-Haute.

"Nick mentioned you found Megan, Frank. I'm sure the situation is complicated, but I'm glad she's safe."

"Thanks. Yeah. Exactly. And the plan now is to keep her safe."

"If there's anything I can do to help, let me know. I'm keeping all of you in my prayers."

"You mean that, Prin?"

"About keeping you in my prayers?"

"No, of course I believe you about that. And I'm grateful. If we ever needed a Hail Mary pass, it's right now. For sure. But did you mean you could *actually* help, too?"

"I can be here until the end of the month, when the park opens, and then I'll go back to Toronto with my family."

"You brought your family with you? They're here?"

"No. Not yet. They're coming down for the park opening."

"Oh. Alright."

"Have you seen it yet, Prin? Looks pretty darned good. Final walk-throughs are this week. Everything's ready except the tunnel," said Nick.

"The tunnel?"

"The Kentucky people are building something in there," said Nick.

"The Dante professors have been emailing me about it. They want to meet me at the arenas."

"They've been after me too. No clue," said Frank.

"I'll talk to them."

"Yeah. That's great. Good job, people. Great kids. So? What about you?"

"What do you mean, Frank?"

"You said you were willing to help, Prin. Will you help?"

"I'll do what I can, Frank."

"Yes or no. Can you take a shift?"

"With your daughter? I'm not sure I'm the right one for that. We've never even met—"

"No. Not with Megan. And not with the girls, either. They can stay with friends, or some high schooler can do her home-work on our couch. I need someone to take my shift at the plant so we can both be with Megan. I think it'll really change things if we're all together, even for a little bit. You're a parent. You're married. You get that, right Prin?"

"I do."

"But what shift at the plant, Frank? It's shut down. It was shut down a month ago. And Prin never worked there. What's going on, man?" said Nick.

"Get in the truck."

Frank's truck was a mess.

And it smelled like gasoline.

There were jerrycans on the backseat, beside me. We

261

followed the perimeter of Tracker Packaging's shuttered buildings—front office, storage warehouse, manufacturing plant. The wood pallets and hazardous waste were still there, the rusty drums painted red, white, and blue from the governor's visit that false spring.

The grass was cut and there was no garbage blowing around. A few lights were on; it didn't look so different from the other times I had visited, just closed. But then I saw the other pick-up trucks. One was parked near the front office. The man inside was holding binoculars against his face that were aimed at the security guard's car across the street.

"Kind of hard for a drug addict to guard a place from drug addicts," said Frank.

Someone honked. It was another older man in a pick-up. He pulled up beside us and lowered the window to ask why Frank was so early for his shift. Frank leaned back so the man could see Nick and me. We waved. The man tipped his baseball hat and kept driving.

"How many people are doing this?" I said.

"We try to have at least three on patrol at all times. One watches the security guard, one maintains the perimeter, and one keeps tabs from behind the bushes."

"What's he looking for? Addicts?" said Nick.

"Dealers. At least a couple drive by every day. You can hear them coming, you know, with the music. No one's claimed this turf yet, but boy did they know it was here for the taking the minute Tracker locked the doors. And he didn't even put any money into a high fence or anything. So it's up to us until he gets back. If he ever comes back."

"Why do you have jerrycans in the backseat?" I said.

"In case I need them."

32

CHARLIE INVITED SOME of us to attend a meeting, the next morning, in the tunnel between the arenas.

Over the summer, the Kentucky people had turned the space
into a guest-services centre. It was very warm inside, and the
air was heavy, close and moist, like we were inside a terrarium.
The central path between Inferno and Paradiso was lined with
dark-green trees on one side. Between the trees were pathways
to display tables and shelves and stands filled with T-shirts,
hats, socks, mugs, keychains, phone and tablet covers, water
bottles, bibs, hard candy, stuffed animals, back pillows, books,
violently bright pants—half were Dante-related, and half came
from Genesis Extreme. Cash registers lined the back wall. On
the other side of the central pathway was a broad basin of shim-
mering water. The opposite back wall had food counters and
more cash registers. In between, raised walkways led to plat-
formed dining tables. The water and the plains and the light-
filled sky above us were all filled with sculpted birds and fish and
lions and sabre-tooth tigers. In the middle of the tunnel was a
massive tree trunk. It was inlaid with mirrors, each topped with
a question lit up by flashing red bulbs.

Am I Adam or Am I Eve?

Above the mirrors was a thick clutch of branches that were
ringed in a long, black serpent, mechanized and perpetually

writing. In place of branches or foliage, the tree of good and evil had four massive screens that showed pairs of beautiful red lips speaking unheard words to each other before biting into apples and becoming broken, bleeding, sobbing mouths screaming at each other.

The video ran in a continuous loop with commercials for Genesis Extreme.

The screens in the tree froze, fuzzed, and went black. Skype-call music started, and the screens showed blue and white swirls. Nick was also here, along with a couple of the Genesis Extreme people as well as crew chiefs and office managers from Tracker Packaging. Frank hadn't been invited.

We walked over to the tree.

Charlie began speaking.

"You're muted!"

"UNMUTE!"

"Still muted!"

"STILL MUTED!"

"Sorry. Can you hear me now? Is the audio on? Can they hear me, Adam? Somebody nod if you can hear me."

We all nodded.

"Alright. So. I know you're probably wondering where I've been for the last little while. I've been on the road, in the air, on the water—you name it, I've been looking all over the place for a new client for the plant. No luck. Then, in a catchup call with Adam, he told me about some friends of his, down here in Brazil, working on something. Well, Adam?"

"We have some good news to share with all of you! I mean, the Good News is always the best news, but this is pretty good, too, I'd say. Right, Charlie?"

Charlie leaned over and whispered.

"Okay. Charlie's pointing out this is long distance so let me get right to it. Back in Dante's time, as many of you know, virtue depended on something called a chastity belt. Fast forward to these days. Obviously no one's wearing one, anymore. But obviously the challenge remains. Some brethren scientists down here in Brazil have been working on a new product that can help young people stay on the straight and narrow path to marriage and family. Charlie can testify. He's seen them at work. Charlie?"

"Sure, though I'm more focused right now on bringing our Brazilian colleagues to Terre-Haute in a couple of days. If the tour goes well, as I expect it will when they see our facility and machines and meet our people, well, then, folks, we'll announce a three-way partnership between Adam's company—"

"Ministry."

"Adam's ministry, Tracker Packaging, and this Brazilian company—"

"Ministry."

"Brazilian ministry. And that, people, will reopen the plant."

Charlie stopped speaking. He looked tired, pouchy, pressed into place, like he was being pushed down and forced up at the same time.

"Let me take it home, Charlie. Jet lag and all. Back home you're probably still wondering what we're talking about, right?"

We all nodded.

He pulled out a blue pill and flashed a V with his other hand.

"A chastity pill?" I said.

"A chastity pill," said Charlie. He'd finally answered one of my calls.

"What's the API?"

"API? Pretty good for an English professor."

"I've spent almost a year in Terre-Haute, Charlie. Pills. Remember?"

"Remember? You're asking me to remember?"

"How is this different from what Hugh was trying to do? Isn't this just another pharmaceutical company?"

"It's a ministry."

"That makes pills?"

"It's called a behaviour-control product. Versions are already being used on teenagers for lots of reasons and they haven't led to major addiction issues. And I'm told they're super-careful about keeping the addictive parts to the absolute minimum, anyway. This one has some kind of ... vascular inhibitor, blood pumper, anti-blood pump, which basically means, without drawing a diagram or anything, that young men take it and don't get too excited around the girls, or even at the idea of girls."

"What does it mean, to keep the addictive parts to the absolute minimum?"

"Fair question, Prin. I asked Adam the same thing."

"And?"

"He says the only thing they'll be addicted to is Jesus."

"Do you believe him?"

"Adam says he has a first-rate addiction ministry operation that he could bring to town, too."

"Charlie—"

"I've been on the road for months, Prin. At my age. And I want to come home. And I told you I wasn't coming home empty-handed."

"Contra—"

"Don't you dare say that to me. This is beyond Dante."

"Do you know about Frank's patrols?"

"I already hired a man to watch the security guard and now he's watching Frank and the other guys, too. I'm worried, same as Frank! And I'm worried, if this doesn't work, that most of those addicts are going to be people who used to work for me. Do you think I want that?"

"No."

"Then help me. I need you, Prin, to keep Frank calm and keep him in place."

"That won't be a problem."

"Why not?"

"He found Megan."

"The, his, daughter?"

"Yes."

"And?"

"He's spending most of his time watching her in a motel, outside town."

He was quiet on the phone.

"Remember what you asked me?"

"About believing Adam?"

"No. When we first met. After lunch at the Steak 'n Shake. Back at the house. Above the garage. In the book room. When you asked me to show you my Dantes, and I did. I told you why I started reading the book. Remember now?"

"Yes. But I don't remember the question."

"You asked me if I looked in the hut. In Vietnam. After my buddy went in and saw the children's bodies and ran off. You asked me if I looked in the hut."

"Yes."

"Do you remember my answer?"

"I don't."

"That's because I didn't give you one. I didn't need to. All that mattered was that my friend needed my help."

He hung up.

The next day, I passed the Dante statue on my way to the arenas. It was a replica of the one I'd seen in Florence, only whiter. Most of the graffiti had been scrubbed from the base. Protesters lined the main drive to the arenas. Not protesters.

Job-seekers. A few were holding out papers.

Were these the area-three people from the job fair, denied positions because Tracker Packaging workers had been hired for daily testing at Inferno and Paradiso?

Not even contrapasso.

I parked and went to meet the Dante professors. They'd asked to meet at the Ferris wheel in Paradiso.

I began in Inferno.

I walked through dry ice to the elevators, which were set into a wall painted like dark woods.

Inside, there was growling: a lion, a wolf, a leopard.

Above me, behind me, beside me.

Lurking.

Stepping out at the top into more dry ice, I went down along the wraparound concourse. The way was lined with molten boulders and scorched, broken walls. Video arcade games where you could slip your hands into studded black glove controllers and punish sinners. Two-person stations where you could take turns.

Strange-coloured smokes and smells and cries for help that played over grinding guitars and driving drums. Barking dogs and moaning contortionists in masks and red leather.

Tall men in high black collars buttoned over their faces. They came out of dark corners holding lamps of human heads to show the way down and down and down.

Roving searchlights moved across the black screening that covered the stadium seats, lighting up the faces and bodies of devils and the damned. On the main floor, a funhouse mirror maze for the vain and false; a train-ride through a haunted house that had a brace of winged devils; a whirling teacup ride for wrongful lovers; a twirling, elfin tree that oozed the fingers and faces of suicides through its cracked, shuddering bark. Laneways of hot coals with scorched feet sticking out, where you could see for yourself what happened when you made money off God; a bubbling black bog lined with fishing rods so you could pull up the raging faces of the wrathful. Those had to be the worst jobs.

Other performers staggered around, split-apart or missing body parts or holding extra body parts. Talking to themselves or asking someone, anyone, to hear their stories through broken teeth and cracked lips.

Paid performers, I prayed.

Inferno's main attraction was still called Geryon, but the rollercoaster's finish had been changed over the summer. The body was now red and gold and the whole thing was barbed like a Chinese dragon. The innocent face at the front looked just like Chairman Mao's. I watched as sparks and smoke shot from the coaster's nostrils before it ran down the main loop, people screaming. Then I made my way towards the giant Satan at the far end of the arena. His three foreheads were red and black and white metal. His eyes were holes of electrified yellow light set in chains and melted tires The ice rink around him was painted black and smoked with more dry ice. His three arms lowered. The massive torsos of upside-down Judas, Brutus, and Cassius had bucket seats inside them. Workers lined up to climb metal stairs bolted along the sides of the traitors' raked, roaring faces and bashed bodies before passing through doors cut into the sides of the betrayers' scorched pelvises. The riders were then strapped in and lifted into one of Satan's chomping mouths— mossy, misting, smoking, flashing red lights and thunder.

I walked past Satan towards the tunnel that led between the parks. It was closed for continuing construction—the Kentucky people's Garden of Eden—so I had to take a temporary path to Paradiso.

This time, the elevators were set into a wall painted to look like a starry galaxy. Inside one was a smiling young woman in a ruby-red velvet gown. One of the Beatrices. Trumpets and French horns filled the air. Glowing constellations and laser lights beamed onto the floors and walls and ceilings. Long, stone-framed glass slabs were set up at intervals along the concourse, onto which were projected holographs of saved souls reciting cantos from Dante and verses from the Bible. Workers were installed at each slab, pressing on screen icons again and again, blank-faced before the muted souls. Like old people on slot machines.

At opposite ends of the arena, just above the floor, were choir lofts full of white-gowned singers with combed-out hair. They were practicing a collective duet. Call and response, back and forth, human voices in harmony, washing and warping. I passed a carousel playing tinny, celestial organ-box music, its horses transformed into heavenly creatures—gryphons, lions, eagles, rams. Beside it was a kiddie ride, individual spaceships zooming around a track inside a bandshell painted as the solar system, held in the massive palms of God. A corner of the arena had a bumper-car pen, each car done up as a winged and laughing baby face. The rest of the floor was full of performers going over their routines: dancers, jumpers, the Alabama dog groomers practicing on cuts of high-pile carpet draped over sawhorses. The arena seats were covered in screens that made nine rings, shaded beige to yellow to gold to bright white.

Every now and then I heard the shuddering and slamming of Geryon as it descended into the next building, trailing shrieks.

The professors were standing in line for the Ferris wheel, which had been painted to look like a shining circle of sunbeams. I joined them.

After we were seated, we went up to the massive Empyrean rose that had been installed in place of the four-sided score-board. Its glowing folds swayed slowly, blowing warm, scented air at us.

I was in the higher car, beside Charlie's rare books guy. The other two were one car down, swinging in the rose-filled air.

"I wasn't able to see what's happening in the tunnel."

"The tunnel?"

"What you've been emailing me about, and also calling Frank, apparently?"

"That's not why we've been calling Frank."

"We have our own cars, Prin. And we're on Facebook."

"Meaning?"

"We'd be willing to drive, too."

"What are you talking about?"

"The shifts. Around Tracker Packaging. We want to help. We want to help Frank. He won't talk to us. Can you talk to him for us? Do you think he'd let us help?"

Behind their beards and glasses, they looked worried, and serious, and hopeful.

I looked down.

How high up before our lives look so fitted?

Young men in cropped angel wings, dropping into bungee-cord dives and pulling up their body-socked partners; cloud-painted ski-lift cars, sailing through the middle air; massage-chair thrones, their buffed, rotating pads catching light; gymnasts in white feathers and brown body-suits, building themselves into a giant eagle and then laughing as they flapped the wings and took flight, leaping and tumbling to the floor. The sound of the choirs. A distant spread of crashing joy.

33

LET ME SHOW you their Dantes.

My last night in Indiana, Frank was at the motel with Megan. Other men were on patrol at the plant. Facebook was saying that Charlie Tracker was coming back. That he was bringing in foreigners for a tour. That no one forgot the last time a Tracker tried this.

Sitting in their trucks, charging their phones and searching and sending. Messaging each other. Declining calls from home. Reading and rereading emails and news stories about what they do down in Brazil with children and pills. Declining calls from home.

The men on patrol had lost jobs and children. The devils could take it all, but not their grandchildren, too.

It got late, darker.

The men on patrol kept jerrycans in their trucks.

Some prayed.

Others drank.

A few did both.

The manufacturing facility had fireproof walls, but the wood pallets caught, and then the oil drums, and then the tailings pond.

By midday, the winds shifted.

The smoke spread.

The evacuation order went out.

Wherever you are, if you can hear this, don't stay there.

Great souls, lost souls, stuck souls. Struck souls.

Where are they?

Find them.

Leave home.

Go home.

Find them.

Where are they?

Find them.

Where are you?

Find them.

Find them and be found.

Acknowledgements

ONE SATURDAY IN Toronto, five years ago, I was vacuuming potato chips out of the car while listening to a BBC Radio adaptation of the *Divine Comedy*. I noticed that the poet and his guide were breathing hard as they made their way through hell. Noxious air and a perilous pathway down to the devil got me thinking about writing a hiker's guide to Dante.

A few months later, under the auspices of the Jackman Humanities Institute at the University of Toronto, I began mapping out *Inferno* as a hiker's guide in the company of five students—Harry Moss, Jonah Shalit, Samuel Hodgkins-Sumner, Joseph Daniel Vedova, and Alex Zutt. Their excellent work was helped along by the time they spent with the Dante Collection at the Kelly Library, St. Michael's College, and with the Dante materials of the Pontifical Institute of Mediaeval Studies. I offer my thanks, respectively, to Noel McFerran and James Farge, CSB, for their generosity towards my students and this idea.

I am a scheming novelist fortunate enough to appear to be a committed researcher. I confess I soon put aside the hiker's guide idea to begin working on this novel, instead. I did so with support from many sources, including the Basilian Chair in Christianity, Arts, and Letters that I held at St. Michael's College from 2016 to 2020, and also research funds

275

associated with my appointment in the English Department at the University of Toronto, and as a vice-dean in the Faculty of Arts and Science. My friends and colleagues in academic leadership, David Cameron, David Mulroney, Paul Stevens, David Sylvester, and Melanie Woodin, were generous with their practical supports and spoken encouragements. I also thank several researchers who have answered very specific questions, about things like the chemistry of addiction and libido-blockers, and also about project managing the construction of a theme park. For protecting crucial time away from my other day jobs, I thank the staff members of the Principal's Office at St. Michael's College and the Dean's Office in Arts and Science.

I thank the students of my undergraduate and graduate courses in English at the University of Toronto, with whom I've had the chance to read and think out loud about contemporary American literature and life while writing this novel, and likewise the students of the Gilson Seminar in Faith and Ideas, with whom I read selections from Dante every year. One of these students bears special mention: Shane Beal amiably lectured me about the importance of the Viségrad Group of countries to the future of the world economy at a campus reception in spring, 2019. I promised him that his argument would figure in this novel. A month later, he unexpectedly died, and remains deeply cherished and missed.

The death of another young man more recently comes to mind. Daunte Wright was fatally shot by a police officer in April 2021, a year after I completed this novel. Unintentionally, this tragic real-life event bears some shuddering resemblance to the death of the character Garyon Jackson in this novel.

I have read and reread several editions of the *Divine Comedy* over the past five years, including translations by Robin Kirkpatrick, Clive James, Charles Edwin Wheeler, and by Robert and Jean Hollander. I also studied visualizations of the poem from across the centuries, most memorably from the holdings of the Zahm Dante Collection in the Hesburgh Library at the University of Notre Dame, with thanks to Tracy Bergstrom. I also want to note the Dante work of contemporary artist Monika Beisner, and two books beyond Dante that were especially important to this novel, Max Hastings's *Vietnam: An Epic History of a Tragic War* and *Dopesick*, by Beth Macy.

Decisive writing time was made possible by a residency at the Sheen Center for Thought and Culture, Archdiocese of New York, in February 2020, with thanks to David DiCerto. I am likewise grateful for the chance to have shared selections from the novel-in-progress with readers thanks to Jessica Johnson and *The Walrus* (2019); Michael Hingston and Natalie Olsen and *The Advent Short-Story Calendar* (2019); via Archbishop Paul Tighe, Richard Rouse and *Culture e Fede* (2020); and Matthew Boudway and *Commonweal* (2021).

I thank the first readers of the novel in its several drafts— T.H. Adamowski, Anna Boyagoda, Michael Czobit, and Charles Foran; I also thank Sam Tanenhaus for being a game, unflagging interlocutor for me and my work. For their tattoo-grade words about the finished book, thank you Aravind Adiga, Junot Díaz, John Irving, and Ian Williams.

Martha Wydysh has been a spirited, thoughtful, and robust advocate for me and my work, and I thank her, and also Ellen Levine, and their colleagues at Trident Media Group.

Dan Wells is the publisher and bookseller that writers and readers alike imagine someday meeting to talk about why we love stories. I am grateful and proud to have this novel brought to public life by Dan and his colleagues at Biblioasis, including Vanessa Stauffer and Michaela Stephen. Michel Vrana is a brilliant book designer, and Emily Donaldson is the copyeditor a writer hopes for (because fears). John Metcalf, my editor, prodded and guided me past many, many lesser versions of this book, amid my many, many infernal thoughts about him.

Finally, my friends and my family—my wife Anna, our daughters Mira, Olive, Ever, and Imogen; my father, Ivor; my mother, June; my sisters and my extended family on both sides of the border and across the seas—have inspired and called me, as Dante does us all, to keep close the hopeful knowledge that on the far side of this life await brighter possibilities.

Don't believe me?

Start with a canto a day, and see where you find yourself, by the end.